M

W9-AUI-942

DISCARD

Love in Bloom

**Center Point
Large Print**

**This Large Print Book carries the
Seal of Approval of N.A.V.H.**

Love in Bloom

SHEILA ROBERTS

CENTER POINT PUBLISHING
THORNDIKE, MAINE

This Center Point Large Print edition
is published in the year 2009 by arrangement with
St. Martin's Press.

Copyright © 2009 by Sheila Rabe.

The text of this Large Print edition is unabridged.
In other aspects, this book may vary
from the original edition.
Printed in the United States of America.
Set in 16-point Times New Roman type.

ISBN: 978-1-60285-471-0

Library of Congress Cataloging-in-Publication Data

Roberts, Sheila.
  Love in bloom / Sheila Roberts.
      p. cm.
  ISBN 978-1-60285-471-0 (library binding : alk. paper)
  1. Florists--Fiction. 2. Breast--Cancer--Patients--Fiction. 3. Female friendship--
Fiction. 4. Large type books. I. Title.

  PS3618.O31625L68 2009
  813'.6--dc22

2009000896

For the Garden Queens:
Jan, Billie, Jenni, Vicki, Alexa, and Katherine.
I thank you for all your help with my garden.
So does everything in there that's still alive.

ACKNOWLEDGMENTS

This was such a fun book to write, especially now that I have caught the gardening bug. Part of what made it fun to write was all the wonderful people who helped me. Huge thanks to Bethany Shippen, owner of the real Changing Seasons, which is on Bainbridge Island, Washington, for all her amazing flower advice and for giving me a glimpse into how a florist works. I'm still not sure I got it all right, but one huge thing I learned from Bethany: There's a lot more to flower arranging than sticking those babies in a vase. Flowers are very labor intensive. Thanks also to Damon Herrick, floral designer at Flowers To Go, for being so willing to answer my last-minute flower questions. I'm greatly indebted to Kathy Defenbaugh and Linda Johnson, the helpful experts at Clear Creek Nursery in Silverdale, Washington, for giving me gardening tips for this book. Thanks, too, to my friends Alexa Darin, Bonnie Westcott, and Anjali Banerjee, who also shared some great tips. I'm hugely indebted to my writing group buddies for their valiant efforts to save me from myself: the Susans, Krysteen, Rose Marie, Lois, PJ, Kate, Suzanne, Elsa, Carol, and

Anjali. Thanks to my friend Kema Bohn for helping me with insight into the mind and heart of a cancer survivor. And to my friend Ruth, who saved me in so many ways, all I can say is, I owe you chocolate. Finally, huge thanks and gratitude to Paige Wheeler and Rose Hilliard, world's best agent and editor. You two are simply awesome. Boy, does it take a lot of people to keep a writer on track! So, with all that help, any boo-boos, anything that doesn't read right, sound right, or smell right . . . my bad.

Love in Bloom

GARDEN SEASON IS HERE AGAIN.
The Heart Lake Park and Recreation Department
is currently reserving plots for all interested
gardeners at the community garden
at Grandview Park.

—from *The Heart Lake Herald*

Seeds

TIPS ON PLANTING

Plant a fifty-cent flower in a five-dollar hole. In other words, invest some money in your soil. Preparing the soil with good nutrients for your plants and flowers will guarantee you a healthy, happy garden.

Feed your soil regularly. Beneficial microbes need organic material to break down and feed the roots of your plants; an annual top dressing of no more than one-half inch of organic compost will help to replenish their banquet table.

Plan ahead. If you plant seeds or bulbs, you will save almost fifty percent over what you'd spend by purchasing the same plant in a pot.

To make your gardening a little easier, keep your plants that are needy divas in one area of the garden. You'll be able to meet their heavier watering and feeding needs in much less time than if they are scattered throughout your garden.

Plants that have been grown in a container sometimes develop encircling roots. These should be stretched out or cut when planting to avoid letting the roots continue circling in the planting hole. These could eventually girdle the plant and kill it.

ONE

I need flowers, dead ones. Have you got any that are starting to wilt?"

"Excuse me?" Hope Walker stared at the scowling woman standing in front of her. She looked like she could scorch a pansy at twenty paces. This was a new one for Changing Seasons Floral. Was this some sort of April Fools' Day joke? Had she just been punked?

"I want to send flowers to my dog," the woman explained. Hope took in the woman's dark hair and angry eyes and thought, Cruella de Vil.

Hope frowned and ran a hand through her hair—all those curls, still hard to get used to. "Excuse me?"

The woman talked right over her. "My ex has custody, so I don't want anything pretty sitting on his doorstep. And I want the card to read, 'These aren't for you, they're for the dog. Condolences, Schatsi, on getting stuck with Daddy.' I'll pay for it with MasterCard."

For everything else, there's MasterCard. But not for this. Life was too short to waste it helping people be bitter.

"I'm afraid I can't help you," said Hope with a smile of faux regret. "All my flowers are fresh."

"Well, you must have something," snapped the woman, making Hope feel like she was twelve instead of thirty.

You are a businesswoman. You can deal with difficult people.

No, she couldn't. If she could, she'd be a lawyer. Or a cop. Or a baseball referee. She went into this business so she could spread love and comfort with pretty flower arrangements.

Hope's heart rate picked up a notch. At five feet five inches, she could look most women in the eye, but this one had a couple of inches on her. And her foul mood made her look seven feet tall.

What to say to someone like this? Hope arranged flowers for happy: weddings, graduations, birthdays. She arranged flowers for sad: funerals, hospital stays. And she arranged flowers for love and sex, and probably not always in that order. But what she didn't arrange flowers for was bitter, angry, or vindictive, and this woman could qualify for all three. It was all Hope could do not to say, "Get visiting rights for the dog and come back when I can help you in a positive way."

"I don't care what you do, just do something that gets the message across. Okay?"

Okay. This was a business. She had to be professional. "How much do you want to spend?"

"Whatever it takes."

Whatever it takes? That wasn't something a woman said when she wanted to prove a point and then move on. That was something a woman said when she was hurt and angry and, deep down, hoping that one desperate gesture would work magic and take her to a Hallmark happy ending.

Now Hope knew these flowers weren't for the dog. She also knew the message this woman really wanted to send and just how she could help. "All right," she said crisply. "I think I can help you. But you need to allow me creative license."

"Do whatever you want," said the woman.

There it was. Permission to do what she did best: speak what was in someone's heart with her flowers. She took the credit card information and Schatsi and Daddy's address, then, after assuring the woman she would get just what she needed, Hope sent her on her way with a little shamrock plant to make her feel better.

Then she slipped behind the thick velvet curtains that hid her work area at the back of the shop and got busy. She combined red carnations, which symbolized an aching heart, with red roses, for love, remembrance, and passion. Ferns made the perfect green for this arrangement because they symbolized sincerity. On the card, she wrote the message behind the message: *Schatsi, I wish things could be different.* She added a quick note explaining the symbolism of the flowers. She'd wait a day before delivering. The flowers wouldn't be wilted, but they wouldn't be fresh, either. It felt like a good compromise.

But would her customer think so? Would the woman call and yell at her? Storm into the shop and threaten to sue her? Had this really been the right thing to do?

She emerged with her masterpiece and looked around her shop, all gussied up in anticipation of Easter with baskets brimming with tulips and daffodils, Easter egg trees and pastel egg garlands. "Well, everyone," she said as she set the bouquet on the counter, "you heard. She insisted. And this will accomplish so much more than what she originally wanted."

Of course, none of the flowers responded, but if they could have, Hope knew they would have cheered her brilliance, clapped their petals even.

The little bell over the shop door jingled and Clarice, her girl Friday, walked in, ten minutes late as usual, a vision in retro hippy clothes, maroon hair, and ear piercings. Clarice was nineteen and very creative, and she liked to make sure people picked up on that at first glance. "Who are you talking to?"

If it had been anyone else, Hope would have been embarrassed. She shrugged. "Just myself. I had the weirdest order. This woman wanted to send a wilted bouquet to her dog."

"Oooh, can I do it?"

Hope pointed to the bouquet next to her. "It's already done."

"Those don't look wilted to me."

"By tomorrow when we deliver, they'll be as close as I can get. If she's not happy, I'll refund her money."

Clarice frowned and shook her head. "It's a good thing you've got the touch with flowers 'cause you suck at business."

"Look who's talking," Hope retorted. "I swear if you ever get a real job, you'll get canned the first week."

Clarice dumped her messenger bag behind the counter with a sigh. "I know I'm late. I overslept. I met the most amazing guy last night." She hugged herself and closed her eyes. "He was like, totally incredible, with the most amazing mouth." She opened her eyes and shrugged. "I was dreaming about him this morning. I just couldn't wake up. Sorry."

A teeny weed of jealousy popped up in Hope's heart. She gave it a mental yank and threw it as far from her as possible. Just because she would probably never find a man didn't mean that she had to resent it when someone else got lucky.

Clarice got lucky a lot.

Another weed. Yank, toss. Sigh.

The bell over the door jingled again and in walked the hunk of the century.

"Wow," breathed Clarice, speaking for both of them.

Hope shot her a look, then asked, "May I help you?" *May I have your children? How soon?*

He looked a little embarrassed, whether from Clarice's unbridled admiration or the fact that he was in a flower shop, who knew? He was tall, with an Arnold Schwarzenegger chest, and fit with the flower shop as well as the proverbial bull in the china closet. Dressed in jeans, a denim shirt, and work boots, he had sandy hair and brown eyes and the tanned skin of a man accustomed to working outside. He belonged on a calendar. Mr. March. No, lose the shirt and make that Mr. July.

"I need to order some flowers," he said, stating the obvious.

Hope walked over to him. He smelled like sawdust and aftershave, a fragrance more enticing than gardenias. "Did you want an arrangement?" She suddenly felt like every bit of estrogen in her body had decided to samba. She smoothed her hands down her jeans in the hope that the rest of her would get the message and stop with the attraction tremors.

He looked around, taking in the Easter frillies, the balloons, and the flowers in the refrigerated case. His gaze rested on Audrey, the shop mascot. "That's quite a plant."

The Christmas cactus that got away. Many people had offered to buy Audrey. With those red glittered heels holding up her pot and her Feed Me sign, she was something. "Audrey's not for sale," Hope said quickly. Audrey had shared her apartment and cheered her up when she went through those nightmare months. Audrey was family. A girl didn't sell her family.

He cocked an eyebrow. "Audrey?"

Hope felt her cheeks warming. "Like in *Little Shop of Horrors*. It was a musical. About a plant that ate people."

He grinned and nodded slowly. "Yeah, I should have got that."

A man who knew about musicals. Was he gay? "You know that musical?"

He shrugged. "I was in it in high school. I played the dentist. Rode a Harley up on stage."

"Awesome," gushed Clarice.

It wasn't hard to picture this guy all studded up in black leather making an entrance on a motorcycle. Hope cleared her throat. The tremors were still there. The hand-smoothing thing hadn't helped.

He shook his head. "The bike's probably the only reason I got the part. Anyway, don't worry about your man-eating plant. I'm looking for something smaller."

"Do you have anything in mind?" Hope asked. She did, but it had nothing to do with flowers.

"I don't know. Some kind of arrangement."

"For your girlfriend?" chirped Clarice from behind the counter. Clarice of the short-term memory loss. So much for the amazing guy she had met the night before.

The customer shook his head. "My mom. It's her birthday."

A hunk who loved his mother. The man had to have a flaw somewhere. Hope walked over to the wrought-iron café table where she kept the book with pictures of all her arrangements and flipped it open. "Would you like to look at some samples?"

He eyed the delicate white chair as if he was wondering whether or not it would hold him. "Uh, I actually have to get back to work. My company's doing the renovations on this building."

The renovations on the long building that housed her flower shop, Something You Need Gifts, and Emma's Quilt Corner had made the sound of hammers and saws familiar background noise as builders shored up some of the sagging structure at the back of the building. So she'd heard him before she'd seen him. Emma was fretting about sawdust filtering into her new shop and coating her fabric, but the idea of sawdust didn't bother Hope. Good topsoil always had some sawdust in it.

"Maybe you can just pick something out," he suggested.

Hope hated it when people said that. Flowers had a language all their own, and every arrangement should say something special that reflected the heart of the giver. Even the angry woman who wanted to send flowers to her dog had had something in mind when she came in.

"Flowers are so personal," Hope told him. "Does your mother have a favorite?"

"She likes roses." His brows knit. "She doesn't

live in Heart Lake. She's closer to Lyndale. Do you deliver that far?"

For you? To the ends of the earth. Hope nodded. "No problem. How much did you want to spend?"

"Cost doesn't matter."

"Dark pink roses symbolize appreciation. You could also add some daffodils, and the color contrast would be striking."

"Do those symbolize something?"

"Every flower does. Daffodils symbolize respect."

He snapped his fingers and pointed at her like she'd just come up with something brilliant. "Perfect. Add those."

"All right then," she said. She moved to the counter and he followed her, pulling out his wallet. She brought up an order form on her computer and took the name and address of the lucky flower recipient. "And how would you like the card to read?"

"Happy birthday."

"You don't want to say anything else?" Hope prompted.

"Happy birthday, Mom?" he guessed.

Clarice snickered and Hope frowned at her.

"Am I missing something here?" he asked.

"Well, women, even moms, sometimes like to receive a special message. We're sentimental that way."

"Words aren't exactly my specialty. I was more of

a math-science guy in college. I appreciate words though," he added. "I'm open to suggestions."

Hope loved this part of her job. She enjoyed helping people with the little cards that accompanied their gifts almost as much as she enjoyed creating the floral arrangements. "Since you're picking such symbolic flowers, it would be nice to tell her what they mean."

He beamed. "Great idea."

"So, how about something like, 'Roses for gratitude, daffodils for respect.'"

"Maybe they'll make up for my neglect," added Clarice, and Hope shot her a silencing look.

"I like it," he said with a nod. "Not the part about neglect though."

"Of course not," Hope said. "And sign it?"

"Love, Jason. Wait. Make that love and gratitude. How's that?"

"Aw, that's sweet," said Clarice, who was now busy watering plants.

He was looking at Hope as if waiting for her approval. "That says it all," she told him. *You're perfect.* For some other woman, not for her. "Now," she said briskly, yanking herself out of her lust trance. "Do you want to put that on your charge card?"

He handed over the card, nodding. She looked at the name on it. Jason Wells. It was a nice, solid-sounding name to go with those nice, solid muscles. *Oh, stop already.*

Their business done, he gave her a nod and a smile and an easy "Thanks," then left the shop.

Hope watched him go.

"Great butt," Clarice said, echoing her thoughts. "No wedding ring. I wonder if he's got a girl-friend."

"Didn't you just meet Mr. Amazing last night?" Hope teased.

Clarice made a face. "Not for me, for you. He's probably at least thirty. That's your age."

"Me?" Hope shook her head. "He's not my type."

"A man like that is anybody's type."

Not anybody's, thought Hope. A man like that needed a perfect woman, not one who was scarred and had an alien implant where her left boob used to be.

Never mind. You may look like the Bride of Frankenstein and have an alien implant, but you have your flower shop, you have your life. And you have a floral arrangement to make.

TWO

*S*eventy-six-year-old Millie Baldwin felt like the Invisible Woman. What did it take to snag a boy's attention these days? "Guess what I did while you were in school?" she asked her twelve-year-old grandson.

No response.

"I stole the Liberty Bell."

Eric gave a grunt and frantically pressed the controls on his video game.

"I buried it in the neighbor's backyard," Millie continued, trying to make herself heard over the sound of gunfire coming from the TV. "Of course, it won't stay over there. That's just temporary, till I can find a buyer. I would have buried it in your backyard, but it would have been too hard to hide all that freshly dug sod under gravel and a bonsai bush."

"Oh, man, he killed me!" cried Eric in disgust.

Millie sighed and let him go on with his game; something called "Halo" that he played on-line with his new best friends who happened to be total strangers. Maybe if she had expressed an interest in killing virtual people when she first came to stay with Debra, she and her grandson would be spending more time together now. Maybe they would talk. Maybe when she talked he would listen. Probably not though. Who wanted to listen to an old woman?

She had tried to figure out the game one afternoon, thinking it would be fun to surprise Eric and challenge him to a duel when he got home from school, but she'd been unable to even make the game start, let alone decipher the purpose of all the buttons on the controller.

"I think I'll just scoot out to the kitchen and make myself a cup of tea, plan my next heist."

"Whoa!" he hooted.

"Would you like something to eat, Eric?" she offered.

"Fritos," he said, and jerked in sympathy as his on-screen action hero dodged a barrage of bullets.

The child had been programmed with selective hearing. Millie fetched the bag of chips, then returned to the living room and stood in front of the couch where her grandson was planted dead center.

"Hey, Gram," he protested, leaning to the right. "I can't see."

"Maybe you've been playing that game so much that you're going blind."

"I don't play that much," he argued, frantically pressing the game controls.

"Your mother wanted me to make sure you did your homework."

"I didn't have any," he said, not missing a beat. His face suddenly crumpled in pain and he dropped the controls and fell over on the couch with a moan. "I'm dead again."

She dropped the chips on the coffee table in front of him. "These should resurrect you."

He sat back up, reaching for the chips while simultaneously punching the game controls.

"You're welcome, dear," she prompted.

"Oh, yeah. Thanks, Gram." He shot her a quick grin and she tousled his hair. He was a cute boy. They used to have fun together when he and his sister came out to visit, playing games like *Sorry* and *Steal the Pack*. But here, on his home turf, those quiet games couldn't compete with the action on the TV screen. Neither could she.

Back in the kitchen, Millie fed Socks the cat, who was winding around her legs, begging for food. Then she put the kettle on to boil and stood looking out the window. She saw a drizzly Pacific Northwest day and a stark landscape of raked rocks, dotted with a few ornamental bushes. Her daughter claimed it was restful. How could a yard with barely any vegetation be restful? And if it was so restful, why was Debra always so tense?

That, of course, was a rhetorical question. Debra was a single, working mother with a stressful job and spoiled children who required the latest of everything. How could she be anything but tense?

Fourteen-year-old Emily bounced into the kitchen, freshly home from school and ready to forage for food. She planted a quick kiss on Millie's cheek and gave her a casual, "Hi, Gram." Like Eric, Emily was a beautiful child, with golden hair and blue eyes. She was two years older than her brother and just as skinny. She also had an equally never-ending appetite. Millie was beginning to suspect these children had tapeworms.

Emily was a multitasker, just like her mom. Right now she was searching the fridge and talking on her shiny, pink cell phone. What did a fourteen-year-old need with a cell phone?

"They all have them, Mom," Debra had informed her. "And, anyway, I like being able to get ahold of her when I need to."

They didn't have cell phones when Debra was growing up, and Millie managed to get ahold of Debra just fine. It was ridiculous if you asked Millie. Not that anyone did.

"I did not say that about her," Emily snarled into her phone. "Is she crazy?"

"I made oatmeal cookies this afternoon," offered Millie.

"Cool, thanks." Emily grabbed a yogurt, piled two cookies on top, and then pulled a spoon from the silverware drawer. "Well, I didn't say that and you need to tell Rachel I didn't say that, and if Brandy doesn't stop telling lies about me, I'm going to nail the skank bitch to the wall."

"Emily," chided Millie. "What nasty words to come out of such a sweet little mouth." Emily had never talked like that as a little girl. She'd been all innocence and curls, and Millie had so enjoyed showing Emily off to her friends on those summer vacation visits. The curls had vanished with adolescence. The sweetness was still there, Millie was sure, just hiding.

"Sorry, Gram," Emily said breezily, and sailed out of the kitchen.

Hiding very well.

The phone rang. Millie checked the caller ID and saw that it was her oldest and dearest friend,

Alice Livingston, calling from Connecticut.

Alice barely gave her time to say hello. "Are you ready to come home yet?"

"This is my home now," Millie said firmly.

Alice gave a snort. "Living in your daughter's house?"

"I like it here," Millie insisted. All right. Perhaps she had made a bit of a hasty decision, but at the time it seemed like the perfect solution for both her daughter and herself. Debra needed help, and Millie needed a home. All those unexpected medical expenses had really upset her financial apple cart. She and Duncan had been the poster couple for why all Americans over the age of sixty should have long-term-care insurance. She was sure that, in the end, Duncan had willed himself to pass on to save what little they had left for her. Sadly, he hadn't saved much.

"Oh, you can't be serious," Alice said, her voice dripping scorn. "Going from your own home to being a dependent."

"I'm not a dependent," Millie said stiffly. "I contribute." Not only did she do the laundry, help with the cooking, and clean up the kitchen after meals, she paid Debra rent from her Social Security check. Debra had balked at taking the money at first, but Millie had insisted. After all, she had her pride.

"You should have moved in with me," Alice said. "We could have had so much fun."

Just thinking about her happy life in Little Haven was enough to bring a sigh—tea parties with her friends of forty years, gardening, attending St. Mark's Episcopal Church, where Debra had been married.

"It's not too late. You could come back," Alice coaxed.

Sounds of kabooms from the TV drifted in from the living room. "No," Millie said firmly. "Going back is never a good idea. I need to move forward."

"Living with your daughter? I call that moving backward."

"Maybe that would be true in your case, but it's not in mine," Millie said. She was needed here. And that was certainly better than staying put, moldering in the past. "Now, dear. I have to go. I have to start dinner."

"Debra's going to work you into an early grave," Alice predicted.

That made Millie smile. Secretly, Alice was jealous. She and her daughter weren't on speaking terms. "I'll talk to you soon, dear," she said, and hung up.

She pulled the teapot from the burner before it could whistle. There was already enough noise in this house. She wasn't about to add to it.

The phone rang again. This time it was Debra. That could mean only one thing. Millie picked up the receiver. "Do you have to work late?"

It happened so much. Millie had thought when she moved out here they'd have more time to talk, do things together. That hadn't quite worked out as planned. Between work and the children, Debra was so busy. And Little League was about to start for Eric, which would make her even busier.

"Sorry, Mom. But don't worry about making dinner. I can pick something up on the way home. The kids don't mind eating late."

That was the trouble with life at Debra's house if you asked Millie, no routine. "You have leftover chicken in the refrigerator. I can make a pot pie."

"No, that's okay. Just leave the chicken. I'm going to make chicken curry with it on the weekend. I'll bring something home. I should be there by quarter to seven."

Almost seven at night. That was too late for Millie to eat. If she ate that late she didn't sleep well.

But this was Debra's house, so she didn't say anything. Instead, she wished her daughter well with the rest of her day and hung up the phone. So much for making dinner. She fixed her tea and then stood in front of the window, looking at the non-view.

Most of Heart Lake was pretty, with its tall evergreens and tangled brush, its homey downtown and converted summer homes. Even the newer houses on the lake had a casual feel that fit the area, and were landscaped in a way that blended with the firs and pines and alders. But the development where her daughter lived camped at the edge of town like an unwanted visitor. It was made up of tract mansions painted in the latest popular colors, bulging like squatting monsters over their small lots. The developer had left a string of fir trees at the back of the development in an attempt to make Heart Lake Estates fit in, but it was plain that whoever planned this suburban ghetto had been given a list of only three landscaping options and told to alternate them: small yard with a couple of rhododendrons and a maple tree in the corner; small yard with a boulder or two at the edge, some pampas grass, and a maple tree in the corner; a gravel Sahara with no front lawn, sparsely dotted with scraggly bonsai and a Japanese maple in the corner. The landscaper on her daughter's house had opted for the latter, both back and front.

Looking at the scene before her, Millie felt far from Zen. Perhaps Alice was right. She didn't fit here. She shouldn't have let Debra persuade her otherwise. At least in Little Haven, she had familiar surroundings and good friends. And a lovely garden.

"Mom, you could live with Randall or me," her son Duncan Jr. had told her. "You don't have to move there just because Deb wants you to."

"I know, dear. But she needs help with the children."

"She needs help. Period. When she's not working you to death, she'll take over your life and boss you around. That's what she did to Ben. That's why he left. She's high-maintenance, Mom."

"I'll be fine," Millie had assured him. Debra was the youngest of her three children, the baby of the family, her change of life baby, and she had brought Millie such joy. Perhaps she'd spoiled Debra just a little, but Debra was her daughter, for heaven's sake. And, yes, Debra could be a little high-maintenance, but Millie didn't have anything else to maintain anyway, so why not? The old house in Little Haven had felt too big for her to rattle around in alone. Just as well it was gone.

But this house felt too small. There was no room for her to squeeze into the lives of the people occupying it. Her daughter barely had time for her, her grandchildren ignored her, and the nonyard mocked her.

She loved to garden. Debra knew that. Where did Debra think her mother was going to garden out there in the Japanese Sahara? Millie longed to feel cheered by an English garden with flowers of all shapes and colors spilling everywhere, a garden she could stand in the middle of and smell the fragrance of new life in bloom. Here at the Heart Lake Bonsai Farm, there wasn't room for so much as a sweet pea.

Millie turned her back on the nonview. "It

doesn't do any good to mope," she told herself. "I need to make some changes."

She took her tea, settled at the kitchen table, and began to look through the weekly edition of *The Heart Lake Herald,* determined to find something with which to build a new life.

The Heart Lake High girls' volleyball team had won their third straight game. Standing O was conducting auditions for *Oklahoma!* The police blotter was full of high crime. A deer had gotten caught in rush-hour traffic at the corner of Lake View and Loveland Lane. The police had been called and the deer escorted to safety. A runner on Lake Drive had found and turned in a silver ring, which was being held until someone came in to claim it. How sweet. So much about this place seemed friendly. Except this house, this yard.

She turned the page and suddenly found exactly what she'd been looking for. *Garden Season Is Here Again,* proclaimed the headline. Millie smiled as she read on. *The Heart Lake Park and Recreation Department is currently reserving plots for all interested gardeners at the community garden at Grandview Park.*

A vision of a little fence hugging delphiniums, petunias, marigolds, and violas, lavender and candytuft formed itself in Millie's mind. And pansies, she couldn't forget pansies with their sweet flower faces. That was the ideal, but alas, some of those flowers were perennials, and a community garden was no place for perennials. But the world was full of flowers. She could make do.

She smiled. Heart Lake had just given her a get out of jail free card.

THREE

I need to leave early," Clarice told Hope as they stood side by side removing thorns from the roses the wholesaler had delivered that morning.

Hope cocked a finger at her. "April Fools, right?"

"No, for real."

She'd come in late and now she wanted to leave early? Hope combed her fingers through her hair. "Do you have to?"

"Look on the bright side. It's an hour you don't have to pay me for."

"I'd rather pay you," Hope said. "Come on, Clarice. I depend on you."

Clarice had the grace to look guilty. But only for a moment. "You can handle things on your own for the last hour, can't you?"

"Barely. We're getting busier all the time."

Word was spreading. Hope Walker was the Picasso of flowers. Between her flower arrangements and the inspiring words she helped customers put on the accompanying gift card, she had probably saved a dozen relationships and cemented another twenty since Valentine's Day. She was already booked for two weddings. This morning alone she'd had a dozen calls for arrangements for everything from birthdays to new babies. And with Heart Lake High's Junior Class Spring Fever Dance coming up on the weekend, orders for corsages and boutonnieres were pouring in. Of course, that was all good, but it was all even better when her help actually stuck around to help. Clarice had to get a grip.

"Clarice," she began, trying to sound firm.

"I promised I'd make dinner for Borg."

Mr. Wonderful, who was responsible for turning Clarice from a flake into a frustration. Of course, she should tell Clarice that she was going to have to make a choice. Either be dependable or go find some other employer to torture. But that was easier said than done. Clarice had been Hope's first employee. Her only employee. Who would she get to replace Clarice?

Any number of people, for crying out loud. Hope put on her sternest expression. "Look," she began again. Clarice was making a pitiful, pleading face she had to have stolen straight from Puss in Boots in the *Shrek* movies. "But you can't cook." *Way to be tough.*

"I know," Clarice moaned. "That's why I need to get off early. It's going to take me hours to figure out how to make spaghetti."

This was why Clarice was ditching her? "Buy

frozen meatballs, canned sauce, and boil some pasta and you're good to go. Trust me."

"And the place is a mess. I need to change the bed."

"TMI," Hope said, holding up a hand.

"Come on, Hope, let me go home early just this once. Haven't you ever been in love?"

When she was Clarice's age, about a million times, and it had been wonderful.

Hope gave up. She still believed in love, if not for herself, then for other people. "Oh, all right. But don't do this to me again. The dance is Saturday, and with all the other orders by Friday we'll be swamped."

Clarice beamed at her. "I'll be here. You can count on me. You know that."

Her words rang mockingly in Hope's ears when on Thursday, with forty-three corsages and almost as many boutonnieres to make (and still counting), two birthday bouquets to get delivered, and the phone ringing off the hook, the clock hit eleven A.M. and there was still no sign of Clarice. Hope had tried Clarice's home phone and her cell only to get her voice mail.

She had finally broken down and put in a desperate call to her younger sister. Bobbi was a disaster in heels, but she had artistic flair and a way with flowers that couldn't be taught. Hope just had to make sure she kept her sister away from the phones and the computer. Nobody could screw up an order like Bobbi. Nobody had a heart like Bobbi, either. God bless her, when someone needed help, she came at a run.

Hope was in the middle of stocking the refrigerator case when the phone rang for what felt like the millionth time. The frazzled, irritated side of her wanted to snarl, "What?," but, professional that she was, she said a calm, "Changing Seasons. May I help you?" Until she heard the voice on the other end of the line. "Clarice! Where in the world are you? If the answer isn't Timbuktu, being held by terrorists, you're dead meat."

"I'm in Vegas. I'm married!"

Hope blinked and gaped at the receiver. "To Borg?"

"I am totally in love. He is amaaaazing."

No, amazing was that Clarice could run away to Vegas with someone she'd known a whole week. And leave her boss stuck up to her neck in flowers. "Why didn't you at least call me and let me know you were going?"

"Well, it was kind of sudden."

Kind of? There was an understatement. Clarice tended to take her whole free-spirit thing too far.

"Borg got laid off and was going down there to check out working at his cousin's garage. And he found this great deal on Travelocity, so we figured, what the hell."

What the hell. No job, no money, just jump and hope a net appears. It sure took all kinds of people to make the world spin. And thanks to Clarice, Hope's was going to be spinning like crazy.

"We're staying at the Bellagio," Clarice continued. "Borg used his whole last paycheck for this. Isn't that sweet? You should see the fountain. It's awesome. This whole place is awesome."

Hope tightened the phone ear bud and went back to her birthday arrangement. "I've heard it's fabulous."

"And the shopping. Oh, my God. We are having so much fun. I'm so happy," Clarice ended on a squeal.

Hope couldn't help smiling. Clarice knew how to live in the moment, that was for sure. She just wished Clarice was living in the moment here at the shop, helping her. "Well, I wish you both the best. Good luck. And let me know where to send your last check."

"Thanks. You're the best. Speaking of luck, I've gotta get back to the slots. Take care. And, Hope?"

"Hmm?" Hope said absently, her mind already on the mountain of orders still waiting to be filled.

"Go for it. Find somebody and just . . . go for it." Before Hope could respond, Clarice was talking to Mr. Wonderful. "Hey, baby. What? You lost how much? Damn." To Hope, "Gotta go!" Then the line went dead.

The bell over the shop door jingled and a familiar voice warbled, "I'm here to save the day."

Thank God. Help. "I'm in the back," Hope called.

A moment later, the red velvet curtains partitioning off the workroom parted and through them stepped her little sister, the reincarnation of Scarlett O'Hara, only with blond hair and bigger boobs. She was wearing jeans, boots, and a black leather jacket over layers of style.

She blew over to Hope and hugged her, enveloping Hope in a mist of DKNY perfume. Bobbi never could put on perfume with a light hand. The parade of men who chased her never seemed to mind.

Normally Hope wouldn't, either. But when she was going through chemo the smell of perfume had made her sick. It still did a little. Now she had to be careful around the thing she loved the most: flowers. She still couldn't come close to the most potent ones like stargazer lilies. And selling potpourri and scented candles was not an option yet, either.

She pulled away and tried not to make a face.

"What?" Bobbi's eyebrows rose with sudden understanding. "The perfume? You can smell it?"

"Um."

"Sorry. If I'd known I was going to be coming here, I wouldn't have put any on. I'll wash it off and go perfume-naked the rest of the day, I promise."

Hope nodded. "Thanks. I hate to cramp your style."

"Nothing cramps my style," Bobbi said with a grin.

"Well, that's good to know, 'cause if you kept dousing yourself with that stuff, I'm afraid I'd have to lock you in the cooler."

Bobbi stuck her tongue out and went off to descent herself.

"Thanks for bailing me out," Hope said when she returned.

"No problem. I'd have just sat around and ate chocolate or something anyway. That's the problem with working nights. You're home all day with nothing to do but fold your laundry and eat."

Who was Bobbi kidding? She never stayed home for long. She was always out, either having coffee with a friend or lunch with some man she'd met at the Last Resort, where she worked as a cocktail waitress while she tried to figure out what she really wanted to do with the rest of her life.

Bobbi plopped her purse under the work counter. "So, how many million corsages do we have left to make?"

The phone rang. "Ask me after this call," Hope said, and took the order. "We're going to be here till midnight," she groaned when she hung up.

"You're going to be here till midnight," Bobbi corrected her, starting on a corsage. "By midnight, I'll be serving drinks and dodging losers trying to cop a feel." She heaved a sigh and shook out the silver bangles at her wrist. "I don't know how long I'm going to last over there."

What to say to that? When it came to careers, Bobbi tended to have a short attention span. In fact, when it came to most things she didn't have a very long attention span. She started books but never finished them (unless they were romance novels, and even those had to be short), and she tried on different hobbies like they were shoes. So far she'd tried hiking (with one of her buff boyfriends—she'd hiked through a nest of wasps and that had ended that), cycling ("Boring," she decided), French cooking (she almost set the kitchen on fire), and knitting (it took too long to see results). Her relationships didn't last long, either—not surprising, considering the undependable guys she picked. If a Hollywood producer decided to make another *Legally Blonde* movie, Bobbi would make the perfect star. She wouldn't even need a script. The producers could just follow her around all day. *Legally Blonde: The Reality Show*. And it would be a hit because everyone would love her.

"What we don't get done today, we'll finish tomorrow." Bobbi put a hand over her heart. "I pledge to make sure that no Heart Lake High School dance queen goes without her flowers." She gave a stack of pink tissue paper a dramatic tug and managed to knock over a container of carnations in the process. "Oops. Don't worry. I'll get it," she said, reaching for the paper towels.

Maybe calling her sister for help hadn't been such a good idea.

"Don't worry," Bobbi assured Hope, as if reading her mind. "I'll get into the rhythm here in a minute."

"It's all good," lied Hope.

"So, have you heard from Clarice yet?"

"She eloped to Vegas."

"Oh, fun!" cried Bobbi. "I so need to go to Vegas. I hear the shopping there is incredible."

"You wouldn't go with someone you'd known only a week would you?"

Bobbi gave a little shrug. "You don't need years to know if it's right."

This coming from the woman who'd had one starter marriage and six boyfriends in the last three years. Talk about starting your twenties with a bang. "Sometimes you worry me, Bobs."

"I know what you're thinking," Bobbi said. "Even though my relationships haven't worked out, I still believe in love at first sight. I just have this way of killing it before it can grow."

"I hate it when you talk like it's all your fault that things didn't work out with those bozos. It takes two to kill love," Hope said, snapping the plastic container shut over a carnation wrist corsage. "You just haven't found the right man yet."

Bobbi sighed. "I need to quit dating losers."

Hallelujah, thought Hope. *It's about time.*

"I need someone who's nice. And responsible.

Someone who doesn't just want to get into my pants."

"Well, for that he'd have to be gay," teased Hope.

Bobbi gave the florist wire holding her carnations together a vicious twist. "I hate men. They only want one thing. Nobody ever cares about your mind."

"Your mind is mostly on *The Bachelor* and *People* magazine. Most guys aren't into that kind of thing," Hope said.

"I like other things," Bobbi protested. "I like dancing and shopping and . . . all kinds of stuff."

"Soap operas and romance novels," Hope supplied.

"So, what's wrong with that?"

"Nothing. I'm just not sure those are subjects most men are interested in talking about."

The shop bell summoned Hope to the front of the shop, and she emerged to find Jason Wells, the hunk, standing in front of the refrigerator case, hands shoved into his jeans back pockets, looking at her premade arrangements. Her body had an instant high-voltage reaction. What cruel joke of fate was this, anyway? *Of all the flower joints in the world, he has to walk into mine.*

"You're back," she said. *Real professional, Hope.*

He smiled at her. It was a friendlier smile than what she'd seen the day before, maybe even a mildly interested smile. "The flowers for my mom

47

were a hit. Now I need something to make a woman feel better."

Was he kidding? All he'd have to do was walk into a room. "Can you give me some details?" *Who's the woman, your girlfriend?* Like it mattered. She was not in the market for a man. But if she was, she'd take this one in a heartbeat.

"You can handle having flowers delivered in another state, right?"

"Sure. We're an FTD florist," Hope said, moving to her computer. "What's the occasion?"

"Well." He cleared his throat. "It's not exactly an occasion."

She raised her eyebrows and looked at him.

"They're for . . ." He stopped mid-sentence, the words falling from his open jaw.

Hope didn't have to turn around to see what he was looking at. She knew. Bobbi had that effect on men.

"Hi," she said from behind Hope. What was Bobbi doing out here anyway? Why wasn't she in the back room where she belonged, toiling away on corsages?

Jason closed his mouth and managed a feeble, "Hi."

Hope tapped the keyboard impatiently with her fingers. "The flowers are for?" she prompted, trying to return some of the oxygen her sister had just sucked out of the room.

He cleared his throat again. "My . . ." He shook

his head as if trying to restart his brain. "They're for my sister."

"For her birthday?" asked Hope.

"No, just because she needs 'em."

"What a nice brother. Sending flowers to your sister," cooed Bobbi.

For a flash, Hope had thought he'd just made up an excuse to come in and see her again. Maybe he had. But now he only had eyes for her sister. She could feel a weed of jealousy growing in her the size of a sunflower. *Yank that out right now. You can't have him anyway.*

"She broke up with her fiancé," Jason said, eyeing Bobbi. "She feels like crap."

"Boy, I know the feeling," muttered Bobbi.

Jason moved closer to the counter where Bobbi stood next to Hope. "I bet you've never had that problem."

She shrugged. "It always hurts to break up."

Hope inserted herself into the conversation. "How much would you like to spend?"

"This man looks like he's got a big heart. I bet if it's for his sister, he doesn't care," said Bobbi, and Jason's face took on a slightly red tint. Gorgeous as he was, he should be used to flattery from women. His embarrassment didn't stop him from smiling at Bobbi. It wasn't a casual smile. It wasn't a mildly interested one, either. It was the kind of smile ignited by the sparks of high-voltage sexual attraction.

"I just want something nice that will make her feel good," he told Hope. "Have you got a flower for that?"

"Let's see," she said, trying to ignore the sudden desire to give her attention-stealing sister poison ivy. A song from her favorite old movie, *White Christmas,* came to mind. "Sisters, sisters," mocked Rosemary Clooney.

You can't have him, she reminded herself, so why not let Bobbi have him? Because even though he wouldn't want Hope, she wanted him. And that was enough reason to balk at sharing with her sister.

But it was a shameful reason, especially since Bobbi had never done anything but look up to her. Oh, and chauffeur her to chemo, and buy her pretty scarves and hats to cover her bald head. Hope felt suddenly hot with shame. She should give herself poison ivy.

She ran a hand through her hair and redirected her brain to the business of selecting just the right flowers for the occasion. "Lily of the valley would be nice. It signifies a return to happiness."

He snapped his fingers. "That'll do."

"I agree," said Bobbi. "Now, how about something for your wife?"

He shook his head. "I don't have a wife."

"Girlfriend?" persisted Bobbi.

Another head shake. "Nope."

"Boyfriend?" Bobbi ventured, looking ready to be thoroughly depressed.

He made a face. "Uh, no."

"Oh," she said cheerily.

"How do you want the card to read?" asked Hope.

"She loves poetry. How about something . . ."

"Poetic?" Hope teased. She loved poetry. She suspected she'd like Jason's sister. "Hmmm." She gave the keyboard a thoughtful tap. "How about this one? *Though lovers be lost love shall not.*"

"I love that one," lied Bobbi.

"That's good. It sounds familiar. Who's the poet?"

"Dylan Thomas," said Hope.

"Love him," Bobbi gushed. The only Dylan she'd ever heard of was Bob Dylan and she was barely familiar with him.

Jason nodded approvingly. "I like him, too. That'll do great."

Next to Hope, Bobbi preened like she'd thought of it.

Jason produced his charge card and they finished the deal.

"Come back again," Bobbi said.

"I will." He smiled at both of them, but when his gaze finally picked one to settle on, it picked Bobbi.

Hope felt a sharp stab deep in her chest, and then she deflated inside as all the happiness drained out of her. Not the happiness of the moment. This hadn't been a particularly happy moment. It was worse than that. She felt like all the happiness she'd ever had, all the happiness she ever would have just rushed away. Plehhhhhh.

She needed to send herself some lily of the valley. Silk ones so they'd last a lifetime. She'd keep them on her vintage yellow Formica table to remind herself every day that she should always be happy just to be alive.

"That man is amazing," said Bobbi.

"He's okay," said Hope. Her pretend lack of interest made her remember the time when they were kids and she tried to convince Bobbi she didn't want any of Hope's Hershey bar. "It's chocolate. You'll hate it. You like Skittles."

But Bobbi had insisted on trying some of that chocolate. And after one bite, there was no going back. Hope had lost half her chocolate bar that day.

Jason Wells is not a chocolate bar, she told herself sternly, and he's certainly not yours.

She sighed inwardly. She wouldn't have gotten this man anyway; she knew that. But it was going to be really hard to watch him fall for her sister.

FOUR

*H*ope was wilted by the end of the day. "I owe you big time," she told Bobbi, giving her a hug.

"Yes, you do owe me," Bobbi said with a sly grin.

Hope knew what that meant. They'd spent most of the afternoon brainstorming ways that Bobbi could interest Jason Wells (as if he wasn't interested already), and Bobbi had finally come up with the perfect plan, one which, naturally, involved her older sister.

"Oh, not now," Hope moaned. "Tell me you don't want to do this now when my feet are about to fall off." She craved home and a bubble bath, followed by an evening on the sofa with her novel. In spite of Bobbi's many runs to Organix for juice and yogurt and anything else she thought would keep her sister going, Hope was drained. "Can we do this first thing tomorrow?"

"I want to do this today, while he still remembers me."

Hope couldn't help smiling. "Trust me. He's not going to forget you."

"I promise I'll be quick." Bobbi produced the grocery bag full of guy junk food she'd picked up at the Safeway store on her last food run. "I can put the gift basket together. I just need you to help me with the card. You're so much better with words than I am. I don't want him to think I'm an airhead."

"He won't care." That hadn't sounded right.

"Well, I'm not an airhead. Okay, not a total one," Bobbi amended. "Come on, you promised you'd help me. This guy looks like a keeper. I need to impress him."

"Bobs, you already did."

"No. I need to impress him with my brain. I can't just send him a basket and say, 'Call me.' That's totally boring."

"But to the point. You want him to call me, er, you."

"I want more than that. I want him to think I'm amazing." Bobbi's gaze dropped. "I've got to brainwash him early, before he finds out I'm just a cocktail waitress."

"There's nothing wrong with being a cocktail waitress," Hope argued. "It's an honest living."

"You don't exactly have to be a genius to serve drinks."

"Yeah, well serving drinks doesn't make you dumb, either. You shouldn't put yourself down."

Bobbi pulled out a big bag of corn chips and nestled them in her basket of shredded paper next to a jar of salsa. She shrugged, keeping her back to Hope. "I'm not you."

Hope gave a disgusted snort. "You don't want to be, believe me."

That made Bobbi whirl around. "Just because you were sick for a while."

"And am now Franken-boob."

Bobbi pointed a scolding finger at her. "Don't go there. There's more to you than your boobs." She smiled. "Just like there's more to me than my body." She sprinkled a bunch of Hershey's Kisses around the basket. "Now, what kind of flower should I add?"

Hope arched an eyebrow. "White mums?"

Bobbi looked at her suspiciously. "That means something bad, doesn't it? I can tell by looking at you. What do they stand for?"

"Truth."

"Ha, ha. Just because I'm having you coach me on my card doesn't mean I'm not being truthful. I picked the stuff for the basket, after all. And, if I do say so myself, it's genius."

"The oysters are subtle."

"Never mind the oysters," Bobbi said, blushing. "What about the flowers?"

"You're off the hook on the mums. We won't stock any until late summer. What about yellow acacia," Hope suggested, "for secret love."

"Oh, I like that!" cried Bobbi. "Do we have any acacia?"

"Yeah, silk ones." Hope started to get up.

"I'll get 'em," said Bobbi. "Which ones are they?"

"They're over in the corner of the west wall. They're the pouffy yellow blooms with the feathery leaves."

"Got it." Bobbi sailed out through the curtains. A moment later she popped her head back in. "Um, which wall is the west wall?"

"Never mind. I'll get them," said Hope.

Bobbi trailed her. "I could have found them. I just needed you to point me in the right direction."

"Never mind," Hope said and plucked a spray.

They returned to the back room and arranged the flowers in the basket, then wrapped it in blue cellophane.

"That looks awesome," Bobbi said with an approving nod. "Now I just need the card."

"What do you want to say?"

"That I think he's hot and I want to go out with him."

"Okay," Hope said, and handed Bobbi a gift card and a pen.

"But I don't want to say it like that." Bobbi tried to hand the card back.

"It should be in your writing," Hope insisted, refusing to take it.

"Okay, help me think."

"You don't need help thinking."

"Yes, I do. Come on. The sooner you help me the sooner you can go home." Bobbi gave her a playful nudge.

Hope sighed. "Okay. Why don't you make a little mystery of it? You know, intrigue him."

"Oh, I like that! How about, '*Guess who?*'"

"You could do that," Hope said. A bit underwhelming, but the basket would make up for what the card lacked in imagination.

Bobbi frowned and chewed the corner of her lip. "That's kind of dumb, isn't it?"

"We could do better." *We.* Now she was an accomplice, caught up in deception by her own cleverness and her soft heart. Was this how Cyrano

56

de Bergerac had felt? *Never mind that. Help your little sister.*

"You're right, we could," Bobbi agreed and looked at her expectantly.

"How about this? Every flower has a meaning, every petal speaks a word."

"Oooh, that's so pretty!" gushed Bobbi. She wrote down the words then looked at the card. "Are you going to make a rhyme out of it? If you do, you'd better not make it a long one. This card isn't that big, you know."

Hope drummed her fingers on the work counter. "Hmmm. I know. Add: But unless you speak their language, something special goes unheard."

"Wow," breathed Bobbi as she wrote.

"Then add: *If you learn what this yellow acacia symbolizes, you'll be halfway to solving the mystery of this basket.*"

"Oh, I love that!" Bobbi stopped writing mid-scrawl and looked up, wearing a fresh frown. "But that doesn't tell him who sent it."

"It's coming from this shop. We were talking about the meaning of flowers earlier today. He's not stupid. He'll figure it out."

"Great." Bobbi slipped the card in an envelope. Then she scooped up the basket. "I'll deliver this on my way home." She hugged Hope, making the cellophane on the gift basket crinkle in protest. "I can help you tomorrow, too, if you want."

That was Bobbi, generous to a fault. She

deserved a great guy like Jason Wells. "You are amazing."

"Aw, you're just saying that 'cause it's true," Bobbi quipped. She gave Hope another quick hug and said, "Go home and get some rest. You look rotten."

"Thanks."

"Any time."

Bobbi left and Hope locked up the shop. Then she drove to her apartment, wondering all the while if Bobbi had found Jason and been able to deliver her basket in person. She made herself some green tea and ran a bath, filling the tub with extra bubble bath. She picked up her well-worn copy of Jane Austen's *Mansfield Park* and climbed into the tub to drink tea and read more about the adventures of her all-time favorite heroine, Fanny Price. Fanny wasn't your typical heroine. She was plain and quiet. But she had a good heart, and in the end Miss Austen rewarded her goodness by giving her the man of her dreams. Hope liked that.

Usually. But tonight Fanny seemed insipid and undeserving—a real little weenie. What man in his right mind would want a Fanny when he could have a Bobbi?

What were Bobbi and Jason doing now?

Hope closed the book and tossed it away from her. She ran a hand through a mountain of bubbles, scooped the frothy summit up and watched it dance and shimmer in her palm. Instead of smiling she blew it to pieces, shook the remainder off her hand and got out of the tub. Bubble baths were overrated. So was green tea. The stuff tasted like grass. She turned her back to the mirror, dried off, dressed in her favorite tee and jammie bottoms, and then wandered out to her living room to slump on the couch. Tea hadn't worked, her book hadn't worked, and her bubble bath had been a failure. She still felt grumpy.

She turned on the TV, found a sitcom, then picked up her knitting and went to work on a half-finished scarf. Okay, she was fine now. Something to create, something to laugh about—life was good again. She could be happy with or without a man.

So there.

Jason Wells sauntered into Changing Seasons Floral on Saturday. If a fish going after a lure could smile, it would look like that, Hope thought. He was dressed in guy casual, wearing jeans, a T-shirt, and a windbreaker, and once again he started those attraction tremors in her.

"Hi. Back for more flowers?" she asked, playing dumb.

"Back to solve a mystery," he replied, and leaned on the counter.

"Oh?" So, Bobbi hadn't found him when she made her gift basket delivery. The little spurt of glee that surfaced in Hope wasn't very sisterly. It wasn't very bright, either. From the look on Jason

Wells's face it was clear that this love rocket was already launched; too late to change its course now.

And she wouldn't even if she could, she told herself firmly. "So, what can I do for you, Sherlock?"

"I got an interesting gift basket from here yesterday. I'm thinking you might know who's responsible for it." He looked past her shoulder and nodded in the direction of the workroom. "Would the person who sent it be back there by any chance?"

She hadn't even made his list of gift basket suspects. That sucked. She forced her smile to stay put. "Sorry, Bobbi's running some errands right now, but she should be back in an hour."

He grinned and gave the counter a little thump. "I'll be back."

He was just turning to go when the door flew open and in blew Bobbi, looking adorable in jeans, a pink sweater, and a red leather jacket. Her face flushed at the sight of him, and she lifted her carefully highlighted hair off her neck as if she was suddenly hot. "Well, hi."

"Hi," he said.

The way they were looking at each other, Hope felt like she was watching a movie. She was painfully present, but not part of the scene. *You love romances,* she reminded herself.

"I got a cool basket," Jason said to Bobbi. "Did you have something to do with that?"

Bobbi smiled. She was the queen of the flirty smile.

Hope decided she had to clean up her work area. She slipped into her workroom, turned on the radio, and began sweeping bits of stems and ribbon off the counter into the garbage, trying to ignore the burble of voices drifting in past the old, velvet curtains.

Bobbi laughed. What had he said to make her laugh?

Oh, what did she care? She plopped down on her work stool and scowled at the row of ribbons hanging in front of her. Pinks, greens, and reds, fat ribbon, skinny ribbon, ribbon so delicate it looked like butterfly wings—so many colors, so many ways to add the perfect finishing touches to her floral arrangements.

She sighed. She was human ribbon, tying up her sister's love life with a pretty bow. Well, why not? Making things beautiful was what she did. She pulled on an end of pink ribbon and twisted it into a tight knot.

The bell over the shop door jangled and a moment later Bobbi was dancing into the workroom. "He loved the basket. And the card." Bobbi hugged Hope. "You're a genius!"

"Yes, I am."

Bobbi pulled away and began playing with one of the ribbons. "We've got a date. We're going out to lunch next week at the Family Inn."

"Great," Hope said encouragingly, concentrating on the corsage she was making.

Bobbi was suddenly quiet. That wasn't normal.

Hope looked up to see her sister gnawing on her lower lip. "Okay, what's wrong?"

"I didn't tell him why I couldn't go out for dinner."

"He's going to find out what you do for a living eventually."

"I know, but meanwhile . . . He, um, thinks I work here."

"Well, you've sure been doing a lot of work the last couple of days. That qualifies." Why was Bobbi looking so guilty?

"He thinks we own this shop together." Bobbi looked at her like she was bracing for Hope to wrap one of the ribbons around her neck.

"What?"

"Please don't be mad. I couldn't tell him I'm a cocktail waitress. I mean, he runs a construction company."

"Oh, for crying out loud," said Hope.

"He runs a company. I just serve booze. I know it was wrong, but I didn't want him to think I'm a nobody."

"You're not a nobody," Hope insisted. "You're gorgeous and creative."

"But I'm not like you. You're smart. You own your own business."

Hope shook her head. "If I had to pick between you and me, I'd pick you in a heartbeat."

"Well, that's because you're nuts."

"What's the point of dating someone if you don't let him know who you really are?" Hope argued.

"I will," Bobbi said. "As soon as he gets to know me better. So, can we please, for a little while, let him think I'm somebody?"

The candy bar, the man, the shop—with sisters it was always about sharing. But this flower shop was Hope's baby. She wasn't sure she wanted to share her baby.

Hmmm. The drives to chemo, the concern, the help—yes, with sisters it was all about sharing. There was nothing wrong with Hope's baby having more than one mommy. She'd already put words in her sister's mouth. Might as well put a feather in her cap, too.

"You are somebody," she told Bobbi, "but if you need this shop to prove it, that's okay."

"Oh, thank you," Bobbi gushed, and hugged her again. "You're the best sister in the whole world."

Not really, but she wanted to be.

And she kept reminding herself of that as she moved through the rest of her day, as she drove home, as she entered her apartment. She'd made it cozy, filling it with books, plants, souvenirs from trips to Ocean Shores, and framed photos she'd taken on hikes in the Cascades. But it was still lacking something. Testosterone.

Never mind that, she told herself and got busy with her juicer making a Hope Walker Cancer

Shield Cocktail, something she'd have started taking a lot earlier if she'd known that a woman could get cancer in her twenties. Parsnips, beets, and wheatgrass—yum, yum.

Blech. She plopped down at her vintage yellow Formica table and opened up the night's issue of *The Heart Lake Herald*. She idly flipped through the pages and suddenly found herself staring at the pictures of newly engaged, smiling couples. How soon till Jason and Bobbi were there?

The features of one of the women on the page suddenly morphed into Bobbi's face. She stuck out her tongue at Hope and taunted, "Nah, nah, nah, nah, nah."

Hope shook her head to clear it and quickly turned the page. "I'm a sick puppy," she scolded herself, "the hogweed queen." Maybe she needed therapy.

And then, like a gift from the flower gods, she found it. Garden therapy. She'd call first thing Monday and reserve a plot at the community garden.

FIVE

*T*he Heart Lake Park and Recreation offices opened at nine A.M., Monday through Friday. At exactly 8:50 A.M. on Friday, Millie Baldwin climbed into her Buick LeSabre to go stake her claim on a garden plot.

She was pleased with her new car, a nice solid used model. "Pre-owned" was the term the car salesman had used. How silly! As if she didn't know what that meant. But it would do her just fine. It should certainly last for the rest of her life. Debra had worried that it was a gas-guzzler. And she didn't see the need for it. Not, she said, when she had a perfectly good car and could take her mother anywhere she needed to go.

"She actually said that?" Millie's friend Alice had asked when Millie repeated their conversation. "Does she think you're in your dotage?"

Apparently. But Millie had shown Debra other-wise. One of the first things she'd done when she arrived in Heart Lake had been to insist her daughter drive her right to the nearest car lot so she could get some safe, dependable transportation.

"I think she was worried I couldn't afford it," Millie had said.

As if Debra was the mother and Millie the child. Really, who was here in Heart Lake to help whom? Millie hadn't come out of Duncan's medical debacle with much, but she had something. And she had been managing money long before her daughter was born. She was going to have her own car and drive it, and she was going to have a life of her own, and a garden of her own, thank you very much.

She smiled as the park came into sight. This was a lovely park. She could easily picture herself spending mornings in a small corner of it among a cozy patch of flowers.

Grandview Park not only offered a peekaboo view of the lake, it came with a view of the Cascade Mountains. Forty acres of land, it had been put to good use, and now the community enjoyed a soccer field, a broad walking path that followed the circumference of the park, a play area for children, tennis courts, a sand volleyball court, and a section of small plots for would-be gardeners.

Just past the entrance sat two small houses, side by side, both painted blue and trimmed with yellow shutters and window boxes filled with plastic geraniums. One belonged to the groundskeeper; the other housed the offices of the Heart Lake Park and Recreational Department. Out front a few angled parking spaces had been reserved for visitors.

Every parking space was full except for one. She hoped all those cars didn't represent people wanting a garden plot.

She had already pulled into the space when she noticed the faded paint that proclaimed it a handicapped parking spot. No wonder there had been so much room. There was nothing for it but to back up and find another spot.

She put the car in reverse, turned the wheel, and started to back up. And suddenly crashed into something unyielding. This couldn't be good.

She let down the window and peered out. Oh, dear, just as she suspected. She had just managed to back into another car. *Millie, you fool!*

She put a hand to her chest to still her fluttering heart and took a deep breath. Calm down, she told herself. In the eternal scheme of things this was nothing.

But this nothing had certainly shaken her up. Well, it served her right. Haste makes waste, and she had been in a hurry to get in and sign up for her garden plot.

She turned off the engine with a shaky hand and got out of her car to inspect the damage. She had managed to effectively crunch both cars. Two for the price of one, as Duncan would have said. Oh, dear. This probably wouldn't be good for her insurance. She could almost hear her daughter pointing that out.

Well, there was nothing for it but to go and see whom she had hit. The sky was blue, but Millie walked into the Park and Recreation offices under a black cloud.

The office was cheery, paneled in pine and smelling of fresh air, thanks to the open windows. Colorful posters and fliers hung on a bulletin board on one wall announcing various community events. Three women sat at desks in a work area behind a long counter, each desk decorated with family pictures and flowers. The long counter held a pile of catalogs for spring classes and community activities, a little bowl of candy, and a pot full of silk flower–tipped pens for people to use. A burble of voices made for welcoming background noise as people waited to register for various classes. A couple of middle-aged women stood chatting over by the bulletin board. At the counter, a young woman wearing jeans and a sweatshirt was conducting business with one of the employees. At her side, a freckle-faced little boy who looked about four hung from the counter, regarding the room as if searching for something to interest him.

So many witnesses—oh, this was embarrassing. Millie cleared her throat. "Excuse me? Does anyone own a white car, rather small? It's parked outside in one of the parking spots."

The two middle-aged women regarded her blankly. The clerk at the counter shook her head and looked sympathetically at Millie as if she somehow knew Millie had a problem.

The younger woman turned around. "A Honda?"

Millie experienced a sudden sinking feeling in her stomach. Not the young mother, please. She probably couldn't afford to be without transportation while her car was getting the dent ironed out.

"I'm not sure about the make," Millie said, "but it's the only white car out there.

"It's mine then," said the woman.

Millie took a deep breath. "I'm terribly sorry, but I'm afraid I've hit it."

The young woman's questioning smile dissolved. She looked like she was experiencing the same sinking feeling Millie had felt out in the parking lot.

"I'm so sorry. Naturally I'll pay for all repairs. I do have insurance," Millie assured her.

"Hey, it could happen to anyone," the woman assured her back. "And the way my luck's been running, I'm not even remotely surprised it happened to me," she muttered, which made Millie feel even worse.

"I think it would be best if we called the police," Millie suggested. "I don't have a cell phone," she told the clerk. She'd always been so proud of the fact that she didn't own one, but right now, not owning the gadget only added to Millie's humiliation.

The clerk smiled kindly at her. "Not a problem. Jean," she said to one of the secretaries manning a desk, "can you ask Tom to send someone out here?"

The secretary nodded and got on the phone.

"Maybe I'd better look at it," the young woman decided. She left the office for the parking lot, the little boy holding her hand and skipping along beside her. Not knowing what else to do, Millie followed them out.

"What happened, Mommy?" the child asked when they reached the cars.

"Just a little boo-boo, Sethie," she said. "It can be fixed," she added, finding a smile for Millie.

"I feel just terrible," Millie told her.

"Don't," said the woman. "I can think of worse places to have an accident."

"Well, thank you," Millie said.

"Mommy, I'm hungry," said the boy.

"I'd love to buy you something to eat as soon as we get this mess squared away," Millie said.

"Oh, you don't need to do that," she said, shaking her head. She was a pretty thing, with long brown hair and big brown eyes. "Like I said, it could happen to anyone."

"Only if they were being careless," Millie said, disgusted with herself all over again. "I was in a big hurry to come in and reserve a garden plot."

"Are you a gardener?" The woman's look turned both speculative and hopeful.

"I am," said Millie.

"I just reserved a plot. We're going to grow our own food, aren't we, Seth?"

The woman said it with such determination Millie had to smile. Ah, the dreams and anticipation that went into planning a garden.

The little boy broke into a grin and nodded. "We're gonna grow punkins for Halloween."

His hair was a lighter brown than his mother's, almost blond. He reminded Millie of her son Duncan Jr. when he was little. "That sounds pretty special," she said to the child.

"They still have several plots left," the woman told her. "Would you like to sign up for one while you're waiting?"

"All right." It was, after all, what she'd come here for. If only she hadn't had that stupid accident and taken the shine off the morning.

"Are you a good gardener?" the woman asked as they walked back to the office.

Millie couldn't remember a time when she hadn't gardened. The sunspots on her hands were like little merit badges. "I certainly have done a lot of it."

"I'm afraid I'm not very good," confessed the woman.

"Maybe I can give you some gardening tips," Millie offered.

The woman nodded. "Thanks. Can you put her next to me?" she asked the clerk as Millie reserved her plot.

"Sure."

"Hello, neighbor," said Millie, offering her hand. "My name is Millie Baldwin. I'm new to the area."

The woman smiled, and this time some of that smile crept into her eyes. "I'm Amber Howell. I'm still new here, too. I work at the bakery."

"Ah. Perhaps I could buy you and your son a treat there."

"I want a treat," piped the child, jumping up and down.

Little boys didn't like to sit still at bakeries while grown-ups talked. "Perhaps we could buy something there and then visit that little lakefront park," Millie suggested.

71

"I want to go to the park." Now the boy was really bouncing.

"I guess that settles it," said Amber, just as a young man in a blue police uniform walked into the office.

It was embarrassing having to explain to the officer how she had managed to bang into poor Amber's car, but he was very respectful. And helpful. He even moved Millie's car for her, saving both vehicles from further damage.

As if sensing Millie was still shaken, Amber offered to drive to their picnic. So they left Millie's car behind, made a stop at the bakery for three bottles of pomegranate juice and half a dozen oatmeal cookies, then went to the park where they enjoyed the sunshine and watched Seth play on the slide.

"What brought you to Washington?" Amber asked.

"My daughter lives here. I moved out to help her."

"Lucky her," Amber said wistfully. "I left my mom in northern California."

It was always hard for a woman to leave her family. Millie felt a strong tug on her heart. "How did you end up here?" she asked, shading her eyes from the sun.

"My husband came up for a job. He's a chef. But the restaurant went belly-up." Amber shrugged. "We found a little place on the lake to rent. A friend of a friend kind of thing."

"Has your husband found a new job?" Millie asked.

Amber's face tightened and Millie could feel the anger bouncing off her. "No."

"I'm sure he will."

"Until he does, we've got my part-time job at the bakery, and cheap rent. And growing our own food should save us some money on groceries."

Millie thought of all the money she'd spent over the years on her gardens and wisely kept her mouth shut.

"So, we'll see you at the garden next month," Amber said an hour later, as she returned Millie to her car.

"Sooner than that," said Millie. "You'll want to fertilize before you plant, get your soil ready."

"Oh."

"Chicken manure works well. Just spread it around, get a shovel, and turn it under," said Millie.

"Chicken manure," repeated Amber. "Just spread it around."

"And turn it under." Millie gave her arm a pat. "You'll be an expert gardener in no time. You'll see."

"Obviously, I need help. With everything," Amber added, frowning. She forced the corners of her mouth back up. "But, hey, things are already looking up. I've got my own garden guru now. I have a feeling my luck is going to change."

"Luck is a lot like the weather this time of year," Millie said, giving Amber an encouraging smile. "It changes often."

Amber nodded. "Thanks. I like you."

"I like you, too," Millie said.

Things had certainly changed for her today, she thought as she drove home. She had started with manure, but out of that had grown hope for new friendship.

Amber returned home to find her husband, Ty, right where she'd left him, his wiry frame sprawled on a chair in their tiny living room in front of the TV as he watched Judge Judy let some hapless fool in her courtroom have it. Ty's chin was still thickly stubbled. He hadn't even bothered to shave yet, and that bothered her even more than the fact that he was parked in front of the TV.

Seth ran over and climbed in his lap. "We got a garden. We're gonna grow punkins. And carrots. Mommy said."

"All right, bud." Ty gave his son's hair a distracted rumpling.

"And I saw a policeman."

That got Ty's attention. "A policeman?" He looked questioningly at Amber.

"And Millie took us to the park," Seth continued.

"Who's Millie?" he asked Amber.

"A woman I met when we went to sign up for our garden plot. She backed into our car."

"What next?" muttered Ty. He grabbed his coat and started for the door to inspect the damage.

"It's not bad," Amber said, following him. "You can still drop off applications."

"Thanks," he said cynically, making her wish she'd bit her lip. Nagging didn't help. It only made him defensive.

Outside, he inspected the back of the car and shook his head in disgust. "Great, just great."

"It could have been worse," Amber offered.

"Yeah?" His voice was tinged with bitterness.

"Yeah. Geez, Ty. Seth and I could have been on the road. We could have been hurt. There are worse things than losing your job, you know."

He scowled. "Thanks for the reminder." He took the keys out of his coat pocket and opened the car door.

"Where are you going?" she demanded.

"To look for a job," he snapped.

He started the engine and she stepped away from the car. "Good idea. If anyone is looking for a depressed, grumpy man who needs a shave you're a shoo-in," she said as he drove off.

She doubted he'd go look for job. It seemed these days all he wanted to do was sit around and mourn the fact that they were broke and going nowhere. Getting to this dead end had started as a team effort. She'd gone along with the dream to own a restaurant. She'd signed those loan papers, too. But, when things had started to sour, the team had dissolved. He turned a deaf ear to her pleas that they try to find a buyer and get out before they got completely burned. Instead, he'd put his dream before her fears. He never saw it that way. He kept telling her she was worrying for nothing.

And nothing was what they wound up with. Ty's confidence and hard work hadn't been enough to save them from disaster. They lost the money their parents had invested and they had to sell their house to pay off their SBA loan. Their first home. Maybe their only home.

Now they were racing toward forty and broke. Failures. At least that was how Ty saw it. And he couldn't get far enough away from everyone who had witnessed the whole ugly mess. The job in Seattle had provided the perfect escape. But then it dried up, and they moved further north. At the rate they were going they'd end up in blippin' Alaska. And at the rate their sex life was going, Seth would be an only child.

At least she had her job at Sweet Somethings, the bakery at the center of town. She hoped someday she'd be baking there, but for now she was just making lattes and ringing up customers. Still, she loved her job. Everyone who came into the place was happy. It felt like a good sign. Even though she was new to Heart Lake, Amber could already tell it was a great community.

And she loved this run-down summer cabin that they'd found to rent. It had been a steal. Right on the water, it was practically encased in sticker bushes, but it had a little porch to sit on and enjoy the view. Watching that water with its changing moods somehow comforted her, especially on a day like this, with the promising spring sun spreading a bright sheen on the water. Given time, she could be happy here. Maybe that wouldn't be with Ty, though, not the way things were going between them.

"Things will work out," her mother kept assuring her.

Things needed to start working out pretty soon or she was going to whack a certain chef with her rolling pin.

Millie's sunny mood lasted until afternoon when her grandchildren came home from school. Like gray clouds on the horizon, they told her it wouldn't be long before a storm arrived.

"Gram, someone creamed your car," Eric informed her as he dropped his backpack on the living room floor.

Millie looked up from her crossword puzzle. "I know, dear. It's all taken care of."

"They sure did a number on it," he observed, and headed for the kitchen.

They sure did.

"Gram, what happened to your car?" Emily asked when she got home.

"I had a little accident," Millie said, and continued calmly peeling carrots.

"Are you okay? Did you get whiplash or anything?"

"No. I'm fine." Exhausted from all the excitement, but at her age that was to be expected.

"You should sue," said Emily. She planted a kiss on Millie's cheek and peered over her shoulder. "What are you making?"

"Carrot cookies," said Millie. Debra had loved carrot cookies.

Emily made a face. "Gross."

Before Millie could assure her that carrot cookies were far from gross, Emily's phone rang, effectively ending their conversation. "No way," Emily gushed into the phone. "Oh my gosh! Shut up." And with that she was gone.

Debra had a little more to say, however. They sat at the table after dinner. The plate of cookies lay untouched between them. "Maybe you shouldn't be driving."

"It could have happened to anyone," Millie insisted. "In fact, most accidents happen in parking lots." She was sure she'd read that somewhere. She hoped Debra didn't ask her where.

Debra heaved a long-suffering sigh. "Mom. There comes a time . . ."

"Well, it hasn't come yet," Millie, said, cutting her off. "I'm only seventy-six."

"Seventy-seven in June," Debra reminded her.

"By today's standards, that's not old."

"Mom, I don't want you getting hurt. Anyway, I

still don't get why you need a car during the day. There are plenty of things you can do here."

Millie frowned. "Is that what you envisioned when you invited me to come stay with you, that I would simply rattle around here alone all day, with no life of my own?"

"You have a life, with us. And the bus stops right down on the corner. If you want to go somewhere, you can take that. Or I can drive you."

"I am perfectly capable of driving a car," Millie said irritably.

"Perfectly capable of wrecking a car," her daughter muttered. "Geez, Mom. Quit while you're ahead. I'll put the car up for sale on craigslist."

"You will do no such thing," Millie said. She took her cup and saucer to the dishwasher. "You don't need to worry about me. I can take care of myself just fine. And now, if you'll excuse me, I'm going to go read my book." She marched from the kitchen, enjoying the satisfaction of having gotten in the last word.

But that satisfaction quickly wore off. Was she that bad a driver? Surely not. She'd never had so much as a ticket.

She made it to her bedroom with her dignity intact, but dignity was highly overrated. "Really, Millie," she said to herself, "here you are pouting in your room like a twelve-year-old girl." It was very immature.

No, no. Immature was behaving in a way that

was completely unjustifiable. Her anger had certainly been justified. Too old to drive. Humph. What would she be too old for next?

She didn't want to think about it, didn't want to think about how a woman's life became a series of shutting doors as she got older. She leaned on the antique dresser that had once resided in Debra's room when she was a girl and regarded the wrinkled woman staring back at her. "I'm not too old," she told the woman in the mirror. That old face was the outside Millie, the casing. The inside Millie was still thirty, and the inside Millie wasn't ready for a rocking chair yet. She had lots of good years left in her, and she intended to make the most of them. Debra could pretend they had reversed their roles all she wanted, but Millie didn't need a mother yet. She was going to have her car, her garden, and her new life.

SIX

*B*obbi arrived at the Family Inn for her lunch date with Jason dressed to kill. She was wearing her favorite top, the black one that showed a hint of cleavage, her short denim skirt, and her Ugg boots. And she'd accessorized with a red denim hobo purse. She'd drenched herself in Vera Wang Princess, her perfume du jour. Before lunch was over Jason Wells would be madly in love with her.

She smiled in anticipation. She had finally found her perfect man. He was hunkalicious, he was kind—ordering flowers for his sis, how sweet—and he was in construction, which meant he would know how to fix anything, a skill that would come in handy when she finally had a house. Heck, it would come in handy now considering how long it took the apartment manager to get around to fixing things. All that remained was to find out if Jason liked kids (which she was sure he must since what kind of man could be so sweet and not like kids?) and if he liked to dance. She simply couldn't be with a man who didn't dance.

She found him waiting in the reception area, looking at the collection of pictures of various families who had frequented the restaurant over the years. They ranged from black and white—showing men in Ward Cleaver suits and women in hats, their children dressed up in their Sunday best—to glossy color photos of people sporting more casual wear like jeans and polo shirts. The food here was far from five star, but it was okay and the price was right. And that was important. If she'd suggested the Two Turtledoves, he'd have died of sticker shock. She didn't want to give the impression that she was high-maintenance.

He turned and his eyes lit up at the sight of her. She had that effect on men. Still, she always seemed to find herself stuck with losers. Not this time though. She knew Jason Wells was a keeper.

And she was going to keep him no matter what it took.

"You look incredible," he said.

And you are incredible, she thought.

"Wells?" called the hostess.

Jason cupped Bobbi's elbow and stepped them forward.

The hostess looked at him appreciatively before leading them past a smattering of retired couples and local workers taking a lunch break to a window table with a view of thick shrubs and bushes, and beyond that, a duck pond.

The best view was sitting right here in front of Bobbi. Jason's Chaps shirt hung open over a blue T-shirt that draped perfect pecs. Yummy.

"You know, the guys are still talking about that basket," he said. "You're pretty damned clever."

She tried to look humble.

"You've got flair. Were you an art major in college?"

College? Which one? She'd done a quarter at Mount Vista Junior College where she'd flunked Math Skills and Science 101, gotten two marriage proposals, and broke her drama prof's nose fighting him off one night back in the costume room. After that, she'd decided she'd rather be a drama queen than take drama. She'd managed a semester's worth of classes at the Northwest Business College where she half mastered typing and flunked her filing test. Who flunked a filing test? Her, of course. She'd always had a fear of testing.

"I should have been an art major," she decided. Why hadn't she thought of that? It wasn't too late to go back to school, but did she really want to study about dead artists who painted cherubs on church ceilings?

Home decorating! She liked making things look pretty. Maybe she should go to school and become an interior decorator. Or sell pretty house things on the home party plan. She loved parties. She could probably make a fortune. And, if she did home parties, she wouldn't have to dodge overly friendly men who were always wanting to grab her butt.

"So, how'd you end up with a flower shop?" Jason wanted to know.

Um. "It was a good thing to do with my sister," she said, thinking fast.

"I'll bet you two have a great time together."

"We do. She's awesome," Bobbi said. "She's always been there for me." She still was.

The waitress came and gave them their menus.

Jason opened his. "What's good on the menu?" he asked the waitress.

"Not much," Bobbi answered, making her frown. "But you can't go wrong with the pizza."

"Okay, pizza it is," Jason decided. "We'll order now. What do you like on yours?" he asked Bobbi.

"Anything but anchovies."

He grinned and ordered a deluxe large and two Cokes. "And we'll do the salad bar," he added, smiling at Bobbi.

Wow, it was like he knew without even asking her. "How did you know?"

"You don't exactly look like the kind of woman who pigs out on pizza." He shrugged. "But I guess I could have been wrong. When I first saw you, you didn't strike me as the kind of woman who'd be into poetry."

"I'm no expert," she said, stretching the truth till it snapped.

She had never in her life, of her own volition, picked up a book of poems. Maybe if she'd been paying less attention to Gregory Wilson in the ninth grade and more attention to her English teacher, she would have developed a taste for that stuff. But she doubted it. Who wanted to read about love when you could live it?

"I'm not much of an expert myself," said Jason. "But I've got my favorites."

He did? What guy liked poetry, anyway? If he was trying to impress her, he could stop now. She suddenly felt fidgety. They were creeping onto dangerous ground here. If she asked him who his favorite poet was, he was bound to ask hers. If she didn't ask, he might think she wasn't interested in him. What to do?

When it came to men, Bobbi's mind was a computer. She inputted her questions and concerns and the answer quickly came back: look interested. Ask him something about poems.

"So, what's your favorite poem?"

"I like a lot of stuff. I really like Robert Service," he said.

"Who?" *Way to sound dumb, Stupid.*

Jason smiled. Her ignorance had amused him. Whew, that was a close one.

"He wrote about life in the Yukon. His most famous poem is 'The Cremation of Sam McGee.' Ever hear of it?"

"Eeew. No." He wasn't going to quote it to her right before they were about to eat, was he?

"Actually, it was a funny poem. I'll tell it to you sometime."

"Like about a hundred years after we've eaten." Before he could ask her who her favorite poet was she stood up, saying, "Let's check out the salad bar."

Now they were done with the subject of poets and they could move on to more fun topics, like TV shows and movies and what they each liked to do for fun.

But oh, no. As they moved along, spooning lettuce and olives and baby corn cobs onto their plates, he picked up the conversation again. "My dad turned me onto Robert Service. I think he figured it would be a good way to whet my appetite. Mom's an English prof and she insisted my brother and I be well rounded, so even though we'd rather have watched football or worked with Dad on construction sites, she forced us to do unguy things, like read poetry and go to musicals. I was even in one once."

"Only once?" He was so good looking he could have been on Broadway. Or at least *American Idol*.

He shook his head. "Once was enough. I sucked. Anyway, sports took most of my time."

Oh, Lord. She hoped he didn't like outdoor sports like hiking. She decided not to ask. Instead, she said, "I like musicals. My favorite is *Phantom of the Opera*; I loved that movie." The phantom had been so sexy. She'd never been able to understand what what's-her-name saw in the wimpy hero when she had that big, bad boy panting after her.

No wonder you end up with losers. You always like bad boys, even in movies.

But no more. She was getting smart and picking smart.

"Most women like the Phantom," he said. "Hard to understand why though. I think it must be the mask."

She smiled. "Women like secrets."

"So do men." He gave her a look that just about set her on fire. "I found out what those flowers stand for."

The acacia. She'd already forgotten. She'd been more into the food goodies that went into the basket. *Pleeeease don't ask me to tell you if you're right.* If he did, she'd run to the bathroom and call Hope.

But he didn't ask her. He did something worse. He brought them back to a subject she thought they were done with. "That was an awesome message on the card. I'm always impressed by people who can do cool things with words. You're quite a poet."

"Oh, not really," Bobbi said, frantically searching her brain for a new topic.

"So, got a favorite?"

"Oh . . ." *Crap.* Her mind was a blank. What kind of guy asked questions like this? Oh, yeah. One who wanted to know more about her, who wasn't a bad boy, one who was perfect. *You have got to impress this man.* She felt her blood pounding in her ears, heating her neck and cheeks.

She should tell him the truth right now, tell him all about how she hadn't paid attention in English class, how she'd jumped from school to school and job to job trying to decide what she wanted to be when she grew up. She should ask him to educate her, teach her to appreciate poetry. And math. Maybe he could teach her how to balance her checkbook.

He was looking at her, waiting for an answer. She tried to pull up some poet's name from her mental computer, but this was hard considering the fact that she had never programmed her computer with this sort of information. She'd never needed it. *Come on, give me something.*

She blurted out the first name that came to mind. "Jane Austen."

His eyes widened in surprise. Uh-oh. Wrong answer.

"I didn't know she wrote poems. You learn something new every day."

"Yeah, you do," Bobbi agreed, all the while hoping that Jane Austen, whoever she was, wrote poems. Why had that name come to mind? Where had she heard of Jane Austen? Somewhere.

Too late to retrieve her misstep now. And he was on to new conversational territory. "I'll bet you're into all those movies they made out of her books."

Of course. Now she remembered, Jane Austen wrote books. Hope loved her books. Well, old Jane probably wrote poems, too. Those writers were always scribbling something.

"My sister is big into those movies," Jason was saying. "She and my mom tried to make me watch one once. Too slow for me. I couldn't keep track of what was going on. I'm more of a *Die Hard* man."

Finally, something she knew. "Me, too," she agreed, leaning forward. "Didn't you love the last one?"

"Oh, yeah." Jason was leaning forward now, too. "I like action."

She knew they had a ton in common. At last they'd found it. "Me, too."

He cocked his head and studied her.

"What?" she prompted.

"I've never met anyone quite like you. You're beautiful, talented, smart—just too good to be true."

"That's me," she said lightly, and vowed to work on getting smart as soon as she found her library card.

After lunch with Bobbi Walker, Jason went to see how things were going at the site of the two duplexes A-1 Construction was building on the outskirts of town. Duke Powers, his right-hand man, looked up from his clipboard and greeted Jason with a jealous smirk. "So, how was it?"

"Great. Did you get ahold of Barrett? Are they delivering the rest of those two-by-fours today or not?"

Duke frowned. "Not. He claims they're short on guys."

"The only thing those clowns are short on is brains," said Jason, disgusted.

"Speaking of brains, what's the verdict?"

Jason smiled. "This one's got 'em."

"So, it looks like you've finally graduated from bimbos," said Duke. "Think you can bring this one home to Mom and Dad?"

"Oh, yeah." This woman had keeper written all over her. She was perfect: easy on the eyes just like her sister, fun, and off-the-charts smart. And obviously the driving force behind the flower shop.

"Hey, if things don't work out and she wants a real man . . ."

Jason looked around. "Where? Anyway, there's no way I'm introducing her to you. She'll take one look at you, see what kind of friends I have, and dump me before we can even have a second date."

"Which I'll bet you already set up."

Jason smiled. "Sunday."

"Sunday? What's wrong with Saturday night? Does she turn into a werewolf or something?"

"Sunday night is some kind of dancing at the Grange Hall."

"Dancing? Since when do you dance?"

"Since now."

Duke shook his head. "A hot chick going out with a klutz foot like you. Man, what a waste."

"She doesn't think so."

"And that makes me think this chick isn't as smart as you think she is," Duke said with a grin.

SEVEN

*E*aster weekend had been soppy, so Amber opted out on the annual egg hunt at Grandview Park, instead giving Seth as elaborate a hunt as she could manage inside their tiny, two-bedroom cabin. Ty had taken the car in to get fixed on Monday, then it had rained again Tuesday and Wednesday, leaving her with a housebound and increasingly cranky little boy.

But this was Thursday, she didn't have to work, and Heart Lake was getting a sun break. It was the perfect day to deal with poop—the garden variety, not what she was dealing with at home. So, she and Seth began their garden adventure with a visit to the Trellis, the town's nursery and one of its oldest businesses.

There was something calming about walking past all those bushes and trees, flats of flowers, and little fountains. A woman could find anything she wanted here, maybe even peace of mind. It was run by the Nakata family, old-time lake residents. In addition to carrying every plant, shrub, and tree known to man, it offered garden art, tools, and soil preparations.

One corner of the shop even offered unique home interior decorations and kitchenware. Amber eyed the yellow polka dot dish setting displayed on a glass patio table with a lustful eye. She would love to have a set of dishes like that. And the patio table. It would have all gone so nicely on their front porch. That house had great potential for entertaining. For a moment, she closed her eyes and envisioned herself as the Rachael Ray of Heart Lake, whipping up meals in minutes for happy guests. No point going there, not yet anyway. She first had to find a way to turn her house into a happy place before she could think about making company happy. *First things first. Tackle the garden.*

"Mommy, look," cried Seth, kneeling in front of a big, stone cat. "Can we have this in our garden?"

She looked at the price sticker. "Not today, Sethie. If we can't use it to grow something to eat, we're not getting it." She spotted a line of little, red wagons and got one for him. "But here. You can pull the wagon for our seeds and things. Okay?"

That satisfied him. Now, if only there was a grown-up version of that red wagon for her. She got another wagon so she could carry their heavier purchases, then, averting her gaze from the plates, she led her son off in search of fertilizer.

It didn't take long to find the rest of the things she needed to become a gardener. It didn't take long to rack up a bill, either. Amber watched the mounting total as the clerk rang up her purchases and tried not to panic: garden gloves, seeds, chicken manure, and two spades—one for her and one for Seth. Yikes! It sure cost a lot of money to save money on food. At least she already had a shovel in her car trunk. It was a rusty old thing that she'd found in the shed behind the house, but it would do fine for working fertilizer into the ground.

As she handed over her charge card, she reminded herself what a good thing this garden was going to be. Fresh air, organic food, something fun to do with Seth—it was all good. And it was better than hanging around the house watching Ty mope in front of the TV. He'd had two interviews in the last couple of days, but neither one had netted a job offer.

She let Seth carry his spade and he bounced ahead of her as they made their way back to the car, singsonging, "We're gonna garden, we're gonna garden."

This will be fun, she told herself, trying to work up to her son's level of enthusiasm. But it wasn't fun, really. The fertilizer bags were heavy and a real pain to haul to their garden plot. And the stuff was stinky. She got some of it in her tennis shoe while dumping it out. Ick! And, good grief, who'd have thought it was such hard work shoveling dirt? The earlier rains had made the ground sodden, and it felt like she was shoveling cement. It wasn't work for Seth. He was having a great time using his new spade to fling soil and manure everywhere.

Just when she thought it couldn't get any better—ha, ha—a fat raindrop hit her nose. Where had the blue sky gone? She looked up. Gray clouds had eaten every scrap of it. And she was only half done. "We'd better hurry," she told Seth.

Taking her at her word, he began to toss spadefuls of dirt in the air. The rain was really coming down now and the dirt was turning to slop. Suddenly, something splattered the side of her head, getting in her hair and on her face. *Oh, please don't let this be what I think it is.* But she knew, even before she put a hand to her cheek, she knew.

"Iiiick," she cried and dropped her shovel. "Ick!" She began dancing around, shaking her head, swatting at her manure-mud-coated curls.

Seth thought she was doing this for his entertainment and began to laugh, going into a Tasmanian devil frenzy, flinging glop every which way.

"Enough, Sethie," she cried, grabbing his hand and stopping him. "This is gross. It's time to go home."

"No," protested Seth, his voice suddenly tearful.

"Yes. It's raining and Mommy is all icky. We'll come back."

In about a million years. People did this for a hobby? People actually thought it was fun to get dirty and stinky like this? At the car, she loaded up the shovel and spades and threw the floral-print gardening gloves into the trunk after them. The pouring rain pelted her and she could feel drips from her hair trickling a river of polluted dirt down her neck. *Ick, ick, ick!*

This was insane and she was going to stop the insanity now. She would see if she could get some more hours at the bakery, or she'd make cookies and sell them at the farmer's market and use the extra money for groceries. But the garden thing was not happening. It was not her. If people had been meant to grow their own vegetables, there'd be no such thing as a produce department.

"I don't want to leave," Seth whined as she climbed behind the wheel.

"Mommy needs a bath," Amber said. *Mommy needs Prozac.*

The car smelled like poop, thanks to her garden hair treatment, making the enclosed space torture. Even though she knew she'd get blasted with cold air and rain, she let down her window. If she didn't get fresh air in this car, she was going to throw up.

The air didn't help. Knowing what was in her hair was making her want to throw up, anyway. A shower, a nice warm, clean shower would be Nirvana. It was all she could do not to speed as they drove along Lake Drive.

"Can we go tomorrow?" asked Seth.

His cheeks were rosy. He looked so cute in his yellow rubber boots. She felt like a rat for not wanting to ever see that stupid garden again. "We'll see," she said. "Here, let's listen to your Veggie Tales songs." She put in the CD to distract him. Now, if only she could find something to distract her. *Shower, shower, shower.* Darn, it was hard to drown out singing tomatoes and cucumbers.

They got back and Seth ran ahead of her into the house. Ty was already making lunch for them. It was something he'd started doing on the days she worked, and the part-time lunch service evolved into an everyday offering. It was one of the few things he did that showed her somewhere, deep inside, he hadn't lost hope, that he wasn't completely ready to give up on life. On them.

He sent Seth to his room to peel off his muddy

clothes. Then he took one look at Amber and his eyes got saucer sized. "Whoa. New look?"

Ha, ha. "I've got poop in my hair," she informed him, and kept on moving to the bathroom, pulling off her jacket as she went.

Ty followed her in. "What happened?"

"We were shoveling in the chicken manure. Seth got carried away. I hate gardening!" She pulled off her sweatshirt. "And I spent a ton of money just to get the stupid, damned, stinky poop for the garden and stupid, damned stinky garden gloves and the stupid, damned stinky seeds. And I'm not saving any money," she finished on a wail.

"Hey, at least you're doing something."

She felt Ty's hand on her shoulder. Next thing she knew he was pulling her to him to comfort her—something he hadn't done since those early days when they first saw trouble looming outside their little restaurant.

It made her cry all the harder, for what they'd had and lost, for where they were now.

"It's okay," he said. "Forget the garden. You're doing enough anyway."

"Mommy?" Seth stood in the doorway, stripped down to his Spider-Man underwear, his round little face tight with worry.

She and Ty pulled apart like they'd been caught doing something wrong. "It's okay, sweetie," she said to Seth. "Go let Daddy feed you lunch while Mommy takes a shower. Okay?"

"Come on, bud," Ty said, steering Seth out of the room.

She piled her dirty clothes on the bathroom floor and charged into the shower. After three doses of shampoo, she almost felt normal again. But normal these days wasn't necessarily that good. She toweled off, put on clean clothes, and joined the boys in the kitchen.

Ty had made panini with some day-old bread she'd brought home from the bakery. This particular sandwich was one of Ty's creations, and it was her all-time favorite sandwich—a panini with mozzarella, red onions, tomatoes, a dash of Dijon mustard, and some fresh basil. Well, almost fresh. She'd found it in the veggie bin on the back porch of Helpline, the local food bank, along with the tomatoes.

She sank her teeth in and felt instantly consoled. "This is great," she said.

"Thanks," he said.

Another bite restored her equilibrium. "I can't quit." She'd already invested in seeds and gardening tools and put down her deposit on the garden plot.

He cocked an eyebrow. "Sure you can. There's nothing wrong with quitting. Isn't that what you told me?"

The bit of sandwich she'd just swallowed stuck in her throat.

He got up, took his plate into the living room, and turned on the TV.

She followed him.

"Mommy?"

"Finish your food, sweetie," she said to Seth, keeping him anchored at the table.

She sat down on the couch opposite her husband, who was staring determinedly at the TV screen. "Are you comparing a garden to that restaurant?" she demanded, her voice low. *That restaurant.* Bad choice of words. She could see his jaw tighten.

"Don't start," he said.

"Mommy?" The lowered voices weren't fooling Seth.

This was pointless, anyway. She left the couch with a smile pasted on her face. "After lunch, we'll take a rest and then when we wake up we'll color. How does that sound?"

Seth smiled, obviously relieved, and nodded.

"Okay then," she said and smiled back at her son with false heartiness. Boy, had she gotten good at that.

Neither she nor her husband mentioned the garden again. Or quitting. Or much of anything. About two in the afternoon, Ty announced, "I'm going out."

She had the good sense not to ask if he was going to pick up applications. Wherever he went, she hoped he didn't use much gas. They had five dollars left till payday.

And she had a fortune in seeds sitting in her trunk. She thought of the old fairy tale about Jack and his beanstalk. Dumb kid, buying magic beans. But look what grew from those beans!

Her hair was coming out of her scrunchy. She pulled the thing out and made a fresh ponytail. She couldn't let her life keep getting away from her like this, she just couldn't.

She grabbed a pencil from the jar of pens and pencils she kept by the phone on the kitchen counter, then marched to the coffee table and picked up the yellow legal pad lying there. She plopped on the couch cross-legged and drew a big square. Over it she wrote: Amber's Garden. Then she began to plan.

EIGHT

*B*y one on Saturday afternoon, all of the Heart Lake High students had been in to pick up their flowers for the dance. Hope expected the afternoon to be relatively quiet, so she gave her sister a thank-you note and a check and set her free to enjoy a much-deserved break.

"Are you sure?" Bobbi asked. "I don't mind staying."

"You have to work tonight. I'd feel guilty if you did. Scram."

"Okay. You talked me into it. Maybe I'll see if Jason Wells likes coffee."

Coffee with Jason, that sounded good to Hope. *You have more important things to do,* she told herself. *Like . . . watering your plants.*

Bobbi was barely out the door when a young couple entered the shop. Even before she saw the ring on the woman's finger, Hope knew they were engaged. Everything about them said it, from the way they held hands like they were glued together to the intimate smile they exchanged. They were here to order flowers for their wedding.

"We've heard you're the best," said the groom-to-be.

Here was a good future husband, already wanting nothing but the best for his wife. "I do love doing flowers for weddings," Hope told them, and seated them at her little wrought-iron table. She fetched her laptop, then pulled up a chair and joined them. "What are your colors?"

"Red and orange," said the bride.

Well, there was a new one. She could only imagine what the bridesmaids' dresses would look like. But red and orange together made for striking floral arrangements. "We could do your bouquet in red and orange roses," she suggested.

"Oh, I like that," said the bride. "Roses are my favorite flower."

It didn't take long to settle on flowers for the boutonnieres, the tossing bouquet, the chapel, and the reception. "I love the idea of using carnival glass as part of the arrangement for the food table," said the woman. "I've never seen that done before. In fact, I never heard of carnival glass," she added, running a finger along the edge of the orange pedestal candy dish Hope had produced.

"It will be unique," said Hope. Everyone was special and the flowers for their event should be special, too.

Her customers left, beaming, and she smiled as she put their deposit check in her cash register. "Life is good," she reminded herself for the umpteenth time that day. Then she happened to look out the window to see Jason Wells walking down the opposite street, talking into his cell phone. He was smiling. He went from smiling to laughing. Was he talking to Bobbi?

If he was, that was a good thing, she told herself. She would be happy for them if they fell in love. Jason would never have a dull moment with Bobbi, and Bobbi would have a dependable man. And Hope would have a nice brother-in-law: a win-win situation for everyone. So, she should feel like a winner. *Okay, feeling like a winner here.* She drummed her fingers on the countertop. *Feeling like an antsy, irritated winner.* It was time to close up shop for the day. It wasn't even two yet and she always stayed open until four on Saturdays, but she needed garden therapy right now, today, or her heart would explode.

She turned the sign on her door to Closed. Under it she taped a note that said, "Sorry. Flower emergency."

Then she drove to the Trellis and bought the goodies for her garden: basil, cilantro, dill, and nasturtiums, which would give her pretty orange blossoms to use in salads. She enjoyed growing garden goodies for cooking, and now that her appetite had returned she was looking forward to spending time in the kitchen again. Others, like the baby's breath and the root beer plant, she'd dry and use for flower arrangements.

She left the nursery with a feeling of anticipation. It was sunny and warm. It would be the perfect day to start her garden.

Her cell phone rang. It was Megan Wales, one of her best customers and also now her lawyer and good friend. "I never heard back. Are you coming tonight?"

Megan's legal chick-flick night—she'd completely forgotten.

"You don't want to miss my salad buffet," Megan added.

A change in lifestyle and a significant weight loss had made Megan the queen of salads. Not only was she a good cook, she was good fun, and being out beat staying home. "You're right, I don't," Hope decided. "I'll be there."

"Good. See you at seven."

Gardening and friends—life was good. Not always perfect, not always what a woman wanted it to be, but good. And for now, good was just fine.

Hope arrived at the community garden to find that she had neighbors. Their plots were to the east of hers, side by side. It looked like they were

102

already on their way to becoming friends as they stood conversing: an old woman and a woman who looked around Hope's age. The younger woman had a little boy beside her, playing in the soil. She was slim, clad in jeans and a black sweatshirt. She had long, brown hair and a slightly long face made pretty by brown eyes and full lips. She looked familiar although Hope couldn't remember where she'd seen her.

The older woman was slender and delicate as a coral bell. She was wearing the kind of smile that said, "You want me for your grandma." She was also wearing purple slacks and a floral blouse topped with an ancient-looking lavender sweatshirt cardigan. A straw sun hat banded by a purple ribbon shaded her eyes from the afternoon sun. *When I'm an old woman, I shall wear purple.* Hope wondered if this woman was a member of that red hat club her grandma had belonged to when she was alive.

Hope walked over and set down her armload of goodies. "Hi," the younger woman greeted her.

"We were wondering who our neighbor might be," said the grandmother, tucking a wandering lock of silver hair behind her ear.

Hope introduced herself.

"I'm Millie Baldwin," said the grandmother, "and this is Amber Howell."

"And this is Seth," Amber said, pointing to her son. "Can you say hi, Sethie?"

The little boy was very busy running a toy truck through the dirt, but he managed a happy hello.

"You look familiar," Hope said to Amber. "I'm trying to figure out where I've seen you."

"Ever come into the bakery?"

And then she knew. "Of course. I've seen you behind the counter."

Amber nodded. "That's me. I'm a lot more at home in the bakery than in the garden, let me tell you. Thank God I met Millie. She's going to be my garden guru and cure me of my disease."

The word made Hope's heart catch. "Disease?"

"*Gardenus ickus.*" Amber raised a hand, thumb up. "I've got the world's biggest black thumb."

Millie chuckled and Hope allowed herself to breathe again.

"The only difference between you and me, my dear, is that I've had many more years of practice," Millie told Amber. She smiled at Hope and peered over at her box. "And what are you growing? Oh, I see herbs!"

Hope ran a loving finger over a feathery dill plant. "I like to cook. And I'm a florist. Some of these I'll dry and use during the year."

"Do you work at that florist shop downtown?" asked Amber.

"Actually, I own it."

"How lovely!" cried Millie. "I always thought it would be fun to have a flower shop. But I must admit that between my family and my garden and my church activities, I don't know when I'd have found the time. Owning your own business is a lot of work."

Amber's genial smile shriveled, and Hope couldn't help wondering what nerve Millie had accidentally hit.

Millie obviously saw the change in Amber. "Well," she said briskly, "now, thanks to Amber, I can get started planting. Although you really didn't need to turn the soil for me," she told Amber. "I could have done it."

Amber brought back some of her smile. "I needed the exercise anyway."

The women set to work laying out their gardens. Hope felt soothed by the sun and the sound of Millie's soft voice as she gently coached Amber. "I think your pumpkin and zucchini would do better if you plant them in little hills. Yes, that looks about the right size. That was nice helping, Seth. Now, make six little holes around the mound. Just like that. Lovely. Now, drop in the seeds. You'll be able to make wonderful zucchini bread with your harvest."

As the day moved on, Hope learned a lot about the other two women. Millie had moved to Heart Lake from back east and was helping her daughter with her two children. But she seemed lonely, happy to have other women to talk to.

"I miss being near my mom," said Amber. She dropped out of the conversation to redirect her son's Tonka truck traffic away from the hill where they had just planted the zucchini.

"Me, too," said Hope. Florida sometimes felt like the other side of the world. But just the day before, during their weekly phone chat, Mom had mentioned the possibility of buying a lot on Heart Lake and putting up a small summer home so they could spend summers near their daughters. "Do you and your daughter do a lot of cool stuff together on the weekends?" she asked Millie.

"Debra is awfully busy," Millie hedged. "Anyway," she added briskly, "a woman should always have a life of her own, no matter how much she loves her children."

Hope could see Amber frowning in disapproval. Their gazes met and an unspoken agreement flashed between them. They would make sure this woman felt wanted and appreciated. That wouldn't be hard. Millie was a sweetie.

Millie was the first to quit. "Well, I think it's about time to go home," she said, straightening and stretching out her back. "I'm afraid I don't have the stamina I did at seventy."

At seventy? How old was this woman?

"You're older than seventy?" asked Amber, voicing Hope's thought.

Millie smiled, obviously flattered. "I'll be seventy-seven come June."

Hope vowed right then to make Millie a special bouquet for her birthday.

"Wow. You're amazing," Amber said. "I hope I'm in as good shape as you when I'm your age."

"I'm sure you will be," Millie said. "You young girls all work so hard at staying fit."

Some of us just work hard at staying alive, Hope thought.

Millie said her good-byes, and the two women watched as she climbed into a big boat of a car with a dented fender and sailed off.

"Wow, she's something else," said Amber. "Do you picture us being like that when we're old?"

"I'm not sure I picture myself being old at all," Hope mused. She didn't want to think about that today though, not here in this place filled with growing things.

"I already feel old," Amber said with a sigh.

"Mommy, I want to go home," said her son. "I'm hungry."

"Okay. Let's go see if Daddy's got dinner ready."

"Your husband cooks for you?" asked Hope.

"Sometimes."

"Lucky you."

"Yeah. Lucky me." Amber's smile was tinged with melancholy. "Okay, Sethie. Pick up your truck. Nice meeting you," she said to Hope. "See you next weekend?"

Hope nodded and watched as Amber led her son away. Interesting neighbors she had here at the community garden.

Playing in the dirt and enjoying the fresh air left Hope refreshed, and enjoying the company of friends left her grateful to be alive. That night she dreamed about her garden. The dill grew waist high, and some of Millie's English garden seeds migrated to her plot and produced a wondrous flower chorus, swaying in the breeze and humming "The Waltz of the Flowers." A beautiful butterfly with lavender wings and a silver body appeared, fluttering from flower to flower. The movie camera of Hope's subconscious zoomed in, showing her that it wasn't a butterfly but a fairy— a beautiful fairy with naked, perfectly formed, rosy-tipped breasts. And her face—the fairy was her! Only more beautiful than she could ever have imagined herself.

She woke up with the morning sun kissing her cheek and sighed, still warm from the aftereffects of the dream. With a dream like that, she simply had to have a wonderful day. How could it be otherwise?

It began with a favorite ritual. On Sundays Bobbi wandered down from Apartment 302 in the Lake Vista Apartments to have lunch with Hope in number 103. Hope always made a soup or salad and served it with homemade oatmeal muffins or whole wheat bread from the bakery, and Bobbi brought dessert to encourage Hope to "live a little." Today's offering was chocolate from the

Chocolate Bar, the new chocolateria in town that specialized in all things chocolate, from truffles to hot cocoa.

"Tonight's the night," Bobbi said, setting out the pink candy box of truffles for dessert. "We are going line dancing at the Grange."

No need to ask who the "we" was. Hope reached for a chocolate. She'd have just one. "So, he's already getting the dance test."

"Why not? Anyway, we couldn't exactly go out last night."

"Did he ask you out for last night?"

"Yeah, but I suggested tonight instead."

"Did you give him a reason for why you couldn't go out last night?"

Bobbi took a truffle. "I played it mysterious and said I had plans. It's good to keep a man intrigued." She closed her eyes and sighed. "He is so gorgeous."

"Amen to that," Hope said. She needed another truffle.

"We talked on the phone for an hour yesterday."

Hope remembered watching Jason walk down the street, smiling as he talked into his cell phone. She popped another truffle. "What did you talk about?"

"Gosh, just silly stuff, you know. Where we grew up, what we like to do for fun." She frowned. "He likes to hike. That is not a plus."

Hope tried not to envision herself and Jason

walking in a meadow at Mount Rainer or hiking to the Sol Duc Hot Springs in the Olympic National Park. *Have another chocolate.*

"Whoa," said Bobbi, watching her put a fourth truffle in her mouth. "Are you on a chocolate bender or something?"

Hope looked at the box. There was only one left. What the heck? She took that and ate it, too. "No. Just in the mood for chocolate. Life's uncertain, eat dessert first."

"Not funny," Bobbi said with a scowl. "Not after what we just went through with you."

"Sorry. I guess I should have said that I'm just trying to live life to the fullest like you're always telling me to do."

"Well, you've got to be full now," Bobbi grumped, looking longingly at the empty box. "I guess I should have bought more."

"Thank God you didn't. That was my sugar quota for the month." How many cancer cells had she just fed?

Bobbi grinned. "Better your hips than mine."

"You're just trying to make me fat 'cause you can't stand the competition," Hope cracked and tried not to think about hungry, out-of-control cells running around her chest, devouring everything in sight like Pac-Man.

"That's it." Bobbi looked at her watch. "I'd better get going. I need to clean my place."

No need to ask why. Of course she'd invite Jason

over after they were done dancing. Well, good for her. *At this rate, she'll be engaged by May and I'll be doing flowers for her wedding in August.* Hope produced a determined smile.

A quick clean-up in the kitchen, a hug, and then Bobbi was gone and the apartment was quiet. Uncomfortably quiet. Hope sat at her vintage Formica table and drummed her fingers. *Don't just sit here, go do something.* The sun was out, the air was spring warm, and she was on chocolate overload. Time for a walk.

She grabbed her sweatshirt and took off, her destination the Grand Forest, a nineteen-acre stretch of land that had been bought by the Heart Lake Land Trust to provide space for wildlife in the growing community. Walking through stands of Douglas-fir, red cedar, hemlock, and broadleaf maple trees always restored her equilibrium and reminded her that the world was a beautiful place. Sometimes she'd see a deer regarding her cautiously from a clearing or catch sight of a pheasant or blue jay. And sometimes she'd meet other people, walkers with a dog on a leash, joggers thundering down the path with iPods plugged in. Today, she encountered . . . oh, good grief. What sick little gremlins were responsible for this?

Jason Wells stopped in front of her, the epitome of masculine in his jeans, a Seahawks sweatshirt, and hiking boots. "Well, hi," he said, giving her a pleasant once-over.

"Hi," she said, and smoothed her suddenly sweaty palms on her thighs. "Nice day to be out," she added. That was lame.

He looked around them, smiling. "Yeah. This is a pretty cool place."

"It's a great place to go mushrooming in the fall."

He raised an eyebrow. "Aren't you afraid you'll poison yourself?"

"On chanterelles? No."

"Whoa. You can find those here?"

"All over the place. It's like Easter egg hunting for grown-ups."

"Sounds like it," he said with a grin. "You must come here a lot."

"When I get a chance."

"Your sister's not with you?"

Bobbi a nature girl? Hope shook her head. "No, she had some things to do. I believe she's getting ready to turn you into Patrick Swayze."

He produced a pained expression. "I think I'm in trouble."

"Don't worry," Hope teased. "She'll make it painless." Suddenly, she was out of words. She managed a breezy, "I'd better get going," and started backing away, giving him a little wave. "Watch out for crazed deer."

Walking backward proved to be more of a challenge than she'd anticipated. Or maybe the challenge was walking backward in front of a hot guy.

Whatever it was, she failed it and lost her straight line. Next thing she knew some sneaky branch had reached out and tripped her. She went over a log with a yelp, landing on the wooded side of the trail with her feet in the air. *Please let him have gotten kidnapped by aliens*, she prayed as she tried to right herself. Getting upright was easier said than done. The underbrush clutched at her and she couldn't seem to get her balance.

Now Jason was leaning over the log, reaching a hand toward her. "Here, let me help."

Okay, the aliens could kidnap *her*.

But no aliens showed up to deliver her from her mortification. Her face flaming like a forest fire, she took his hand and he pulled her to her feet. The forest fire was still raging. She tried to put it out by focusing on brushing off her bottom.

Jason took a helpful sweep at her back. "You okay?"

No. I want to turn invisible right now. No, scratch that. I want to rocket back in time and turn invisible two minutes ago. "I guess I need to get my steering checked," she said, making him smile. "I'm not normally clumsy," she added.

"You sure you're okay? You didn't sprain anything?"

"Only my pride. I'm fine. Thanks. Nice running away from . . . into you," she stammered, and felt a fresh flush of embarrassment run up her neck and flood her cheeks.

He grinned. "Same here."

She started walking—forward this time, no going backward. She could hear him striding away, his feet landing on the path with sureness and confidence. The temptation to turn and watch him was strong, but she resisted. It would be just her luck that he'd look over his shoulder and catch her gawking at him like a lovesick tweenie.

Get a grip, she scolded herself. *So, you fell on your butt in front of your sister's boyfriend. You don't need to impress him. You couldn't if you tried.* Well, that was a nice, depressing pep talk.

Hope realized she was suddenly tired, so she turned and retraced her steps. What she needed was an afternoon with a cup of herbal tea and a good book. No Jane Austen today. A murder mystery, a gory one.

In his jeans, white shirt, and boots, Jason Wells looked like he was born to dance. Boy, are looks deceiving, thought Bobbi. Even the steps of the simple Ah Si eluded him. But he was good-natured, laughing as he turned the wrong way or bumped into someone. And at least he was trying.

"I think I need private lessons," he said as they sat back down at their table and dived into their lemonades.

"I think that could be arranged," she said coyly.

"Tonight?"

She hadn't cleaned her apartment for nothing. "Maybe."

Half an hour later they were on their way to her place. "I was walking not far from here today," he said as he parked his truck in the guest parking. "In your Grand Forest."

"Oh," she said, trying to sound interested.

"I ran into your sister."

That wasn't surprising. Bobbi had never understood what Hope found so exciting about wandering around in the woods. She liked flowers as much as her sister, but flowers were meant to be enjoyed like nature intended, in pretty arrangements sitting on your table, not out in the wild where you could get lost or stung by bees. Or both.

"I thought maybe I'd see you with her. Do you like to hike?"

"Oh . . ." *Crap.* "Who doesn't?" There. She hadn't lied. Further into their relationship, she'd explain to him about the dangers of bees and sticker bushes and other nasty things.

Inside her apartment, she settled Jason at the kitchen table, then set out milk paired with cookies from Sweet Somethings Bakery.

"These are good," he said, holding up a half-consumed ginger cookie. "Did you make them?"

"I love to bake." She was a whiz when it came to whipping that refrigerator case cookie dough onto a cookie sheet. She slid the plate toward him. "Have another."

He swallowed the last of his cookie and reached for a second. "You know what this reminds me of?"

She shook her head.

"A scene from *Stranger than Fiction*."

"Yeah? I like Will Ferrell, but I didn't see that movie." Her friend Anna from the Last Resort had said it was weird so she hadn't bothered.

"It was pretty good."

She propped her elbows on the kitchen table. "So, tell me about it."

"Well, it's about a guy whose life is going nowhere. And suddenly there's this voice narrating everything he does."

"Like God or something?"

"No, just a voice."

"Oh, so he's crazy."

Jason shook his head. "Just dull. He's an IRS agent and he winds up auditing this woman who's a baker. She bakes him cookies." Jason smiled and sat back in his seat. "It's a cool scene. It's like the guy's life starts with a cookie. And a perfect woman."

Okay, she got the connection. She cocked her head and smiled at him. "And he's the perfect guy for her."

"Oh, yeah." Jason got up slowly. "So, how about that dance lesson?"

"Okay." She got up, too, and led him to the middle of the living room. "Maybe we should try it without music first so we can go slow."

She placed herself by his side, ready to help him master the concept of heel-toe, but he caught her around the waist and pulled her to him and started them swaying. "What if I don't want to go slow?"

"We could speed things up a little," she said with a smile. But not too much too quickly. That spoiled a man's appetite for commitment. She turned her face up to him and let him kiss her.

And that was the end of the dance lesson.

By the time he left, Bobbi was dizzy with love. This man was perfect. Well, other than the fact that he had two left feet that he liked to use to stomp around in the woods—oh, and the fact that he now thought she was the queen of the kitchen—they were a perfect match.

Jason drove home buzzing like a power saw. Bobbi Walker was amazing. He loved her sense of fun and enthusiasm. He was amazed at how much they had in common. And beautiful? She was the woman in Byron's poem: *She walks in beauty, like the night.* Except Bobbi Walker wasn't night. She was broad daylight, dazzling sunshine. He'd hit the jackpot this time.

He went home, tossed his coat on a chair, and got a beer out of the fridge. Cookies and milk; that had been so cute. He called back the mental image of her in that hot, red top and those butt-hugging jeans. He backed off from mentally stripping her out of them. If he did he'd never get any sleep, and he did have to go to work in the morning. No virtual stripping.

No real stripping, either. This time he wasn't going to rush things. No doing it wrong with Miss Right.

He took another swig of beer, plopped on his couch, and picked up his Tony Hillerman mystery.

He'd read two pages when a fresh image popped into his mind: her apartment. It had been cozy with chick stuff: paintings of flowers, knick-knacks, some kind of handmade blanket thrown over the couch, ferns and flowers. But where were the books? No matter how hard he tried, he couldn't bring up an image of a book anywhere. No bookcase, no book lying on the coffee table. Magazines, but no books. Strange.

NINE

*O*n Monday at Changing Seasons Floral, Hope had Easter inventory to mark down another ten percent, a cooler case to stock, and orders to fill. And it seemed like everyone in Heart Lake wanted to stop in to visit.

"The flowers you did for my mom's ninetieth birthday were gorgeous," said Judy Livingston, one of her favorite customers. "And I can't believe how long they lasted."

Judy was sixty-nine, but other than some wrinkles and a few age spots, she didn't look it. She still kept her hair blond and cut in the latest style, and wore jeans and tops with cheeky sayings. Today her shirt read, "You're a bad boy. Now go to my room." Judy taught water aerobics and golfed once a week, and on weekends she took trips to the ocean with her boyfriend. Every time she came into the shop, Hope prepared to laugh. And when Hope was sick, Judy had made sure she laughed as much as possible, always dropping DVDs of classic comedies on her doorstep.

"And was the party a big hit?" Hope asked.

"With my chocolate-fudge cake? How could it not be? In fact . . ." Judy produced a foil-wrapped package. "I saved you a piece."

The last thing Hope wanted was more chocolate. She'd give it to Bobbi—restitution for eating all the truffles. "That was really sweet of you. You're great."

Judy smiled, making herself look like a senior citizen pixie. "I know."

They were still talking when a plump little woman about Judy's age entered the shop bearing a huge, sick-looking potted ivy. It trailed behind her like a dragon's tail, leaving who knew what kind of bugs and disease in its wake. *Typhoid Mary.*

"Carol. What are you doing bringing that sick thing in here? You want to kill all Hope's plants?" Judy scolded.

The woman stopped in her tracks and looked

chagrined. "I thought you might know what's wrong with it," she said to Hope. "I think it's dying. I figured if anyone could tell me what's wrong it's you." She almost sounded like she was going to start crying. She was such a gentle soul. Hope didn't have the heart to scold her, especially after Carol had elevated her from floral designer to plant whisperer.

"Let's take it outside in the sunlight where I can get a better look," Hope said, turning her around and guiding her and her plaguey plant out the door. Outside she examined the leaves. Oh, boy, just as she'd feared. The leaves were dry and yellowed. And it looked like the plant was completely root bound. "Okay," Hope said crisply. "Here's what I'd do. I'd repot it. Then I'd go to the Trellis and get some insecticidal soap. I think you've got a whitefly problem."

"Will it live?"

"I'm sure it'll be fine," Hope said.

"Thank you," Carol breathed. She turned and hurried off down the street, her ivy plant sweeping the sidewalk. And probably dropping little bugs everywhere.

Bugs. Hope hurried back inside the shop. Judy was still there, waiting at the counter, a stone soap dish in her hand. "Do you need to fumigate?"

"I think I'm going to vacuum," Hope said as she rang up the sale.

She'd barely gotten Judy out of the shop and

vacuumed (and sprayed the floor with organic insecticide, just to be sure) when two more customers wandered in. "It's so gloomy out today. We need flowers," said one.

"Tulips," said the other.

"Tulips are perfect for a gloomy day," Hope said with a smile.

"Especially if they come from Changing Seasons. I swear, your flowers last forever."

"Only if they're silk," Hope quipped.

Bobbi arrived at noon, ready and willing to work. But first . . . "I want to send a card," she said, holding up a pink envelope. The front of the card was crammed with a collage of flowers. The inside was blank. "I need to write something really brilliant. What would you say to a man if you'd had an incredible evening together?"

Hope swallowed a little bud of envy. "The possibilities are endless. So, you had a good time. Does that mean he can dance?"

Bobbi made a face. "Barely." Her expression turned dreamy. "But he has no problem with slow dancing. So, I thought something about dancing." She scrambled around in her purse and came up with a pen.

"Hmmm." Hope drummed the counter with her fingertips, trying to focus on being brilliant. "Two bodies swaying."

"Oooh, that's good," Bobbi approved, and began to write.

"Two hearts feeling the same beat, moving as one." Hope closed her eyes and got a sudden vision of herself in Jason's arms. She forced her eyelids back up.

"That's good. What next?"

"I don't know." She was suddenly out of words, her brain stalled.

" 'I don't know'? That's not very poetic."

"I didn't mean write that. I meant I don't know. I'm out of ideas."

"Impossible. You're never out of ideas. Come on. Let's come up with something that says I want to see him again. Something about dancing, maybe?"

"Hmm. Okay, how about this? We're just learning the steps, we've barely begun."

"Oh, yeah. It rhymes! That's great."

"And maybe sign it, 'Let's keep dancing.' "

"Aw, that's nice," Bobbi said with a sigh, and finished writing.

She was just stuffing the card in the envelope when the door of the shop jangled and in walked Jason himself, wearing his standard sexy denim work clothes. Bobbi gave a start and hid the card behind her back.

"You look like a woman with a secret," he teased her. "What are you ladies up to?"

Bobbi produced the card and handed it to him. "I was going to mail you this."

"Yeah?" Now he was looking at her like he suspected she was about to give him the keys to a new Jaguar. He opened the envelope, pulled out the card, and read, a grin spreading across his face. "That's awesome." He pointed a finger at Bobbi. "You've really got a gift. You know that?"

Her cheeks turned rose-petal pink. "Oh, not really," she said with a little flick of her hand. "So, what brings you to the shop?"

He tapped his watch. "Lunchtime. I thought maybe you could take a break." He smiled at Hope. "How about it?"

He was asking her to join them? Of course she'd be a good sister and turn down the offer. But her spirits lifted all the same.

"You wouldn't mind watching the shop for an hour, would you?" he continued. "I promise I'll bring her back by one."

Of course he hadn't been inviting her along. What had she been thinking? Just as well. She didn't want to be rolling along as a third wheel. "No problem," she said.

"Are you sure?" asked Bobbi.

"You've got to eat," Jason urged.

Hope nodded and shooed them on their way. "Have fun."

They barely heard her as they sailed out the door.

She plopped on the little stool she kept behind the counter, grabbed a floral card and began doodling on it, drawing a Patience Brewster–styled rose girl, all dolled up and ready for a ball. Hope loved to dance, too. The doodling turned to writing. *I teach the steps. She dances. I wish I could dance. With him.*

Pathetic. *You are such a hogweed. Get over yourself. You don't need a partner to dance.*

She brought out the old radio she kept in the workroom, set it on the counter, and plugged it in. Then she cranked it up full blast.

She walked over to where Audrey the Christmas cactus sat. "May I have this dance?"

Audrey seemed reluctant.

"What, you don't dance? You don't know what you're missing. Dancing is good therapy."

Great therapy. Hope let the music wash away the little vines of self-pity trying to wrap around her heart and danced around the shop, watering her potted plants as she went. Halfway through the first song she was lost in the music. Life was good. She needed to always remember that.

"So, how about going out with me this weekend?" Jason asked Bobbi as they sat in Sweet Somethings, digging into sandwiches made on freshly baked sourdough bread.

"How about Sunday?" Bobbi offered.

"Friday," he countered. "I was thinking we could catch a movie."

"I'm kind of booked Friday." Now he'd try for Saturday. She inputted this information, along with the chances of getting Saturday night off. *No chance for Saturday,* came the answer. *Take Friday. If you turn him down for both days, he'll want to know why.* "But I think I can change my plans," she added with a smile and a flip of her hair. She'd find someone to cover for her.

"Great," he said.

"That new movie, *Bomb Squad,* is opening," Bobbi suggested. There was also a chick flick opening, but she could see that with Hope. Jason would want to see the action movie.

She could tell by his expression that she'd hit it on the nose. "Works for me. Meanwhile, how about lunch tomorrow?"

Okay, now she was making it all too easy for him. She stuck out her lower lip. "Sorry. I've got plans." She would have as soon as she got back to the shop. She and Hope hadn't been out to lunch in ages. "We'll have fun Friday," she added, rewarding him with a dimpled smile.

He gave a fatalistic shrug and smiled in return. "I guess I'll have to wait till Friday then."

Anticipation was a good thing. Men loved the thrill of the hunt, and she didn't want to deny him that.

Funny, she was so good at hooking men, but keeping them on the hook was another matter. Probably because she never seemed to find the perfect man.

This time you have, she reminded herself.

• • •

Jason was certainly hooked Friday night. He had no desire to end their date with just a movie—a very good sign.

But his choice of how to continue the evening nearly gave her a heart attack. "How about going over to the Last Resort for a drink? I've been meaning to check the place out. I hear they have karaoke on Friday nights."

All she needed was to come in there with Jason in tow and have the other waitresses greeting her and asking her how she was enjoying her night off. "I've got a better idea," she said. "How about coming back to my place? I've got chocolate cake." Thank God she'd made a bakery run earlier.

"That's even better," he said with a smile.

She was feeling pretty smug about how she'd dodged that bullet, watching him devour the cake she'd picked up from the bakery, when he pointed to her *People* magazine and idly observed, "So, you like to read."

She thought of the romance novel on her nightstand. "Oh, yeah."

He looked around the apartment. "Where are your books?"

Books? As in a whole bunch? "I . . ." *Umm.* "They're still in boxes," she improvised.

"Oh, you haven't been here that long?" He looked confused. Probably wondering how she could be new in town and own a flower shop at the same time.

"Not in this apartment. I was living someplace else." That was no lie. This apartment had become available and the idea of being neighbors with her sister had sounded like fun. "I need to get a book-case," she added.

"I could make you one. I make all kinds of stuff."

"Well, then, I'll take one. Thanks. That's so sweet." What was she going to fill it with?

"I've got some nice cedar left over from a project I did last month."

"Great," she said. *Just Great. DON'T ANYBODY PANIC!*

Saturday morning found Bobbi at the Heart Lake Library for the Friends of the Library book sale, frantically stocking up on books to supplement her meager supply. Brainy books. So far she'd found a money management one for dummies (she needed that), two fitness books, a Martha Stewart tome on decorating, and a great cookbook that was nothing but chocolate recipes. She'd even picked up a Jane Austen novel—*Pride and Prejudice.*

"Hi there," she said to the woman taking her money. "I'm Bobbi, your new best friend."

"The library always needs new friends," the woman said with a smile.

"So, friend to friend, what do you think of this

book?" Bobbi held up her Jane Austen novel.

"It's the perfect introduction to Jane Austen," the woman assured her. "That will be six dollars."

"For all these?" Wow.

"A steal," said a deep voice behind Bobbi.

She gave a guilty start and turned to see Jason Wells. He was wearing long, baggy shorts, a sweatshirt with the sleeves ripped off, and tennis shoes. He looked like he was getting ready to go running or work out at the gym—both preferable options to being here, catching her buying props for her apartment.

"Hi." How long had he been standing there? What had he heard?

"I see you're taking advantage of the sale," he said.

"Absolutely." She nodded vigorously. "You, too?"

"Yep. I was on my way to the gym when I saw the sign outside. By the way, your bookcase should be done by next Saturday. Want me to come over and help you fill it?"

"Sure," she said. What she had here was not going to fill a bookcase.

Then she remembered her sister's book-overflow problem. Hope had just filled a box to donate to the library. Maybe a few of those books could take a little detour to Bobbi's apartment.

Bobbi left Hope's apartment after lunch Sunday carrying a box of books and vowing to read every one.

"Do you really think you can sit still long enough?" Hope teased.

"I can try," Bobbi replied with a grin.

Hope shut her apartment door with a sigh and a shake of the head. This was nuts. Her sister was slipping from make-a-good-impression mode into romantic fraud, and she was becoming an accomplice. Bobbi needed to just be herself. If the man didn't like Bobbi for who she was (and how could he not?), then he wasn't the right one. It was silly to build up a false image.

Hope thought of her fake breast. That was different, she told herself. She wasn't trying to get a man. With the ugly scars and the Franken-boob, there was no chance of that. The second operation after the capsular contracture had gone better, but it wasn't hard to spot which boob was the patch job and which one was the original. Still, she wasn't out to do any false advertising. She was just trying to feel like herself again and get her life back.

And she was glad to be alive. Glad. To prove it, she got her gardening tools and drove to the community garden.

She arrived to find Millie Baldwin there, tending her patch. "Hello," Millie greeted her. She pointed to Hope's pale green sweatshirt. "That's almost too pretty for the garden. And such a flattering color."

Garden therapy was the best. Millie made it sound like Hope really looked special. That was stretching it. Even before the cancer she'd been just okay. She had nice eyes to make up for the snub nose she hated, an okay mouth. Good legs. But stand her next to Bobbi and she disappeared.

"Thanks," she murmured. "Do you have all your flowers planted now?" She motioned to the little stakes capped with empty seed packets delineating tiny flower neighborhoods.

"Almost. I'd love to plant some lavender, but it's silly to plant a perennial in a community garden. Such a shame though. I have the best recipe for lavender cookies."

"If it's any consolation, you can get lavender sugar at Kizzy's Kitchen," Hope said.

"I'll remember that," said Millie. "Although I'm not sure lavender cookies will go over that big with my grandchildren. Carrot cookies certainly didn't."

Hope wasn't sure carrot cookies would go over that well with her, either, but she kept her mouth shut.

"Or maybe I'll give the recipe to Amber, our resident baker," Millie added. "I'd love to be able to pass it on to someone."

"Your daughter?" Hope suggested.

Millie got suddenly busy with her flowers. "Oh, Debra's much too busy to fuss with baking."

"Well, I'm sure Amber would love the recipe, and so would I," said Hope.

Millie looked at her and smiled. "Thank you."

As they chatted, Hope felt her frustrations slipping away. The sun fought off the occasional chilly breeze and kept them warm. A couple of mothers had brought their children to the play area, and the sound of laughter danced on the air and lulled her.

And then the lull ended. "I imagine a pretty girl like you has got a boyfriend waiting for you to finish up here and go do something with him," said Millie.

"No boyfriend," said Hope, shaking her head. "I'm too busy with my shop."

"Oh." Millie appeared nonplussed.

Hope could feel Millie studying her. "I . . ." She had no idea how to finish her sentence.

"It's none of my business," Millie said quickly.

Now Millie thought she was a loser. She didn't want that. "I'm still putting my life back together. I was sick."

"Oh, I'm sorry," Millie said, her voice filled with concern. She offered a gentle smile. "You look the picture of health now."

Hope shrugged. "So far, so good."

"I hope it's not something that can come back."

"It could. Right now I'm in remission." Hope regretted the words the minute they slipped out. Such a dead giveaway. And what was she doing sharing so much personal stuff with someone she hardly knew? Except Millie didn't feel like a stranger. She felt more like a newly found grandmother.

Millie's face donned that oh-no expression all

women wore when confronted with even a whiff of the *C* word. "What kind of cancer did you have, dear?"

Hope got suddenly very busy pressing earth down around her seeds. "Breast."

"I'm so sorry you had to go through something so horrible at a young age."

Suddenly, bitter words wanted to spill out of Hope's mouth. It wasn't fair. Who in her twenties got cancer? That happened to older women, women who'd had a chance for husbands and children and . . . Hope bit down on her lower lip.

"You've been very blessed," Millie said. "You're still here. God must have important things for you to do in that little flower shop of yours."

Millie's gentle reminder sweetened the bitter waters. Hope wasn't sure about many things, but the fact that she was doing something good with her life was one she was sure of.

"And someone very special waiting in the wings."

Right. To want someone with a scarred body and a questionable life span, the guy would have to be way beyond special. Hope shook her head. "I don't know about that."

"I do," Millie said, a smile in her voice. "You'll see."

Hope didn't say anything. Not that she wanted to be rude. She'd simply run out of words.

TEN

After a string of soppy days, April bowed out to May, which entered Heart Lake bearing perfect weather. Amber came home from work to find her son antsy, with an overload of energy needing to be burned, and her husband ready for a break. Of course, getting a job would get him a break on a regular basis, but she decided against pointing that out to him. There was no sense in starting a fight on such a pretty day. Instead, she decided to take Seth to the park and check their garden.

They arrived to find Millie already there, kneeling on a bright yellow foam pad, digging away in the damp earth with her garden spade, visiting with her neighbor on the other side of her garden, a scrawny old man with an old fishing hat mashed onto a wiry nest of gray hair, who was busy hoeing.

She smiled and waved at the sight of Amber and Seth. "Happy May. Isn't the sunshine wonderful?" she greeted them.

"Absolutely. I'm ready for some nice weather. How are our gardens?" Amber looked at her plot. Lots of little green things were popping out. "Wow, Sethie, look at all the veggies we've got growing!"

"I'm afraid many of those are weeds," Millie

informed her. "And it looks like the slugs have gotten to some of your crop."

Amber took a closer look and saw nibbled down greens. All around them lay the shiny slime trail left behind by the Northwest's infamous garden pest. "Gross," she said in disgust.

"Bring home some of the grounds from all those coffee drinks you're making and sprinkle them around your plants," suggested Millie. "That will keep the slugs away."

"Really?"

"Old wives' tale," muttered the man.

"Oh, Henry," Millie said pleasantly. And then introduced Amber.

Amber said a polite hello, but she wasn't going to give old Henry any more than that. She already had one grumpy man in her life. She didn't need another.

"I got my truck," Seth announced before Millie could say more. He held up his prized Tonka truck for Millie to see.

She nodded her approval. "Very handy for hauling away weeds."

He beamed. But the truck didn't divert his attention for long. "Look, Mommy, a bunny!" he cried.

Amber looked to where he was pointing. Sure enough. A little brown rabbit sat at the edge of a tangle of ferns and thimbleberry bushes, regarding them with a twitching nose. Peter Rabbit. "Oh, how cute!"

Of course, Seth ran toward it, crying, "Here, bunny."

The rabbit took off as if Mr. McGregor was after it, and Seth dragged back to the garden plot, disappointed.

"Damned rabbits," muttered Henry.

"But it's so cute," Amber said to him.

"You won't think that when it's eating your garden down to the nub," retorted the man.

"Well, Henry, we'll just have to take precautions," Millie said to him. "Don't worry," she told Seth. "It will be back."

"Rabbits at the park?" wondered Amber.

Millie pursed her lips and shook her head. "Probably pet owners dumping them. People get a cute little bunny for Easter and then realize that, like all pets, the animal requires care. I'm sure later this spring, that little guy will have a lot more friends to keep him company. And Henry's right. They'll all be by to sample your lettuce."

Amber frowned. Suddenly the bunny wasn't quite so cute.

"Invest in some chicken wire," Millie advised.

"Great. One more thing to buy so I can save money," Amber grumbled.

"Can I go look for the bunny?" asked Seth.

"Yeah, and if you find it, kill it," muttered Henry.

Amber frowned at him, but he was too busy hoeing to see. "Stay right around here where I can see you," she said to Seth, and he scampered to the far end of the row of garden plots and began peering under bushes.

"He's a sweet child," Millie commented. "And all those lovely golden curls. I never did ask. Does he take after his father?"

"Well, in looks. Thank God that's all," Amber said, feeling suddenly as grumpy as Henry.

"If you women are going to start male bashing, I'm leaving," announced Henry, opening his garden gate.

Amber immediately felt like a heel.

"'Bye, Henry," Millie said pleasantly. "See you next week. He was finished anyway," she said to Amber as Henry hobbled off on stiff hips.

But Henry had been right. That hadn't been fair. Even if she was mad at Ty, he didn't deserve getting publicly villainized at the community garden. "I shouldn't say that. Ty's not a bad guy. Right now he's just not much fun to be around is all. He still hasn't found a job. And he's not looking very hard, either," she added miserably.

"Well," Millie said thoughtfully, "didn't you tell me that your restaurant closed down?"

"Yeah. And we were supposed to come up here to make a new start. The only one really making any kind of new start is me. He's sitting in front of the TV and feeling sorry for himself. Oh, I take that back. He makes lunch every day. Big whoop."

"Considering how depressed he probably is, I

think it might actually be a big whoop," Millie said thoughtfully.

"I'm the one who's working," Amber protested. "*I'm* at the bakery three days a week at eight A.M. *I'm* growing the garden. I'm even going to start selling cookies at the farmer's market. What's he doing?" With each word she could hear the anger building in her like lava in a volcano. She gave a weed a vicious stab with her spade, cutting it in half.

Millie sighed. "It's hard when the man you love lets you down. When our children were little, Duncan got a stock tip from one of his friends at the office." She shook her head. "We lost ten thousand dollars. Not much by today's standards, I suppose, but to us it was a fortune." She gave a mirthless chuckle. "I wanted to kill him."

Amber stared at her. "The way you talked about your husband last time we were together I thought he was a saint."

"He was, a saint who made mistakes. They all do."

"Well, I bet Duncan didn't sit around moping every day," said Amber. "Ty only went out to look for a job once last week."

"Maybe that's because he's battle weary and he's lost his armor."

Surely Millie wasn't comparing Ty to a knight in shining armor. "Oh, come on."

"I know it sounds corny, but every man wants to

provide for his family and protect them. Your husband is no exception. He's failed at both. That has to have hit him pretty hard."

"I get that he's bummed, but that's no excuse for doing nothing."

"Of course not," Millie agreed. "But it is an explanation. It's hard for a person who is seriously depressed to motivate himself to do anything."

"Hey, I'm seriously depressed, too," protested Amber.

"There are some things we women simply don't understand about our men. They need to be able to provide for us, even in this day and age when women work. If a man can't provide for his family, he doesn't feel like a man. It's as if he's gone to war and lost a limb."

"Lots of men learn to cope without an arm or leg," Amber said unsympathetically.

"Yes, they do. But I suspect what your husband really needs before he can go out and fight the world again is his armor."

That again. "Well, tell me where the nearest shining armor shop is and I'll be happy to get him some."

Seth had returned. "I can't find the bunny anywhere."

"I guess he's playing hide and seek," said Amber. She handed Seth his spade. "How about helping me weed?" She set him to work at the far corner of the plot, then turned to Millie. "Okay, tell me about the armor." What the heck? Millie had been around the marriage block. And they had to talk about something.

Millie beamed at her like she was a willing pupil. "Well, it's quite simple really. The armor is your faith in him, your encouragement."

Amber yanked out another weed. Okay, maybe she didn't want to hear what Millie had to say after all. "Why me? I'm tired of being strong. I'm doing everything."

"You are doing a lot," Millie agreed. "And I know that seems awfully unfair right now. And, of course, I could be all wrong, but maybe you're not doing what's needed the most."

That wasn't fun to digest. Amber spent the next ten minutes stabbing the dirt, pulling weeds, and brooding. Millie wisely kept quiet. "I don't see why I have to be the one to make all the effort," Amber said at last. "He needs to man up."

"It's been my experience that men sometimes need a little help with that. Did you ever hear the story of Samson, from the Bible?"

"The guy with long hair? Of course."

"Then you remember what happened to him when his hair got cut."

Amber chewed her lip. Where were they going with this? Probably no place she wanted to go.

"He had no strength until his hair grew back."

This was dumb. "So, now we're comparing Ty to Samson?"

"They're both men, aren't they? What was your husband like before your restaurant failed?"

Amber took in a deep breath of spring air. The groundskeeper was cutting shaggy lawn in one area of the park, and the fragrance of newly mowed grass drifted their way along with the hum of the mower. She could close her eyes and remember other smells—the smells in the kitchen of their little restaurant: garlic and seared beef and salmon. She could almost hear the hiss and crackle of the pots on the big stove, and Ty's laughter.

His grandfather had been a chef who'd owned his own restaurant. Ty had inherited the prized black and white photo of Grandpa Tyler posing next to John Wayne's table, the Duke shaking hands with Grandpa, giving his compliments to the chef. He'd also inherited his grandfather's flair for food. His dad had become a teacher, but he loved the idea of his son owning a restaurant. In fact, both families had been more than happy to support them, both emotionally and financially. In spite of all the hands willing to catch them, the fall from that lofty, hopeful high had been horrible, humiliating.

Amber took in a deep breath. "He was a happy man. Lots of big dreams, you know. He wasn't a football star or anything in high school, but he was fun to be around. Everybody hung out at his house after school. He made better nachos than Red Robin. Everybody liked him."

"Including you."

"Including me. I don't like him much right now, though. In fact, I don't even know if I love him anymore."

"Well, it seems to me that love is ninety-nine percent doing. If you keep doing love, the feeling might just grow back," said Millie.

Seth came over with a handful of what Amber hoped were weeds. "Look at all the weeds I got, Mommy."

"Good job, Sethie," she told him. She regarded her little garden kingdom. Tiny green things had popped up everywhere, many of them uninvited. She'd be here forever. "I hate weeding," she said with a sigh.

"Weeds don't go away instantly," Millie said. "But don't worry, you'll get a handle on it. Gardening, like so many things, takes time and patience."

"That was subtle," said Amber, giving her a reluctant smile.

"I thought so." Millie let out a tired sigh and pulled back a garden glove to check her watch. "Oh, look at the time. I need to get going." She picked up her yellow kneeling pad. "Don't forget about the coffee grounds."

"I won't. And thanks. For everything."

Millie smiled down on her. "You're going to be fine, my dear. I know it."

"I hope you know as much as you think you

know," she murmured as Millie climbed into her car.

She stayed at the community garden a little longer, idly pulling weeds and thinking about the man she'd married. For better or for worse. Things couldn't get much worse. Did she have enough energy to try just a little harder to make them better? She sure had nothing to lose.

They returned home to find Ty brooding on the couch, scowling over an old issue of *Bon Appétit*.

"Daddy, we saw a bunny today," Seth announced as she pulled off his dirty shoes at the front door.

Ty rubbed a hand across his thickly stubbled chin. "The Easter Bunny, huh? He's probably got his Easter egg factory somewhere nearby."

"Easter eggs?" Seth asked eagerly.

"You'll never find them," Amber told him. "Not until next Easter when he's ready for you to. Now, go take off those dirty pants," she added, giving him a pat on the bottom.

"A rabbit, that'll be good for your garden," Ty said, turning back to his magazine.

His negative words didn't do much for her new determination to take Millie's advice. She had to force herself to walk over to the couch. She pulled out the memory of their first night back from their honeymoon and in their new apartment, envisioned Ty and herself making chicken pesto pizza for their first dinner, then eating it while they unpacked boxes. And kissed. And kissed some more. They never ate much of that pizza, and they didn't get very many boxes unpacked. Or so she'd thought. But after she went to bed, he stayed up half the night setting up her kitchen for her.

Her husband had a good heart. She bent down and kissed him on the cheek.

"What was that for?" he asked suspiciously.

"Just a thank you for being a good man."

He looked at her with eyebrows raised. "Uh. Thanks."

She didn't say anything more. She simply turned and went to the bedroom to change. She hadn't exactly given her husband an entire emotional suit of armor, but it was a beginning.

It dawned on Millie when her grandson came home that it wouldn't hurt her to take some of her own advice. Did it matter whose fault it was that she was feeling a little left out here in her new home? What mattered was rolling up her sleeves and doing something about it.

When he plopped down on the couch to play his video game, she plopped down right next to him. "You know, that looks like fun," she lied.

The expression on his face told her he thought she'd gone around the bend.

"How about showing me how to play?"

"Sure," he agreed with a shrug that said, "Whatever," but his smile said, "All right!" He plugged in a second set of controls and walked her through the intricate how-tos.

And, of course, once they started playing, she couldn't even begin to keep up. So many buttons to push, so much to remember! It seemed she barely got her man on the screen when Eric found him and killed him. "Eric the Punisher strikes again," she moaned, making him laugh.

The game was ridiculous and she didn't have the fast reflexes for it, but she didn't care. She was sitting beside her grandson, doing something together. That was priceless.

Emily came in the door with her best friend, Sarah. "Gram, what are you doing?" She gawked at Millie as if she was running around the room in her underwear.

"Just playing a game," Millie said. She probably should have been lying down, resting. But she could rest anytime.

"Okay," Emily said dubiously. "Come on," she said to Sarah, and they disappeared up the stairs.

At five o'clock the phone rang. Millie knew before she answered it that it was Debra, calling to say she'd be home late.

"Some of the women in my department are going out for dinner. Ben won't be coming to get the kids until tomorrow. Do you mind feeding them and keeping an eye on things tonight?"

"Not at all. You need to get out."

Although Debra hadn't been home much all week. The excuses came fast and furious. She had to work late. She had to run errands. She had to get her haircut. She had to go shopping. Home was not a place of refuge for her daughter. It was a reminder of failure and a yoke of responsibility to be borne alone. Not totally true, since her ex-husband took the children every other weekend. But he wasn't there in the trenches with her every day. Millie knew that hurt, and it wasn't the kind of hurt a mother could heal.

"Thanks," said Debra. "Oh, and Emily had asked if Sarah could spend the night, but if it's going to be a problem having an extra kid around till I get home, you can tell her no."

"That's not a problem," said Millie.

"Thanks, Mom. I really need this."

"I know you do."

"Don't wait up for me. Love you."

Millie could hear the gratitude in her daughter's voice and it made her feel good that she could help. Still, she hung up with a sigh. She'd still hardly had any quality time with Debra. That was another garden that needed some serious tending.

But for now she had children to feed. She'd thawed hamburger earlier and she made it into meatloaf. She half considered making baked pota-toes to go with it, along with green beans from the freezer. She decided instead on substituting frozen French fries and making a green bean casserole. Everyone would eat that, she knew.

And they did, along with ice cream for dessert.

Millie remembered her daughter's sleepovers

and slumber parties. Even then girls wanted to look and act like supermodels, but they always reverted back to simply being young girls, eager for evening treats. Emily and her friend would be hungry for something more in an hour.

So, Millie found the makings for chocolate chip cookies and got to work as soon as she'd loaded the dinner dishes. Fifteen minutes later, the house was filled with the fragrance of chocolate.

Carrot cookies hadn't been a hit, but chocolate chip were another matter altogether.

Eric raided the first batch out of the oven while they were almost too hot to handle. "These are good," he said, and snitched another. The phone rang and he snagged it. "Hey. Yeah? Cool," he said to the mystery caller. Then to Millie, "Can I spend the night at Mike's house? His mom will come get me."

"Are you tired of me beating you at that Halo game?" she teased.

That made him guffaw.

Mike was Eric's best friend. Debra would have okayed it, so Millie said, "Of course."

Now it would be just her and the girls. Maybe she could lure them downstairs to play Steal the Pack.

Eric was off in a flash to grab his coat . . . and a toothbrush and clean underwear with a little prompting from his grandmother. Ten minutes later, he was gone and she was taking cookies up to the girls.

"Wow," said Sarah. She stopped painting her toenails and grabbed for a cookie. "These look awesome." At least that was what Millie thought she said. The music was turned up so high she couldn't be positive.

Emily smiled at her and called, "Thanks," then went back to turning her toenails blue.

Somehow, it didn't seem like the right time to suggest a girl party. A girl party was already going on, one for young girls. And that is as it should be, Millie told herself. She was too tired to play Steal the Pack anyway.

Emily and her friend came down twice, once for milk to go with the cookies, another to make microwave popcorn. The first time they were too busy talking to even notice Millie sitting on the couch with her book. The second time Emily was on her phone, having some kind of important conversation while Sarah coached her through it as the microwave popped. And then they vanished.

The girls were having fun, Millie told herself, and that was the main thing. And they liked the cookies.

And she was a long ways from Little Haven. She wondered what her friend Alice was doing. This would be the perfect time for a chat.

Except back in Little Haven, it was now after ten at night and Alice would be in bed. So would all of her old gardening buddies. Well, maybe she'd just give the boys a call. But her sons weren't home. Of course not. It was Friday night. People were out having fun. Having a life.

With a sigh, Millie turned on the TV to the home and garden channel. Her daughter's living room looked so big and empty when only one person was sitting in it. And there was nothing on the home and garden channel.

"Bah," she said in disgust, and started flipping channels in search of something more exciting.

ELEVEN

*D*ebra was grumpy on Saturday morning, refusing the offer of pancakes and yelling at Emily, who was chasing her friend up and down the stairs in pursuit of the pink cell phone that held treasure—a boy on the other end of the line. Millie watched with concern as Debra poured herself a cup of coffee, then leaned against the kitchen counter gripping her cup like it held the elixir of life.

"I know I'm a grump. I had too much to drink last night," Debra confessed.

It wasn't a hangover that was responsible for her daughter's mood. Debra's ex-husband was due to pick up the children for the weekend. Millie made a wide berth around that subject. "Did one of your friends bring you home?" she asked as she put the frying pan in the sink.

"Yeah. I'll have to take the bus on Monday. I'm not sure last night was worth that."

Debra had been such a pretty girl. But this morning with the dark circles under her eyes and the deepening frown lines between her brows and around her mouth, the prettiness was slipping away. And she was letting herself get too thin. It made her look gaunt. Pancakes would have been good for both her soul and her hips. "But you had a good time?" Millie prompted.

"It was okay," Debra said. Rather a lackluster account of her big evening out. "Thanks for staying with the kids," she added.

Squeals and thumping penetrated through the ceiling. Debra moaned and took another sip of her coffee. "I know I was like this at that age. Poor you."

Millie shook her head. "I loved every minute of it."

"Then you were nuts." Debra rubbed her forehead. She pushed away from the counter with a world-weary sigh. "I'm going to shower. Ben should be here soon."

"I'll clean up," Millie said, and started loading the breakfast plates into the dishwasher.

"Thanks, Mom," Debra said, and kissed her cheek.

It was a small, daughterly gesture, but it warmed Millie's heart like summer sunshine. She hummed as she cleaned up and rolled leftover pancakes into little jam sandwiches.

She had just finished in the kitchen when the

doorbell rang. It was Sarah's mother coming to collect her. Since Debra was still showering and dressing, Millie did the farewell honors.

"Thanks for making cookies," Sarah told her. "They were great. Text me," she said to Emily.

Emily nodded, then, as soon as the door was shut, ran up the stairs to pack for her weekend with her dad.

Next, Debra's ex arrived. Eric still hadn't returned from his sleepover, so there was nothing for it but to invite him in. "Emily, your father's here," Millie called up the stairs, and hoped Emily would come right down.

But she didn't. And Debra was still nowhere in sight. It looked like Millie was going to be left in charge of entertaining her former son-in-law.

They stood there in the hallway, enveloped in awkward silence. "Would you like to sit down?" she offered.

He looked up the stairway as if hoping his kids would instantly materialize so he could escape but said, "Sure. Thanks."

He followed her into the living room and they took up positions on opposite ends of the couch.

Millie hadn't seen her son-in-law without the buffer of other people since the divorce, and she found herself at a complete loss for words. What did one discuss with the man who had once been a son and was now an outcast?

"I told Eric to be back by ten. I'll just call and

make sure he's on his way," she said. That took a whole minute. Yes, Eric was en route. She returned to the living room, wishing she could have hidden out in the kitchen. But that would have been rude. "Would you like some coffee?"

"No, thanks. I'm fine."

And, from what Millie knew, he was. According to the children, their father had acquired a new girl-friend since the divorce. Someone had stepped in and taken her daughter's place. It didn't seem right.

He cleared his throat and gave the keys in his hand a flip. "Are you settling in out here okay?"

So, they were going to keep things light. Of course, there was no point talking about disappointments and regrets. "Oh, yes." And then, she couldn't help herself. "Ben, I'm so sorry you and Debra couldn't work things out."

"Maybe if she was more like you, we could have," Ben said, his jaw tight.

"Yeah, and maybe if you weren't a bastard, I would be more like my mother," came an angry voice from the stairs.

Ben stood. Politely. Reluctantly. "I see you're your normal happy self."

Debra walked into the room. She'd put on makeup and was wearing her tightest jeans, but the angry expression on her face ruined the effect. "You missed a whole night with your kids."

"I told you, it couldn't be helped," Ben snapped.

Debra rolled her eyes. "Right."

Emily thumped down the stairs, dragging an overnight bag behind her. "Daddy!" she cried, and left the bag at the bottom of the stairs and ran to her father for a hug.

"Hey, Princess," he said. "Ready for some fun?"

"Oh, yeah."

She lit up like a firefly when she was around her dad. Watching her brought back happy memories of Debra hanging on Duncan's arm when he stood visiting in the church narthex or running to greet him when he came home from a business trip. Little girls adored their daddies no matter what. Why did they have such a hard time feeling the same way about their husbands?

Now Eric had blown in the door, and he was equally glad to see his dad, and ready to turn right around and head out the door. With no clean underwear.

Debra sent him to his room to collect fresh clothes, and the three adults stood awkwardly together while Emily prattled on about her adventures at school.

This, Millie decided, was not the place for her. She could be no help to either her daughter or her former son-in-law at this point. She slipped away to hide in the kitchen. Surely something in there needed cleaning.

Five minutes later, both the children were gone and Debra was in the kitchen, too. "I'm going to run some errands," she said, her voice tight.

"Would you like some company?" Millie offered.

Debra shook her head. She heaved a sigh.

"Why don't we do something fun today instead, maybe go out for lunch?"

"I can't, Mom. I've got too much to do."

"I'm here to help."

"I know. You're doing enough already." She sighed again. "God, I hate my life."

Millie set down her sponge and hugged her daughter. "It will get better, baby."

"Yeah? When?" Debra replied bitterly, pulling away. "He skips off into the sunset with his new girlfriend and I'm left taking care of the kids. Why do I have to be the responsible one? Why does everyone have to depend on me?"

Everyone. Suddenly the breakfast pancakes weren't setting well in Millie's tummy. Was she one of the everyones?

Debra shook her head. "Don't mind me. I'm just hungover."

And hangovers had a way of bringing out what people were really feeling. Before Millie could ask her daughter if she had regrets over inviting Millie to live with them, Debra was leaving the kitchen. "I don't know when I'll be back. Don't wait on me for dinner."

A moment later, Millie heard the front door shut, and she was standing alone in the empty kitchen and looking out at the bonsai desert. What was she doing here? She threw the sponge in the sink and went to put on her garden clothes.

Amber was already at the community garden when she arrived. She greeted Millie with a smile.

"You look happy," Millie said to her. "Where's your son?"

"Home, playing with Dad."

"That's a good thing," said Millie.

"Yes, it is. They haven't done that in a while." She suddenly got busy examining her garden glove. "I probably didn't seem real open to advice yesterday, but I'm glad you gave it anyway. I think you were right. In fact, if you keep counseling me, you may just save my marriage."

Too bad she couldn't have saved her own daughter's.

"Anyway, I just wanted to thank you. I came today, hoping you'd be here."

Just a few words, but they acted like soul vitamins. Someone appreciated her. She still wasn't sure what she was doing at her daughter's house, but she knew why she was here at this garden.

TWELVE

At 11 A.M. sharp on Saturday morning, Jason was on Bobbi's apartment building doorstep with the bookcase he'd made for her, a cedar contemporary ladder style where she could put both books and plants. She opened the door and gave him a real feast for the eyes: hot legs in tight jeans, blond hair caught up in a ponytail, and pouty lips tinted pink, waiting to get kissed. He was ready for that.

He was also ready to learn more about how her mind worked. So far they'd been having a great time together. But he wanted more than a great time. He wanted depth. Those cards she kept giving him told him it was there somewhere under all that froth. Getting a chance to help her load up her new bookcase was going to give him the perfect place to look.

She pointed to it and asked with a tinge of awe in her voice, "You made that?"

He nodded, feeling as pleased as a little kid whose teacher had just raved over his crayon art.

Bobbi stepped onto the porch and ran a hand along the smooth surface of the top shelf. "It's gorgeous," she breathed. "I love it."

He could feel himself puffing up like a bullfrog. "I'm glad you like it. Let's see what it looks like with your books on it."

She stepped aside so he could carry it up to her apartment.

"I thought it might look good on that wall over there, by the window." She pointed to the far side of the room where a box of books already sat. Next to that he saw another small stack of books. Where had those been before?

"Can I get you something? Coffee, iced tea, Coke?"

"A Coke would be great," he said.

As he settled the bookcase in its new home, she poured the cola into a tall glass full of ice and then set it on her coffee table.

That was when he noticed the novel on the table with a bookmark sticking out. He picked it up. Jane Austen, of course. "Reading an old favorite?"

She blushed and nodded. There was something about a woman blushing. He felt a sudden urge to forget about loading the bookcase and start kissing off that pink lipstick right then.

But before he could, she turned around and began to dig books out of the box. "I hope they'll all fit."

"If not, I'll just have to make another bookcase," he said, and reached into the box. "Do you have a particular order you want these to go in?"

"Order?" she repeated.

"Alphabetical? By category?"

"Oh, that. Just, well, um." She began digging out books.

"You've got a lot of books on gardening," he observed, and wondered where the heck she gardened in an apartment.

"There's a community garden at Grandview Park," Bobbi said.

Gardening and reading were solitary pursuits. Somehow, he had a hard time matching those hobbies with the vivacious Bobbi, especially after seeing her in action at the Grange Hall when they'd gone line dancing. She was a people person, a real party girl. Keeping track of all the people she'd introduced him to had been almost harder than trying to keep up with her on the dance floor.

But this was nice. Perfect, in fact. She had a quiet side, too. He flipped open a book. Inside he saw the name Hope Walker. "This has your sister's name on it."

Bobbi looked over her shoulder and read it. Her cheeks turned pink again, making him wonder if she'd snitched the book from her sis. She shrugged and said, "We borrow back and forth a lot. Hope's a bookaholic. Just like me."

He scooped up a trio of self-help books on time management and goal setting, and self-actualization. "Which one of you read these?"

He was about to open one when Bobbi snatched them away. "I was going through a phase."

"A good phase to go through when you're starting a business," he observed. "So, are you an expert at goal setting? Got your whole life mapped out?"

"I wish," she said with a sigh. "I'm just not sure what I want to do."

"You mean the flower shop isn't what you want to do?"

"Oh, I love the shop," she said quickly. "I mean, well . . . it's complicated." She pulled out some more books and set them on the floor.

"Life is like that, isn't it?" she added breezily, shutting the door on the topic.

Now, that was interesting. Why didn't she want to talk more about her complicated life? Women always wanted to talk about their problems. In fact, most of the women he'd dated talked until his ears fell off.

He picked up a handful of books and began to sort through them. Here was one on herbal medicine, another on origami. And, what was this? *Beating Breast Cancer with a Positive Attitude.* Whoa. Was this what she meant by complicated? No name inside, so it couldn't be her sister's. Had Bobbi had breast cancer? Other than the pink ribbons he saw everywhere and those ads for the three-day walk, Jason didn't know much about the disease. His mom and sister were healthy. It had never touched his door. But when he thought of cancer, he thought of older women with grown kids or families at least half-raised.

He studied Bobbi as she burrowed in the box, now pulling out mostly novels. She was so sexy and full of energy. Jason thought it was pretty damned cool that she owned her own business, but maybe after having survived the disease she was re-evaluating her life. It was too early in the relationship to ask all the details he suddenly wanted to know, but he hoped she'd tell him soon. To go through what she'd gone through and stay so sunny, it took spunk.

The doorbell rang and she ran to get it.

She opened the door and there stood her sister, Hope, holding a cardboard box. "I found some more books." She caught sight of Jason and got suddenly pink cheeked. "Oh, sorry. I came up the back stairs. I didn't know you had company already."

"Come on in," said Bobbi. She turned to Jason. "We were just . . ."

"Putting together some donations for the library," Hope finished.

"Yeah," Bobbi nodded.

Jason crossed the floor and took the box from Hope. "So, you live nearby?"

"Thanks. Just downstairs." She ran a hand across her brow, which was damp from exertion, and stepped into the apartment.

"Where do you want this?" Jason asked Bobbi.

"Put it by the bookcase. I'll sort through it later. Want some iced tea?" Bobbi asked her sister.

"Um, sure," said Hope, sounding uncertain. She turned and followed Bobbi into the kitchen.

Nice asses ran in the family, Jason thought, watching her. Hope Walker had a great set of legs, too. Unlike her sister, though, she didn't dress to show off the goods. He found himself idly wondering if she had a boyfriend.

"Don't you love the bookcase Jason made?" Bobbi asked her.

Hope moved to the bookcase and ran her hand

along a smooth shelf. "It's gorgeous. You've got a real talent," she said to Jason. "What else have you made?" She knelt in front of the books and began looking through them, separating them into piles.

He joined her. "Not a lot. A couple things for myself. I made a bed for my sister, and a rocking chair for my mom. I've done some wood carving." He shrugged like it was no big deal even though to him it was. He knew he'd never be great with words. But his hands, that was a different matter.

"That's amazing," said Hope.

She was so earnest. Jason liked earnest in a woman. "Thanks."

"I love a man who can use his hands," added Bobbi, plopping down next to Jason. Between the two of them, the sisters were going to make his head so fat he'd never be able to get it through the apartment door.

He shrugged, trying to look modest. It was hard with two women fussing over you. "Everybody's got talent. You ladies work magic in that flower shop of yours."

"We try," said Hope, and Bobbi smiled at her.

Obviously these two were close. Had Hope been there for Bobbi when she had cancer? Probably. "Looks like you've got a system going here," he said, pointing to the growing piles in front of Hope.

"I like to sort books by category and then author," she said. "It's a lot easier to find what you're looking for that way, especially the nonfiction. And I keep the hardbacks and paperbacks separate. It looks better visually."

"Great idea," said Jason.

"That's how I like to do it, too." Bobbi picked up a book and looked at it, considering.

"How about putting that one over here with your fiction?" Hope suggested.

Bobbi nodded and handed it over. "I was just going to do that. You know, I think we should have some lunch," she decided, jumping up. "I've got pizza in the freezer. I'll throw it in the oven."

"Oh, I can't stay," Hope said. "I've got things to do."

"Are you sure?" asked Bobbi.

Jason could tell it was halfhearted, and he couldn't help smiling. Bobbi didn't want to share. He liked that.

"Yeah. Nice to see you," Hope said to him, and smiled. She had a nice smile. It wasn't a thousand-watt one like her sister's, but it was enough to get a guy's attention. It was quiet and warm, and reminded Jason of Glenn Close in *The Natural*.

"Same here," he said, standing and lifting a hand in casual salute.

He settled back on the couch as Bobbi walked her to the door. Pizza for lunch sounded good. The sun was shining. Maybe he could parlay lunch into an afternoon hike in the Grand Forest. And then dinner afterward.

"So," he said later, shoving the paper plate away from him, "what do you think about working off some of that pizza?"

"What did you have in mind?" she asked.

"How about a hike in the Grand Forest?" Okay, her lips were still turned up at the corners, but the smile had died from her eyes. "You like to hike, right?" Hadn't she said that?

"Oh, yeah. It's just that . . ."

"What?"

"Well, I have to be somewhere tonight and . . ."

Where did she have to be tonight, and with whom? It was still too early to be asking those kind of questions. They hadn't slept together. They hadn't talked about being exclusive. Right now he didn't have a right to ask. But that didn't mean he wasn't dying to know who his competition was. "Tonight is a long ways away," he said.

"You're right." She stood up like a woman who had made a decision and was ready to act on it. "Let's do it."

It wasn't quite as good a response as "Cool" or "Sounds like fun," but it was still a yes, so Jason decided he was good with that. He couldn't help wondering why she hadn't jumped at the chance to go hiking with him. They were having fun, she was interested in him, so what was the problem? And what did she have going on tonight?

Never mind. It didn't matter. He hated to think he had competition, but it shouldn't surprise him if he did. He'd just have to outdo the competition, that was all.

As they meandered along various trails under tall firs and cedars, she plied him with questions about the different hikes he'd done and where. Had he ever seen a bear? Had he ever gotten stung by bees? Did he ever worry about getting mugged? Not exactly the conversation of a seasoned hiker.

"Don't tell me you've gotten mugged hiking?" he teased.

"Does getting groped count?"

That wasn't surprising to hear. He could hardly keep his hands off her.

"It can be dangerous for a woman in the woods," Bobbi continued.

"Not in these woods," he scoffed. Suddenly, a vision of his encounter with her sister came to mind. Hope had been flushed and smiling, walking along the trail, lost in the experience. She sure hadn't been afraid.

"And bees. You can get stung."

"Yeah, I got stung once," Jason admitted.

"It's not fun," Bobbi said, her mouth turning down. She started chewing her lip as if working on a big decision. "I should tell you, I haven't gone hiking since I got stung by bees."

Jason scratched the back of his head. Hmmm. She'd led him to believe she was into this kind of thing. Well, maybe she had been before she got stung. A bad experience could turn a woman off.

"You can get stung by bees in the garden, too," he pointed out.

"Not a whole nest of them." She shuddered. "But this is nice," she added in a small voice. "I'm having a good time."

He smiled down at her. "I'm glad." He gently pulled her to him and kissed her.

She came willingly enough, but the kiss got cut short by other approaching hikers. Just as well, he decided. He didn't want to be numbered with those other gropers she'd encountered in the woods in the past. He reminded himself that he wasn't in a hurry. *Don't let your brains go south this time around. The big head tells the little head what to do, not the other way around.*

Half an hour later they had reached the end of the trail. "I think you helped me conquer my fear of bees," Bobbi told him, giving him a dimpled smile.

"Good. What do you say we go out to dinner tonight and celebrate?" The answer was going to be no. He could see it in her eyes.

She shook her head. "I'm sorry. I've got a commitment I can't get out of."

"Every Saturday?"

"For a while. But I'm free on Sunday. Want to try your hand at line dancing again?"

Not really, but for her he would. "Why not?" he said, trying to sound excited about the prospect of making a fool of himself in public again.

He was about as excited over that as he was over

having nothing to do on a Saturday night. Maybe he should have just come right out and asked Bobbi if he had competition. Much more of this settling for a date on Sundays and he was going to feel like a second-string player.

"Still can't make the A-list, huh?" teased Duke when Jason called to see if he wanted to go out for a beer.

"You're funny," said Jason. "Maybe I should take that smart lip of yours and wrap it over your head."

"You can try," Duke said amiably. "Meanwhile, why dontcha come check out the action at the Last Resort? The scenery over there beats the Sticks and Balls to hell. Those cocktail waitresses are hot."

Jason wasn't interested in hot cocktail waitresses, not when he'd found the perfect woman. But he wasn't interested in sitting around watching the tube on a Saturday night, either. And he was ready to branch out beyond the tavern at the edge of town they often haunted after work. "I'm down with that."

So, nine o'clock found him threading his way through a sea of tables that looked like they'd been stolen from the set of some old fifties flick to where Duke sat, dredging handfuls of beer nuts out of one of the biggest, ugliest old ashtrays Jason had ever seen.

"Hey, man," Duke greeted him.

They bumped fists and Jason sat down and looked around, checking the place out. The point of entry had a huge fish tank running all along the wall, dividing the lobby area from the rest of the lounge. The bar took up the entire far end of the room. The dance floor wasn't big, and tonight the little stage above it was set up with a podium and microphone—trivia night, Duke had said. The place was dim, and packed with a mix of mostly twenty-something couples and singles looking to end up as a couple before the evening was over. A Blake Lewis song blasted out of the speakers, wrapping the hip hangout in an audio blanket of cool. Two women sat at a table nearby nursing drinks and pretending to visit as they checked out the neighboring tables. One of them winked at him.

"Yeah, they're here for the trivia contest," Duke cracked.

"I'm surprised you haven't offered to team up with them," said Jason.

Duke smirked. "I might give 'em a thrill. After I get this chick's phone number." He nodded at the approaching waitress, all decked out in a short, black skirt and a plunging black halter top. "Now there's some hot cheese. Don't be getting any ideas about this one. She's got Duke written all over her."

Jason stared at the waitress and felt his lower jaw dropping. "What the hell?"

THIRTEEN

*B*obbi had been approaching the table at a good clip. Jason watched as she put on the brakes and stared at him like he was a cross between the grim reaper and the taxman.

She made a fast recovery though, smiling at him and closing the distance. "Fancy meeting you here."

Her recovery was quicker than his. All he could do was gawk at her, his brain frozen. What was Bobbi Walker the florist doing working as a cocktail waitress? He turned to Duke as if his friend somehow had an explanation for why his perfect woman was slinging drinks in the local pickup place instead of . . . what? What should she be doing? Sitting home reading poetry? At least he now knew there wasn't somebody else.

"You guys know each other?" Duke asked, looking from one to the other.

"Yeah," Jason said slowly. "Why didn't you just tell me you worked on Saturday nights?" he asked Bobbi. "I was beginning to think I had competition."

"This is the Sunday-night chick?" Duke asked, dismayed.

"I thought you wouldn't be real impressed if you knew I was a cocktail waitress." She lifted one shoulder in an embarrassed shrug. "But . . . I've got bills."

Jason remembered the book on cancer he'd seen at her apartment. Of course, that explained what she was doing here dressed up like a fifties pin-up girl. The poor kid was moonlighting to pay off medical bills. "How do you manage to do this and work at the shop every day?" She was going to jeopardize her health with all that nonstop work. This woman needed someone to step in and take care of her.

She smiled her dimpled smile. "Working at the shop's not working. That's fun." And then she turned the thousand-watt charm on Duke, too. "So is working here. What can I get you?"

"Heineken," said Duke. He sounded like a man who wanted a Harley and had to settle for a Honda.

"I'll have a Hale's Pale Amber," said Jason.

"Coming right up," she said and hurried off.

Jason frowned as Duke watched her retreating posterior. "Hey."

Now Duke was frowning, too. "I can't believe that's the woman you've been seeing. I thought she owned a flower shop. What's she doing working here?"

"You heard her. She's got bills."

"What, she's got a shopping addiction?"

"She's got medical bills."

Duke's eyebrows shot up. "Medical bills?"

"I was helping her set up her bookcase today. She had a book on cancer."

Duke let out a soft whistle and shook his head. "I can't believe it."

"Me, either," said Jason. "She's got so much energy."

They both watched as Bobbi stopped at other tables, collecting empty glasses and fresh orders. Neither one said anything, not until after she'd returned with their beers and started their tab.

"I don't know," Duke said as she walked away. "It can't have been breast cancer. I'd stake my life on it. Those are real."

"Hey, keep your eyes off the boobs," Jason snapped.

"Sorry," Duke muttered, and took a swig of his beer. "I just can't believe my cocktail babe is your flower chick. Man, that sucks."

She'd known this was coming. Sooner or later, Jason had to come here. But why, oh why, couldn't he have come after she'd moved on to something else, something better, brainier, more impressive? This was so embarrassing. Of course, he'd been too polite to say anything rude, but he hadn't had to. She'd known what he thought of her when she saw that shocked expression on his face. Everyone thought cocktail waitresses were dumb. It wasn't fair. A girl could do this to put herself through school, but if it was her real job, well then, all people saw when they looked at her was a bod with no brain. But she had a brain and she'd prove it to him. She was going to read that Jane Austen book first thing when she got home tonight.

For now, she needed to pay attention to what she was doing. She went to turn in her orders to Don, the owner, who was tending bar. "I need a Scotch rocks, two Red Hooks, a Sex on the Beach, a Heineken, and a Hale's Pale Amber."

Anna Lane, another one of the waitresses, was frowning as she loaded up her cocktail tray. Like Bobbi, she spent a lot of time dodging gropers. Unlike Bobbi, she wasn't very good at it.

"If that creep puts his hands on my butt one more time . . ." She left the sentence unfinished.

"Is he drunk?" asked Bobbi.

"If he's had too much we can refuse to serve him," said Don.

"No, he's had just enough to make him a jerk," Anna said.

"After this, I'm cutting him off," Don said. "We don't need a problem."

Bobbi turned to look at Anna's section. It wasn't difficult to locate the creep. He was sitting with a couple of other guys and a woman who looked like she needed the table to hold her up. He had chin-length hair tucked behind his ears and was wearing jeans and a white shirt unbuttoned low enough to show off his spray-tanned and freshly waxed chest, and he was tipped back in his chair, ogling the women a couple of tables over.

"God's gift to the cocktail waitress," Bobbi said in disgust.

"Sometimes I hate this job," Anna said, her voice wobbly. "Everyone thinks we're sluts."

"Well, we're not," Bobbi said firmly, but she couldn't help sneaking a look in Jason's direction. Now that he saw what she did for a living, would he think in stereotypes and decide she was a slut? "Why don't you let me take that table?" she offered.

"He'd grope you, too," Anna predicted. "No, I can handle him."

Bobbi wasn't so sure about that, so she kept an eye out as she served her tables. If that slimeball made one false move . . .

And there it was. Anna leaned over to lay a drink in front of his friend and got her butt patted in the process.

Anna straightened and looked down at Slimeball and said something. He held up both hands and shook his head, feigning innocence.

Somebody needed to clue this guy in. Bobbi sailed off across the lounge, riding to the rescue as Jerry, who ran the trivia contest, took his place up at the mike and said, "Okay, people, how smart do you all think you are tonight?"

She arrived at the table just in time to hear Anna say to the slimeball, "You did, too, touch me."

"If I did it must have been an accident," Slimeball said, and winked at his buddy.

"You apologize to her right now," Bobbi demanded.

"Whoa, it's Wonder Babe." Chuckling, he picked up his drink and raised it to his lips.

"Yeah. Wonder Babe meets Slimeball," Bobbi growled. She still had a drink on her cocktail tray. Perfect. She dumped it into his lap. "Oh, my bad."

Her surprise attack made him jump up. In the process, he bumped the table and sent his drink flying into the woman sitting with him and his friends. "Hey," she cried, and jumped up, too, like a human domino.

"Sorry," Bobbi said. "I guess that's what you get for hanging out with slime."

"That's not slime. That's my brother," the woman snarled.

"I want an apology," yelled Slimeball.

"Maybe you should learn how to give one before you ask for one," Bobbi retorted.

"Hey," said his friend. He made a grab for Bobbi, but she danced out of reach.

"Oh, dear," fretted Anna.

Suddenly, there was another player. Jason had Bobbi firmly by the arm and was trying to lead her away, saying, "My friend and I are ready for another drink."

But the tipsy woman caught her other arm. "Where do you think you're going? I want an apology."

Two more guys from a neighboring table joined

the fray. "Why don't you pick on someone your own size?" one growled at Slimeball.

"What would you know about size?" he shot back.

Now they had a major testosterone spill at the Last Resort, with male fists starting to fly in all directions.

"I think it would be a good idea if you went home sick," Jason said, urging Bobbi along.

She tried to keep going with him, but the tipsy woman still had a hold of her other arm and was trying to drag her across the table. "I feel like a wishbone," she groaned. This was like playing tug-of-war. Only she was the rope. She had a sudden vision of herself with droopy arms stretched out to twice their normal length. By the time she got loose, she'd not only be putting pumice cream on her heels, she'd be putting it on her knuckles, too.

She made one final, superhuman effort to break free. The woman lost her grip and fell over the table, bringing it down. Someone threw a chair. Outside she could hear a police siren.

Jason's friend was with him now, running interference. Brawlers bounced off him as Jason hustled Bobbi toward the door.

They were about to go out when the police came in.

"Just as well," Jason's friend told her. "You can tell the cops what happened. We saw everything. We'll back you up."

And they did, which was good enough for the cops. But not good enough for Bobbi's boss.

"Bobbi, we need to talk," Don told her after things had finally settled down.

She knew what that meant. With tears in her eyes and her chin held high, she followed Don to the liquor room in back of the club. The small storage room with its boxes and bottles of booze closed in on her as Don turned on the light and shut the door. Bobbi wedged herself in between a couple of boxes of beer and tried to will the axe not to fall.

"You know I like you," he began.

How many hard breakups had she tried to soften with those very same words? "Then don't fire me," she pleaded.

"That was strike two tonight. The cops come one more time and I'm out of business." Don scratched his shaved head. "I wish I didn't have to let you go, I really do. But I've sunk everything into this place and I can't lose it. And that guy you dumped the drink on . . ."

"The one who was harassing Anna," Bobbi reminded him.

"You know who that was?"

Uh-oh. "Someone important?" Bobbi's stomach was feeling queasy now.

"The mayor's kid."

Bobbi fell back against the shelves, making the beer bottles rattle. "Oh, no."

"Oh, yes."

"I'm sorry, Don. I'm really sorry." If only she'd known. Why hadn't she known? She knew half of Heart Lake, for crying out loud. Obviously, not the important half.

"Me, too," Don said. "But I still have to let you go."

Bobbi nodded, tears slipping down her cheeks. "I understand." At least he hadn't yelled at her, or pointed a finger and said, "You're fired," like Donald Trump on that TV show.

When she finally left the Last Resort, she was no longer an employee.

"Your boss is a moron," seethed Jason's friend as they walked her to her car. "You're the reason I come in there. They're not getting my business anymore."

Bobbi blew her nose into the tissue he'd offered and tried to smile her thanks. That muscle-filled black T-shirt, those black jeans, and the leather jacket just cried bad boy. And now here he was, being a bad boy with a good heart.

But his kind words didn't make her feel any better. "That's sweet of you to say," she managed, her voice quavering.

"At least you still have the flower shop," Jason said, giving her a hug.

It was the final straw. Her stream of tears became a river. What, oh, what was she going to do? How was she going to pay her rent?

● ● ●

"I know exactly what you're going to do," Hope said when Bobbi told her the news the next day. "You can move in with me. I'm not using that extra bedroom for anything but junk anyway." Hope regarded her sister, who sat slumped at her little Formica table. Normally Bobbi was like the crocus, ready to shrug off winter and rush into spring. Right now she looked more like a wilted pansy. It was unnerving. Hope decided the African violets on her kitchen table needed watering. She got up and filled a glass with water. "There's still the flower shop. Now you can work for me full time."

"You can't afford that," Bobbi said.

"Sure, I can. I was paying Clarice to work there four days a week. What's one more day? And the way the business is growing I really need the help. You'd be doing me a favor."

Bobbi gave a snort. "I know I'm not the smart one, but I'm not that dumb."

"I'm not snowing you," Hope insisted. "We can do twice the volume with you there all the time. And, now that you're not working nights, you could take a course and become a floral designer."

"A floral designer," Bobbi breathed. "That sounds impressive."

"You've already got the gift. You may as well develop it," Hope said.

"You'd really do this for me?"

"It's no more than you'd do for me."

176

"Wow," breathed Bobbi. "You've saved me."

"It's not much compared to how you saved me when I was sick," said Hope.

"It's a lot to me," Bobbi assured her. She jumped out of her chair and hugged Hope. "You're the best sister in the universe." Hope had barely hugged her back before Bobbi was racing for the door, saying, "I've got to go."

"Where are you going?"

"I have to start packing, sign up for my first class . . ." Her words echoed behind her. A moment later, the door shut, leaving Hope smiling. She'd done a good thing. This was awesome. She and Bobbi would get to be in the shop together all the time. And they'd be roommates.

And every time she turned around she'd see Jason Wells.

Early afternoon sun was streaming in through the kitchen window, spotlighting the pot of flowers. She could almost hear them whispering, "Let's go to the garden."

Good idea.

FOURTEEN

*M*illie had tried to convince her daughter to go to church with her in the morning, but Debra had insisted she wasn't up to it.

"I don't want to go sit all by myself in a church full of strangers," she'd said.

"You won't be by yourself. You'll be with me."

"I mean without a husband." Debra poured herself a cup of coffee and retreated to the living room, her bedroom slippers scuff-scuffing over the kitchen vinyl as she went.

Millie followed her. "A lot of women don't have husbands. Surely you don't want to wait until you have a new man to have a life."

Debra fell onto the couch, put her mug on the coffee table, and stared into it as if she could see her future in there.

Millie understood about loss. A woman had to swim through deep, dark waters before she got safely to shore. But swimming was the operative word. Debra was barely treading water. Working long hours, drinking afterward with her coworkers, and spending money on things she didn't need wasn't going to get her safely to dry land.

Millie sat down opposite her. "Debra," she said firmly. "You have got to start looking ahead. You're still a young woman. Your life is not over."

Debra took a deep drink, then frowned as if her coffee was bitter. "We haven't even been divorced a year and he's already got a girlfriend."

"You're not married anymore. Was he supposed to carry a torch forever?" Millie asked reasonably.

That made Debra glower. "He's just skipping off into the sunset and I'm here making the house payments and raising the kids."

"With child support he's giving you. You can't have it both ways. You can't turn a man loose and then expect him to hang around. You didn't want to be married to him anymore."

"I didn't want to be married to him the way he was acting. If he'd gone to counseling, we'd still be together. Whose side are you on, anyway?" Debra shot off the couch and went to the kitchen to pour herself a fresh mug of bitterness.

Millie remained in her chair and sighed. She loved her daughter dearly, but sometimes Debra exhausted her. Had she exhausted Ben, too? Millie looked out the window at the stark front yard. How could she help Debra plant something right now that would give her the future she wanted? It was a question worth asking, but not today. In her present mood, Debra wasn't open to advice from her mother. Come to think of it, Debra had rarely been open to advice from her mother.

Millie felt suddenly tired, but she planted both hands on her thighs and leveraged herself out of the chair. She was going to church. And then she was going to spend some time in her garden, where things wanted to grow.

By the time she got to the community garden, Amber and her son were already there. Amber sat in the spring sunshine pulling weeds, while Seth squatted in front of some nearby thimbleberry bushes looking for the rabbit.

179

Amber raised a hand in greeting. "We've got things coming up," she announced. "How cool is that?"

"Very," Millie said with a smile. She looked around at the other patches. Green things were flourishing everywhere. She could hear birds singing. She stepped through her garden gate and set down the containers of pansies she'd picked up on sale at Safeway's garden department.

"And look," Amber added, pointing to the little coffee grounds fence she was building around her plants. "No slugs. You're a genius, Millie."

Tell that to my daughter, Millie thought.

Seth came running back. "Mommy, I saw the bunny."

"Did you leave him the carrot?"

Seth nodded eagerly and pointed to where the carrot lay on the ground in front of the tangle of bushes.

"Well, then, watch from here and let's see if he comes out and eats it."

"He won't be tempted by that. They like the greens," said Millie. "And I'm not sure bribing him with carrots is going to keep him out of your garden. He seems to have found a way past the fence. I do think you're going to have to add that chicken wire."

Amber heaved a sigh. "This garden is going to cost me a fortune."

"Think of it as an investment," Millie told her.

"You get so much from a garden, things that you can't put a price on."

"I want to go look for the bunny," Seth said, marching out of the garden.

"You can, but he'll probably be too scared to come out and get the carrot if he sees you sitting there," Amber cautioned him.

"But I won't hurt him," said Seth.

"I know that and you know that, but he doesn't. We're a lot bigger than him and he's scared. He needs time to get brave."

Seth sighed and plopped down in the dirt.

"Would you like to help me plant my pansies, Seth?" Millie offered.

The child lit up at that and nodded eagerly.

"Well, come back inside the fence and we'll settle these in their new home."

He was in her garden in a second, trampling the flowers in his eagerness.

"Seth, watch where you're stepping," Amber said.

"He's fine," Millie said, pulling on her garden gloves. She could still remember Debra in the garden with her, patting down soil with pudgy, little hands. As she got older, Debra drifted away from the garden, setting up her headquarters on the lawn and sunning herself on a blanket, painting her nails, reading magazines about beautiful people.

"I did the farmer's market yesterday," Amber announced.

"Oh? And how did that go?"

Amber gave a one-shouldered shrug. "Okay. I didn't realize how many people would be there selling—everything from honey to candles. A lot of people selling baked stuff."

"So, the competition was fierce?" guessed Millie.

Amber gave a half-frown. "You could say that. I think I need to sell something besides banana bread and oatmeal cookies."

Millie took a moment to direct Seth in digging a home for the pansies. She looked at them thoughtfully.

"Got any suggestions?"

"As a matter of fact, yes," Millie said slowly. "What about trying something more unique?"

"Okay," Amber prompted.

"Maybe take advantage of garden season. So many flowers are edible, pansies for instance, and they make lovely decorations. Of course, you have to make sure they haven't been sprayed. I bet you could find some at the Trellis."

"Great idea! I could sugar them, put them on cupcakes," said Amber, catching on.

"There you go. And maybe incorporate some lavender in your baking? I have a wonderful recipe for lavender cookies I could give you, if you'd like it," Millie offered.

"I'll take it," said Amber with a decisive nod. "Can you e-mail it to me?"

"I'm afraid I'm not much good on the computer," Millie said. "But I'll copy it out for you, and you can come by one day this week and pick it up if you like. I'll make tea. How does that sound?"

"That sounds like a deal," Amber said, beaming. She looked around the garden, suddenly stumped. "Um. We're not growing any lavender, are we?"

"I'm afraid not," Millie said sadly. "But Hope says that little kitchen shop in town sells lavender sugar."

"Perfect. I'll make a batch of cookies to sell this weekend." Amber smiled at her. "Millie, I'm sure glad I met you. You're amazing."

It was nice that someone thought so. "I'm happy to help," she murmured.

They worked on, Seth chattering happily, the birds serenading them. At last Amber sat back, turned her face up to the sun, and sighed. "You know, I never thought I'd like being in the garden, but there's something about this that's, I don't know, peaceful. I feel like I'm building my own world here." She shot Millie a mischievous grin. "Do you think that's what God felt when He was making the Garden of Eden?"

Millie smiled back. "I wouldn't doubt it."

"Here comes our neighbor," Amber said, pointing to Hope Walker, who was striding their way, resplendent in jeans and a sleeveless pink top and carrying a little basket full of gardening tools. "It's about time you got here," Amber greeted her. "We've been at this for hours."

Hope waved her hand in salute. "I'll bet."

"You look like spring," Millie said.

"Thanks," said Hope. "I can't think of anything I'd rather look like."

"How's life?" added Amber.

"Crazy," said Hope. "My sister's moving in with me. And I have a new employee."

"Really. Who?" asked Millie.

"My sister."

"Wow, that's a lot of togetherness," Amber observed.

"But great fun," added Millie.

"It will be," Hope said, almost sounding like she was still convincing herself of it.

"I like to have fun," put in Seth, who was now done with the pansies. He stood up and looked over to the thimbleberry bushes. "Look!"

The little rabbit had crept out from under the bushes and was now investigating the carrot.

"I guess the bunny was ready for lunch," said Amber. "Better that carrot than our veggies."

"Oh, he'll get around to those eventually," Hope said. "It looks like he's already snitched some of that lettuce that's coming up."

Amber sighed. "That thing is not a rabbit. It's a pig dressed up in bunny fur."

"I want to go see him," Seth said.

"Go really slow," Amber cautioned. "And don't get too close. You'll scare him."

Seth nodded and was out of the garden in a bound, then running on tiptoe toward the rabbit.

Amber returned her attention to Hope. "How did all this stuff with your sister happen?"

Hope set down her gardening basket. "Well, she lost her job."

Amber got suddenly quiet, leaving Millie to carry on the conversation. "It's really sweet of you to help her out."

"She'd do the same for me," Hope said. "In fact, she's done a lot for me. I owe her big time. But that's not why I'm doing this," she added quickly. "I love my sister. I'm happy to have her working with me. Bobbi does gorgeous arrangements. She's got a real gift. And people love her. She'll be wonderful with the customers. And the shop's getting busier all the time, so I need the help."

Millie set down her spade and studied Hope. She was saying all the right things, but . . . "Taking on a full-time employee is a big step."

"But it's a good step. If I get sick again . . ."

"Sick?" Amber looked questioningly at Hope. "Were you sick?"

Hope bit her lip.

Millie kept quiet. It wasn't her place to say anything. If Hope wanted to share, she would.

Hope gnawed on her lower lip.

"Not that it's any of my business," Amber said quickly. "Sorry. I didn't mean to pry."

"No, that's okay. It's just . . . I had cancer."

Amber stared at her. "Oh, no. But you're too young."

Hope ran a hand through the soil in front of her. "I guess somebody forgot to card those cancer cells."

"Gosh, I'm sorry," said Amber. "You've had it tough." She lowered her gaze. "It makes losing our restaurant seem like nothing."

Hope looked at her in surprise. "You had a restaurant?"

"Once upon a bad time."

"That couldn't have been easy," said Hope. "I can't imagine losing my business."

"I don't want to go through it again, that's for sure. One time on that ride was enough."

"I hear you," Hope murmured.

Millie regarded the two women working companionably alongside her. Debra could learn something from them.

The women tinkered in their gardens another hour, then Amber threw down her spade and said, "Okay, I've had enough. Anybody feel like getting something to drink at Crazy Eric's? I have a whole six dollars to spend."

Hope drew an arm across her damp brow. "That sounds good to me. I'm ready for a break."

A break sounded good to Millie, too. Actually,

she'd been ready to quit an hour ago, but she'd stayed for the companionship. That probably hadn't been wise. She felt a little shaky as she got up. You need to pace yourself, she thought, you're not fifty anymore. But when she was with these girls she could almost believe she was.

Fifteen minutes later, they were all at Heart Lake's one-and-only burger joint, nursing diet root beers and watching Seth consume what looked like the world's largest root beer float.

Millie wondered what Debra was doing right now. She was probably at the mall, engaging in what she called retail therapy, trying to find the cure for her frustration inside a new purse.

If you asked Millie, this was true therapy. Enjoying the company of women who were working hard to make their lives better, listening to a child's laughter.

A sudden thought hit Millie. When had it become more rewarding to spend time with relative strangers than with her own flesh and blood? And how was it that relative strangers could so quickly begin to feel like relatives?

It was a bittersweet mystery. Maybe someday she'd solve it. Meanwhile, she'd enjoy this new blessing that was blooming in her life.

FIFTEEN

Amber returned home carrying a heart full of hope. She loved it here at Heart Lake. She loved her new friends. And she loved gardening. Okay, not the getting dirty part, and if it wasn't for the companionship at the community garden, she would die from the tedium of weeding. But feeling the sun on her back, seeing Seth thriving in the fresh air, visiting with her new friends, planning new baking adventures—it all worked like some magical tonic. It filled her with energy, drove her to roll down her car window and sing along with her son's Veggie Tales CD at the top of her lungs. She couldn't carry a tune in a flowerpot, but that didn't bother Seth. He sang right along with her.

They were still singing when they got out of the car. They came into the house with pink cheeks and smelling like the great outdoors to find Ty stationed at his usual post in front of the TV, looking as white as bread dough.

"You should come to the garden with us," said Amber.

He held up a hand in a no-thanks gesture. "That's okay."

"You look like a zombie." What a coincidence. He practically was one.

Or not quite. She noticed the Sunday paper open

to the classifieds. Maybe he'd been doing more than chopping vegetables while they were gone.

He made a face. "Thanks." Then, "Are you hungry? I've got stuff cut up for stir-fry."

"That sounds good," she said. What she'd really wanted to say was, "So, have you been looking for work? Did you check anything out on-line?" But she didn't. The sore subject of Ty's unemployment was becoming the elephant in the room nobody wanted to acknowledge.

Actually, there was more than one elephant stomping through the Howell house. Talking about their marriage was even scarier than talking about Ty's job situation. Better to let that particular elephant crash around and hope that eventually it would move on to someone else's home. Maybe if she kept following Millie's advice, it would.

"This is good," she said later as they ate Ty's stir-fry. "Did you make this up?"

He shrugged. "I just threw in a bunch of stuff."

"You throw good," she said, and managed an encouraging smile.

"Can I have some more?" asked Seth.

"Sure, bud," he said.

"Pretty soon we'll have spinach from our garden to cook with, won't we, Sethie?" said Amber. "Spinach salad, spinach quiche, spinach pie. Spinach cake," she added, tickling Seth and making him giggle.

"You've actually got things growing?"

Amber frowned at her husband. Cute. Building up your mate didn't seem to be a two-way street around here. "Yeah, as a matter of fact, I do."

He acknowledged her accomplishment with a grunt.

She let it go without saying anything, but inside she fumed. At least she was doing something. What was he doing?

She found out after she'd cleaned up the dinner mess and they'd put Seth to bed.

"What do you think about moving to Seattle?" Ty said as she turned on the radio.

Think? She couldn't think. She could only sit there in shock while Taylor Swift sang about tears on her guitar. "Why?"

"More restaurants."

"It's not that far to drive from here."

He didn't say anything, just looked out the window at the lake.

Now that the sun had gone down, Heart Lake had turned into a dark mirror, reflecting the lights from houses on the other side. It looked cozy and romantic, like something out of a Thomas Kinkade painting. Only the other day she'd been considering pulling up the sticker bushes and trying to plant some flowers around the house, make it look like one of those little cottages that made her want to escape into the picture.

"Do you have something lined up in Seattle?" she asked, bracing herself.

He shook his head. "Not yet."

"Then I don't understand why you want to move." Why was he doing this to her?

"I'm just throwing out ideas," he said, his voice defensive.

"Well, can't you throw out some other ideas? I like it here. I don't want to move again."

That stopped the dialogue. Ty clamped his mouth tighter than the proverbial clam. She could see the muscles along his jaw clenching, a sure sign that he was mad. She supposed if Millie were here she'd advise Amber to go over to where he sat on the couch and give him a hug, tell him that if they wound up having to move she'd go, she'd be there for him. But she didn't want to move. And right now, she didn't want to be there for him, either. And she didn't want to tiptoe around this damned elephant one second longer.

"You know what," she said, her voice a snotty dare. "You find a job first and then let's talk about where we're going to live. But right now, I'm the only one who's working. And I'm working here. And I like it here." This little house wasn't much, but she had made it her own, hanging her pictures on the wall, scraping together enough money to paint the kitchen a pretty sage green. And she was just finding her feet in this new community. Now he wanted to knock her off her feet. She'd be damned if she'd help him do it.

She snatched up the latest well-worn issue of *Bon*

Appétit from the coffee table and marched to the bedroom to read, leaving Ty alone with Taylor Swift.

She read the magazine cover to cover, then turned to her library paperback romance to read about real heroes while Ty sat moping in the living room. The sound of music was long gone and Amber could hear the drone of the TV.

He never used to watch TV, other than the World Series or an occasional movie. Too much to do, he used to joke. Now watching the tube was the only thing he did. For all she cared, he could get sucked in there and never come out.

At ten, she turned off the light and burrowed under the covers, hugging her pillow. Her day had started out so great. Why did he have to go and spoil it?

He came to bed not long after her. She could sense him leaning over her to see if she was awake, but she kept her eyes shut until he settled down with his back to her. The last thing she wanted right now was to talk about her future, and the last person she wanted to talk about it with was him.

When his breathing finally became deeper and steadier, she opened her eyes and stared into the dark at the everyday things that took on new identities with the night. The old dresser lurked against the wall like a monster waiting to pounce. The chair next to the bed with her clothes draped over it felt like some entity crouching next to her. Sleep, that blessed shield, lay a million blinks away.

She used to sleep great at night, but those were the days when she snuggled into bed next to Ty wearing nothing but a smile. She squeezed her eyes shut, determined to conk out. She started by counting sheep. Somewhere along the way, the sheep morphed into giant bunnies with big, veggie-devouring fangs.

Okay, that did it. Time to get up. She padded to the kitchen and made herself a cup of chamomile tea, then stood drinking it and looking out the window. If only she could gather all the bad feelings dirtying up the house and throw them in the lake.

She poured the last half of her tea down the sink with a sigh. What she needed to sleep well couldn't be put in a mug. She went back to bed and slipped in next to Ty. Then she hugged her pillow and shut her eyes. At least she could pretend to sleep, and maybe, if she pretended long enough, she would.

At some point she did, but she woke up the next morning feeling unrested and grumpy. She needed mommy R & R. "I've got some errands to run," she told Ty. Her voice was still full of leftover snottiness from the night before, but she didn't care.

"Are you taking Seth?" he asked. He sounded stiff, like his jaw had locked in its clenched condition.

She shook her head. "You guys are on your own."

"I was going to drop off some apps."

Sure he was. "I'll be back by noon," she said. If she didn't return to find him camped in front of the tube, it would be a miracle.

Her first stop was Kizzy's Kitchen, the place to look for lavender sugar to use in her baking. The kitchen shop occupied space in one of the buildings on Lake Way, the downtown's main street, between Front Porch Furnishings and Something You Need. As with all the shops in town, the street number was painted on a flat, pink, wood heart positioned to the left of the front door. Amber looked at that little heart and thought of one of her mother's favorite sayings: *Home is where the heart is.* If that was the case, she and Ty were on the verge of being homeless.

The kitchen shop was a cook's dream, full of goodies, gadgets, cookbooks, tea towels, aprons, and oven mitts that Martha Stewart would kill for. A cheery display of copper pots and pans hung in one corner. Now, that was what Amber wanted in her kitchen someday, if she ever could afford a house again—lots and lots of copper cookware. She'd buy out the whole display. And she'd have a big kitchen with granite countertops and stainless steel appliances, and an island where she could whip up incredible desserts.

For now, all she'd be buying was lavender sugar. She drifted to the section of the store that had been set aside for baking and immediately got sucked in by the row of bins housing every kind of cookie cutter imaginable. Amber loved cookie cutters. She owned everything from alphabet letters to angels. Of course, she had all the traditional holiday cookie cutters, too. But here was one she didn't have. Shaped like a tulip in full bloom, it was perfect for her new life. And it would be perfect for lavender cookies. Now, if she could just find some lavender sugar.

Kizzy, the shop owner, was more than happy to help her. In her full-length red apron with its heart appliqué, she looked like she should be on a cooking show. Amber guessed this woman was somewhere around her mother's age, but she had no gray hair and her skin was smooth and dark as carved mahogany.

"Are you new in town?" she asked as she rang up Amber's purchases. "I could have sworn I knew every baker in Heart Lake."

"I am, as a matter of fact, but I'm loving it here. And I love to bake. If these cookies turn out, I'm going to sell them at the farmer's market."

"Maybe you should be making them at Sweet Somethings Bakery. Sarah Goodwin is a friend of mine. I could speak to her."

"How about telling her to give me a raise?" Amber joked.

Kizzy threw up her hands. "I should have known if there was new talent in town Sarah would find it."

"Well, I don't know if she's quite discovered my

talent. Right now I'm ringing up orders and making lattes."

"You come up with some good stuff and she'll have you chained to the oven in no time, I can guarantee it," Kizzy said, handing over the bag with Amber's purchases. "And you come back and see me again soon. Let me know how those cookies turn out."

"I'll do better than that. I'll bring you some," Amber offered.

Kizzy made the sign of the cross and shook her head violently. "I couldn't. I'm a member of Cookies Anonymous. One bite and I'd be under the kitchen table with crumbs on my face. But they sound wonderful," she added. "I'm sure they'll be a hit."

Millie's house was Amber's next stop. She had to double-check the address when she pulled up in front of the place. What kind of bad karma was this? The house was big and boring, and it had no yard. Millie belonged in a little English cottage, or a farmhouse with flowers everywhere and a front walk made of paving stones. No wonder she was at the community garden so much.

Millie was ready for her. "I've got the water on," she said, leading the way to the kitchen.

Amber followed her through a living room with big, leather furniture and a flat-panel TV. A black cat with white front paws trotted out from behind a chair and followed them into the kitchen.

"Now, you know you've been fed. Nothing more until tonight," Millie told it.

But once they were in the kitchen, she caved and dished a couple of spoonfuls into the cat's bowl. "I'm a bit of a pushover," she confessed.

Amber couldn't help wondering if that was how Millie had wound up out here at her daughter's house in the first place.

"These used to be the hit of my garden club meetings," she said, handing over a sheet of paper with a beautifully scripted recipe. "I'm so happy a whole new generation is going to be enjoying them. You know, for a while, lavender was considered rather an old-fashioned herb, but it's making a comeback."

"I hope so," Amber said.

"I'll give you my carrot cookie recipe, too. People will love those and come back for more."

"Good. I need to make a pot of cash."

"I'm sure you will. And before long, your husband will have a job and then you can keep what you make for pin money."

That wiped the smile off Amber's face. "Only if he can move to Seattle."

Millie wasn't looking so cheerful herself all of a sudden. "Oh. You're moving?"

"He wants to."

"Does he have a job offer?" Millie became suddenly very busy setting the teapot and their cups and saucers on the kitchen table.

Amber perched on a kitchen chair and eyed the frosted cookies Millie had set out on a salad plate. "No. Seattle is just the latest plot of green grass."

"Ah. The grass is always greener?"

"Something like that. But I like it here. I don't want to move, so I hope you're not going to suggest I just pick up and follow him."

Millie nudged the plate her direction. "Have a carrot cookie."

Amber took a cookie and bit into it. And was pleasantly surprised. "You're right. People will love these."

Millie smiled as she settled herself at the table and poured tea into their cups. "They're perfect with a nice cup of tea. Constant Comment, my favorite," she murmured. "I think it's a comforting tea."

"I could use some comfort." Emotion gathered in a tight ball in Amber's throat and she suddenly found it hard to swallow.

Millie leaned across the table and placed a hand on her arm. "Be patient, dear. These difficult times always feel like they'll never end. But trust me, they do."

"I don't want to move again." Amber could feel the tears rising in her eyes. She gave them an angry swipe. "I'm such a baby."

"No, you're not." Millie patted her arm. "And this will all work out, you'll see."

"How do you know?"

"Because I'm going to pray about it," Millie said firmly.

"Well, good luck with that," Amber said, her voice seasoned with bitterness. "I think we've done something to piss God off."

Millie settled back in her seat and took a sip of tea. "Oh, I don't know about that. I have a feeling it's about time for some good things to happen in your life."

"I hope you're right."

"I know I'm right. Don't get discouraged. Your life is like your garden."

"That's a scary thought," Amber said, looking warily at her.

"You plant your seeds, but it takes time for them to germinate. You don't see vegetables or even the promise of vegetables for a while, but they're still busy growing beneath the soil, getting ready to produce something wonderful for you. I think life is like that. At least, I hope it is."

"Is that how it's worked for you?" Amber asked. If so, why did Millie look kind of sad all of a sudden?

"That's how I try to make it work," Millie said. "It's the best I can do."

"Well," Amber said with a sigh, "all I can do is keep planting, I guess. I've got too much invested to quit."

She thought of Hope Walker, working hard to

turn her back on a scary past and seed her life with new, good things. And here was Millie, making friends in a new place. If they can keep working at it, so can I, she told herself.

SIXTEEN

*J*ason stopped by the flower shop on Tuesday to see how Bobbi was doing.

As he leaned on the counter, spotlighted by mid-morning sunshine, Hope couldn't help lusting just a little over her sister's boyfriend. In his dusty jeans and work shirt, he was so very lustible. All that maleness, it charged her flower shop with electricity. Or maybe it was just her who was getting the charge.

Bobbi didn't seem to feel it all that much. Her smile was standard Bobbi issue. Yes, she wanted Jason Wells, but did she really WANT him?

"So, you're doing okay?" Jason asked Bobbi.

"Absolutely." She slung an arm over Hope's shoulder. "Who needs the Last Resort anyway? I'm happy here with my sis, making art." She turned to Hope. "That's what we're doing, isn't it?"

Hope nodded. *Way to be brilliant.* She was willing for Bobbi to get Jason, totally willing. But just once she'd like to come across as more than a common dandelion. Hard to do when your sister was a stargazer lily.

Dandelions were pretty, too, she told herself. And useful, with edible leaves and petals that could be turned into wine.

"And my money problems are solved," Bobbi was saying. "We're going to be roommates."

Jason smiled at that. "That's got to be a chick thing."

"What do you mean?" asked Bobbi.

"I tried being roommates with my brother. It lasted two months. We almost killed each other."

"That's not going to happen to us," Bobbi insisted. "We're not just sisters, we're best friends." She gave Hope a squeeze.

"Absolutely," Hope agreed, and squeezed back. And sisters shared. Everything. Except in the case of Jason, she could hardly call it sharing since he was all Bobbi's.

The phone rang. "I'll get it," Bobbi said, picking up the receiver.

While she talked on the phone, Jason turned to Hope and asked in a low voice, "Is she going to be okay?"

"She'll be fine," Hope assured him.

He drummed the counter, calling Hope's attention to his hands. They were big and work roughened. Strong hands. He looked to where Bobbi stood with her back to them, still busy on the phone. "I don't want to rush her to share personal stuff with me, but if she's got a problem, if she's got a big bill she can't pay . . ."

Thanks to her skill with a charge card, Bobbi always had bills, but they weren't anything she couldn't handle, especially with her rent now cut in half. She was doing fine. Hope shook her head, confused.

"Hospital bills?" he prompted.

"Hospital bills?" Hope repeated. What could her sister have told Jason to make him believe she had hospital bills? Someone in this shop had them, but it sure wasn't Bobbi.

"Look, I saw a book when we were helping her load her bookcase, the one about cancer."

Hope felt her cheeks warming. If she'd seen that book first, she'd have ditched it.

"When I saw her Saturday, she talked about having bills to pay. I assumed . . . ."

Hope wasn't about to step forward and say, "I'm the one who had the big *C*." But she couldn't let him think Bobbi had had it. "It wasn't her. It was . . . someone else in our family. Bobbi was helping her."

Jason looked at Bobbi like he was watching a saint in action. "Is this person okay now?"

"She's doing fine," Hope said.

"A fighter, huh?"

"She is." At least on some levels.

Bobbi hung up and announced, "We just got an order for a fiftieth birthday. They want an over-the-hill theme, but not a mean one. How do we do that?"

"We'll . . . you'll think of something," Hope corrected herself, conscious of Jason standing there, listening.

Bobbi's cheeks turned pink. "Oh, yeah."

Jason gave the counter a thump. "Well, I'd better get back to work. Just thought I'd see how you were doing, if you needed anything."

"As a matter of fact, I do," said Bobbi. "I need your body."

Who didn't? Hope kept her features neutral.

That got his interest.

"And any other help you can find. Bring your friend. This Saturday is moving day, and I need to take a bunch of stuff to storage. I'll feed you," she added.

A corner of his lip lifted. "Food is good."

"Okay then. Ten A.M?"

"Ten A.M.," he repeated, and left the store, giving them a quick salute as he went.

Bobbi turned and beamed at her sister. "There. That takes care of the muscle. Jason's got a really cute friend. Maybe he'll bring him."

"Getting greedy?" Hope teased.

"Not for me, for you."

"I'm not interested," Hope said, and slipped behind the velvet curtain to the work area.

Bobbi followed her. "You will be when you see him. He's gorgeous, *Phantom of the Opera* gorgeous."

Hope made a face. "I wasn't the one who had the hots for the Phantom. Remember?"

"Well, you'll have the hots for this guy, trust me."

"Speaking of trust," Hope began.

"What?"

"Jason saw one of my books."

Bobbi gave a snort. "He saw a lot of your books."

"The one on cancer."

"Oh." Bobbi gave her lower lip a good gnawing.

"I told him someone in our family had it, so I don't think he'll bring up the subject again. But if he does, don't tell him it was me." She wasn't exactly on Jason's radar, but she didn't want to suddenly pop up there as Miss Cancer of Heart Lake. Too humiliating.

Bobbi nodded, her face serious. "Don't worry. I won't. If the subject comes up, I'll tell him it was a cousin or something. And you know what else I'll tell him? That woman is my hero."

Hope just shook her head. "Oh, Bobs, you need to get out more."

Bobbi grinned. "That is definitely not my problem."

The day drifted pleasantly by, like so many dandelion seeds on the wind. The sisters got their orders filled and, that afternoon, while Hope was doing paperwork, Bobbi delivered them.

Bobbi wasn't the world's best driver, so Hope spent much of the afternoon imagining her sister in a ditch somewhere, all the arrangements spilled and ruined. But Bobbi made it back, mission accomplished, and Hope decided she didn't need to worry so much. This was all working out beautifully.

The rest of the week followed the same pleasant pattern until Friday, when Jason came in at noon with sub sandwiches from the Safeway deli. Hope was ready to slip into the back room to give them some privacy, but both Bobbi and Jason insisted she stay and eat.

"There's plenty," he said easily.

And so she stayed and played third wheel, listening while he and Bobbi compared growing up stories. He regaled them with tales of the many fights he and his brother had growing up, and the creative ways they managed to torture each other. "One Christmas my buddies and I tied him up with a string of Christmas lights and stuck him in the closet."

"That's terrible," said Bobbi.

"It could have been worse," Jason said with a shrug. "I wanted to plug the lights in."

"What happened?" asked Hope.

"One of my other friends felt sorry and set him free while we were playing a video game. He told my mom. I was grounded for two weeks."

"Well, at least you didn't have a school newsletter where you published his private information," Bobbi said, looking accusingly at Hope. "She got mad at me one time for using all her new makeup to give my friend makeovers and published some stuff about me that got her on restriction for a whole month."

"Let's not go into that," Hope said quickly, her face hot. Jason didn't need to learn that she'd published an ode to her thirteen-year-old sister's bra size.

He flashed a puckish grin at her as he said to Bobbi, "I had a sister. I can imagine what yours published."

"She got her revenge," Hope said. "She stole my journal and read the most embarrassing parts to all her friends at lunch."

"Not that you ever did much to be embarrassed about," put in Bobbi, "since you were the perfect one."

"I *thought* enough to be embarrassed about," Hope retorted.

"Of course, she told Mom, and then I was on restriction, too," Bobbi said.

And they'd spent the rest of the month with a social life that consisted of only each other. They'd watched movies and played board games and forgotten that they hated each other.

Jason said to Hope, "Journals, newsletters—looks like you've got a way with words, like your sister."

"I guess," Hope said, feeling suddenly squirmy.

"So, how come you didn't end up as a writer?" he asked.

206

Hope toyed with a flower-tipped pen. "I guess I like speaking with flowers more. And I can still dabble in writing when I help people with their gift cards." Wait. That was probably TMI.

He pointed a finger at her. "I remember how you helped me when I first came in here."

Hope felt her face warming. Definitely TMI. She felt like a criminal boxed into a verbal corner by a clever detective. She sneaked a look at Bobbi. Her cheeks were tea rose pink.

"You did most of the work on that," she told him, sending the awkward moment slinking away.

She'd been having so much fun turning Jason's visit into a threesome that it took a while for Hope to remember to make herself scarce. As she ducked behind the velvet curtain to start the birthday arrangement, she told herself in no uncertain terms that she was not going to make a habit of hanging around every time he visited her sister. This could prove hard when he came to the apartment, but she'd manage it.

And then she realized that it was only a matter of time before Jason wouldn't be coming over to the apartment at all. He and Bobbi would want privacy, and Bobbi would be at his place all the time. And then she'd be moving out, just as quickly as she moved in.

And you'll be glad, she told herself firmly. *Bobbi will finally get settled with a good man. You'll have the flower shop. Everyone will be happy.*

• • •

Hope was at Bobbi's apartment on Saturday, helping Bobbi finish packing her dishes, when the moving team showed up. Jason was his usual delicious self, wearing his favorite outfit of jeans and T-shirt. Those brown eyes, that smile—every time he entered a room, she had to fight the tremors. The other guy was even more muscled than him, with swarthy skin and dark hair and Johnny Depp eyes. The newcomer was wearing black jeans and a ripped gray T-shirt, partially covered by a black leather jacket. And black boots, the kind guys wore to drive Harleys. Next to her, Hope was aware of Bobbi smoothing her hands on her jeans. She'd never done that when Jason came into the shop.

The men had brought an intriguing scent into the apartment, that mix of musk and sawdust that Hope always smelled on Jason, and something else. Motor oil? This new addition had to come from Duke, Hope thought as Jason introduced them.

Duke gave her a genial smile, but when he looked at Bobbi, lightning flashed. He quickly looked away, but not before Hope spied a dangerous answering flicker from her sister. Oh, no. What was brewing here? What happened to picking Mr. Right, to no more bad boys?

This man couldn't be all bad if he was friends with Jason. Then again, men weren't always that discerning when it came to friends. Hope sneaked a look in her sister's direction. Bobbi was looking at Duke like he was the last piece of chocolate left in the world. This was not good. Her sister needed to stay on track, especially now that she had Mr. Right's heart in the palm of her hand, not only for her sake but for Jason's, too. He would be so hurt if Bobbi dumped him for his friend.

"We've got my truck outside," Jason said. "What goes to storage?"

As he was talking, Duke slipped off his jacket and tossed it over a chair, revealing a tattoo: a skull with a scorpion twisted around it and the word *Scorpio* written below it in blood red. Hope had to forcibly pull her eyes back from bug-out mode.

This was Bobbi's favorite type of man, the bad boy kind who always broke her heart. Concern now joined the jumble of feelings Hope had been dancing with ever since Bobbi pulled her in as a secret weapon in her campaign to win Jason.

Bobbi set the men to work loading up her couch, and, as soon as they were out of the apartment, Hope gave her a low-voiced third degree. "What are you doing?"

"What do you mean what am I doing?" Bobbi quickly got busy wrapping a glass in newsprint.

"I saw how you looked at Jason's friend."

Bobbi stared at her, faking affront. "I just looked at him. There was no *how* to it."

"What happened to picking Mr. Right?" Hope hissed. *What happened to all the work and sacrifice?*

Bobbi's eyebrows dipped down in a scowl. "I have picked Mr. Right. I don't want Duke."

"You just remember that," Hope warned as the guys came back in for more.

By five o'clock, all Bobbi's possessions were either in storage or at Hope's apartment.

"Okay, time for burgers," Bobbi said, and went to the kitchen of her new home. "And we've got beer."

"I could definitely use one of those," said Duke, following her. "Need help?"

Hope watched as Bobbi smiled up at him. Yes, her sister definitely needed help. Professional help. "I'll make some oatmeal cookies," she offered, joining Bobbi and Duke in the kitchen. It was too small for three people, especially when one of them was a six-foot-tall construction worker, but Duke didn't seem in a hurry to leave. So Hope helped him on his way, accidentally on purpose pulling the silverware drawer into his hip. "Oops. Sorry."

"No problem," he said, looking at her like she was a lethal weapon. But he moved to the other side of the kitchen counter.

Both he and Jason were back underfoot the minute the cookies came out of the oven.

"Hey, these are good," Duke said, spitting crumbs as he talked.

"You're a good cook," Jason told Hope.

"I'm good at a lot things," she said coyly, and turned to pull salad makings from the fridge. Now, where had that come from? Shades of the good old days when she actually dated.

"All right, we're ready," Bobbi announced, and set out a platter piled with burgers.

Duke moved to her side, like one of Pavlov's dogs. "These look good," he said, but Hope couldn't tell if he was talking about the burgers or the view he was enjoying looking down Bobbi's top.

Jason seemed oblivious. He was helping himself to another cookie. Well, he was either confident or clueless. Probably clueless, Hope decided. Lucky for him, she was there.

As they ate, she tried to gently interrogate the newcomer. "So, have you got family around here?" she asked. Obviously, he didn't have a girlfriend.

"Nope," Duke said, and took a swig from his second beer. "I'm really up here because Jace convinced me the area's growing. Lots of construction work."

"How do you two know each other?" Mr. Dependable and Mr. Grunge Tattoo.

"We went to high school together," Jason said.

"Yeah, then I split for California. Did the beach bum thing, played in a band."

Got tattooed. Hope pointed to his arm. "Is that where you got this?"

He gave her a John Malkovich kind of grin. "That was the name of my band."

"I like it," said Bobbi, and he turned his Malkovich grin on her.

If Hope could have reached her sister from under the table, she would have kicked her. Why were they working so hard to snag Jason for Bobbi if she was going to blow it all by drooling over this guy?

After they'd eaten, they found enough energy to play Spoons, a wild card game that involved diving for and fighting over a limited supply of spoons. Bobbi managed to gouge both men with her fingernails before the game was over. Hope was the first one out and it gave her a chance to observe her sister's behavior carefully. She laughed and flirted with both men, but the way she looked at Duke made Hope nervous.

Still, she breathed easier when the guys finally stood by the front door, ready to leave, and Bobbi hung on Jason's arm. "Thanks for being so awesome," she told him.

"That's what we do best," Duke answered for him, and sauntered out the door.

At least he'd had the grace to leave. Hope did the same, all the while, sending her sister a psychic message. *Don't be a fool. Mr. Perfect wants you. Take him.*

A moment later, Hope heard Jason's big truck roar to life, and the front door shut and Bobbi came into the living room, wearing the smile of a woman who had just been thoroughly kissed. Okay, good. Her sister was back on track. She could quit worrying.

But she couldn't quit remembering Jason's smile as he ate that oatmeal cookie.

SEVENTEEN

$\mathcal{H}$ope's first customer on Monday was Amber Howell. The shop was a jungle of tempting goodies: teacups brimming with silk tea roses, beribboned baskets full of potted flowers, garden art, and wind chimes made by a local artist. Amber looked around her like a woman hungry to spend money—a good thing for business, but probably not a good thing for a family with a husband out of work. As Hope greeted her, she silently vowed not to let Amber throw herself under the financial bus.

"I need to order an arrangement," Amber announced.

"How about this?" Hope said, picking up an affordable pot of irises.

Amber shook her head. "Nope. It needs to be something special. It's for Millie. I owe her big time." She reached into her purse and pulled out a fistful of bills. "Thanks to her lavender and carrot cookie recipes, I am rolling in the dough, and I need to majorly thank her."

Okay, she didn't want to talk Amber out of a nice gesture. "How about a bouquet of yellow roses. They symbolize joy and friendship."

"Perfect! Can we tell her that in the card?"

"Absolutely," said Hope.

"On second thought. Don't. Maybe when we're

at the garden again, I'll have her guess." Amber began peeling bills off her wad.

Hope didn't let her peel very far. "That should cover it just fine."

Amber looked at her suspiciously. "This is not enough for roses."

"It is today. I'm running a special."

Amber cocked an eyebrow. "Yeah? Since when?"

"Since you walked in. Don't give me grief," she added. "Otherwise I'll make you go to the grocery store, and those flowers won't be nearly as nice as mine."

Amber shook her head. "You're a tough businesswoman, you know that?"

Hope shrugged. "I know. I'm a killer."

Amber pulled off one more ten and pressed it into Hope's palm. "Me, too. Can it go out today?"

"Absolutely," Hope promised.

Amber was barely out the door when Bobbi entered, bringing coffee—decaf for Hope—from the Coffee Stop. She nodded at Amber, walking off down the street. "So, was that an order?"

"As a matter of fact, it was. You are going to be a busy bee today. We've got a lot of important orders to deliver."

"Busy is good. I need to earn my keep."

"You already are," Hope assured her. "Believe me."

They worked companionably for the next two

hours, the creative process interrupted by a handful of phone orders and a woman who came into the shop needing a bouquet sent to her sister ASAP.

Bobbi had been helping her, but she quickly pulled Hope out of the back room, saying, "We need expert advice out here."

That was an understatement. This customer needed Dr. Phil. Her eyes were bloodshot and she looked like she would happily ingest belladonna.

"She's really mad. If she ever speaks to me again, it will be a miracle," the woman moaned.

"I'm not sure we can guarantee a miracle," Hope told her, "but we can guarantee a lovely arrangement that will help you get your message across. Purple hyacinths say 'I'm sorry,' and we have some in the cooler. And I often use camellia for greens. Camellia symbolizes admiration. How would that work?"

The woman's eyes were tearing up. She didn't speak, probably couldn't for the lump in her throat. But she nodded vigorously.

Hope typed up the order. "How would you like the card to read?"

"Please forgive me." It came out as a whisper.

"And would you like me to add what the flowers mean?"

The woman nodded and produced her charge card.

"I think we can get those out today," said Hope.

"Absolutely," said Bobbi. She laid a comforting

hand on the woman's arm. "And you know what? I'll bet, deep down, your sister feels as bad as you. Things will work out. Sisters are like treasure, and who wants to lose treasure?"

"Thank you," the woman breathed. She smiled at Bobbi, then looked at Hope like she was Mother Teresa, Joan of Arc, and Oprah all rolled into one.

No pressure. "I hope it works out," Hope managed.

"I'm not sure we should be making those kind of promises," she said to Bobbi after their customer had left.

Bobbi looked at her, mystified. "What kind of promises?"

"Like that it will all be okay."

Bobbi chewed her lip for a moment, considering, then said, "But I think it will. You know why?"

"You're psychic?"

"Nope. Just smart. That woman was so miserable. She wouldn't be if she and her sis weren't close. I'll make a great bouquet and you can write something really cool on the card. By tomorrow, she'll be back in here kissing your feet."

Hope just shook her head. "Okay, let's get this finished, then after lunch we can load up the wagon."

The wagon was a used PT Cruiser, yellow with Changing Seasons Floral scripted on its side in green. Impossible to miss, it was like a billboard on wheels.

"Okay now, remember, drive carefully," Hope cautioned as Bobbi slipped in behind the wheel.

They had a lot of inventory stashed back there: three birthday arrangements, one anniversary special, something to celebrate a new baby, a delivery to welcome a newcomer to Heart Lake, Amber's thank-you gift to Millie, and the all-important reconciliation arrangement for the angry sister. But probably the most valuable thing in the truck was a showy arrangement for a booksellers' reception Hope's friend Erin Rockwell was in charge of. The event was a big deal. So were the flowers. If all went well, Erin would give Hope more business as her new event-planning company grew.

Bobbi was now no stranger to making deliveries, Hope reminded herself. Still, she couldn't help reminding her sister one last time to drive carefully.

Bobbi gave a snort of disgust. "What? You think I don't know I'm carrying valuable stuff here? Of course I'll drive carefully. I always drive carefully."

Hope nodded and stepped away from the car. She'll be fine, she told herself.

She had barely sent Bobbi off when the shop bell jangled and in walked—"Clarice?"

Her hair was blue now instead of maroon, but other than that, she was the same old Clarice, pierced and grinning. "Have you missed me?"

Missed the coming in late and leaving early? "Of course. But what are you doing here?"

Clarice spread her arms wide. "I'm back."

"What happened to Vegas?"

"Vegas is history," Clarice said with a shrug. "Anyway, what happens in Vegas stays in Vegas. Right?" she added with a grin. She crossed the room and squatted in front of Audrey and gave the giant Christmas cactus a friendly rumple. "Hey, Audrey."

"Did you leave Bork in Vegas?" Hope asked.

"Borg," Clarice corrected her. "Of course not. He's back, too, job hunting."

"What happened to the one at his cousin's garage?"

"It didn't work out. Anyway, we decided we'd rather live here." Clarice straightened slowly. "Uh, speaking of jobs, I thought maybe you could use some help."

Hope was torn between regret that she couldn't hire Clarice back and relief that she didn't have to. "Gosh, I'm sorry. My sister's working with me now."

Clarice's casual expression melted into disappointment. "Oh." But, being Clarice, it was only momentary. She shrugged. "Oh, well. I just thought I'd give you first dibs."

"Thanks."

"I figured I owed you," Clarice added, "after leaving so, uh . . ."

"Suddenly?" Hope supplied.

"Yeah. I felt bad, by the way, really. But what can you do? It's stupid to let love get away."

The words buzzed around the back of Hope's mind after Clarice left. Too bad Bobbi hadn't been around to hear them. A little positive reinforcement would have been good for her.

Really, Bobbi thought as she tooled along Lake Way, Hope was such a worrywart. What did she think was going to happen anyway?

Bobbi decided to make the new baby delivery first since that was the farthest away, on a side road off the far end of one of the curves at the top end of the lake. Heart Lake was shaped like a two-mile-long valentine, and, at this end, the roads tended to be a tangle and the addresses often didn't make sense. Even though she'd MapQuested the address, she still got lost. Clouds had taken over the morning's blue sky and now it was raining, which wasn't great for visibility. At the rate she was going, she'd be driving around in the dark, delivering flowers right along with people's dessert. And Hope wouldn't be happy about that.

Bobbi was relieved when she finally found the address. The house was hidden at the end of a tree-encased gravel drive that could easily get an award for the most potholes ever put on one road. She didn't waste any time getting the flowers to the front door.

The new mommy's eyes lit up like Bobbi was holding out a tray of diamonds instead of an arrangement of blue carnations and baby's breath. "For me?"

"For sure. Happy baby."

"Thanks. They're gorgeous."

"That's what we do," Bobbi told her. Lord, she loved this job. Except for the running back and forth from the car to the houses in the rain. Yuck.

She hopped into the car, then bumped her way back down the potholed drive. Once she was on paved road again, she floored it, making up for lost time.

She'd barely gone a quarter mile when her cell phone rang with her latest ring tone: Blondie singing "Call Me."

Of course, she would never talk on the cell phone while driving. She picked it up off the front seat and did a quick look to see who it was. And then things got bad. Even as she was looking at the phone, she saw the dog, an old dog, limping out onto the road in front of her. "Noooooo!" She stomped on the brakes and cranked the wheel to the right. The Cruiser fishtailed like she was in the middle of a chase scene with Jason Bourne, the phone went flying, and Bobbi let out a screech. She could hear tires squealing, gravel spitting, and Blondie shrieking, "Call me!" And, in the back of the Cruiser, things were going thump, thump, thump. When the car came to a stop, she was on the shoulder of the road and her heart was racing ninety miles an hour. And the dog, where was the dog? She jumped out of the car and ran to the front. No dead dog under the wheels. Her anxious gaze swept the road.

There went the old guy limping off into the bushes. *Thank God.* She leaned against the car and let out a sigh of relief.

The relief was short-lived. The front wheels were as close as they could come to being off the shoulder. And the flowers, what about the flowers? She ran to the back of the Cruiser and pulled it open. *Oh, no.*

Flowers lay on their sides everywhere, their little boxes upended, many of them had slid right into the side of the car and the little plastic forks that held the gift card envelopes had been snapped. Rivulets of water snaked toward three cards that had managed to get dislodged.

"Oh, crap!" Bobbi growled. "Crap, crap, crap!" She scooped up the envelopes, one just as a finger of water scraped across its corner. Meanwhile, at the front of the Cruiser, Blondie was back. "Call me!" Bobbi didn't even have to look. She knew it would be Hope again. *CRAP!*

She wiped off an envelope and then began righting the arrangements, all the while chanting, "Please be okay, please be okay." Hope was going to fire her, for sure. Fired twice in one week, and once by your sister. Did it get any worse than that? Stay calm, she advised herself.

But she didn't listen. Instead, she did some

serious crying, wailing loud enough to be heard from one end of the lake to the other. It took her a full five minutes to calm herself down. And to realize the engine was still on.

She turned it off and went back to examining the arrangements, heedless of the chilly spring rain that was pelting her. Thank God, no vases had broken. A couple of the hyacinths had taken a beating. She pulled them out and threw them in the gully beneath the shoulder of the road, then rearranged the flowers. There, you couldn't even tell it was missing a couple. A rose in another one of the arrangements had suffered a broken neck. It followed the hyacinths into the gully. There, that took care of that. She fluffed the rest of the flowers and coaxed the arrangements back into place. Good as new. She'd stop by the gas station and refill the vases and everyone would be fine.

And now, the cards. What went where? Some she knew, like the showy arrangement for the reception. Some . . . *crap*. She got her clipboard with names and addresses from the front seat. Nothing had changed there. It still gave her only names and addresses. There'd been no need to note who was getting what, not when the cards with the recipients' names on them were in the arrangements, and the clipboard had the names matched with addresses. Everything had been fine until the merchandise went flying. Boy, that practice had to change.

Blondie was singing again. Bobbi knew she had to answer.

"How's it going?" asked Hope.

Bobbi got a look at herself in the rearview mirror. Her hair was plastered to her head, her eyes were red from crying, and her eyeliner was running down her face. She looked like an escapee from a horror movie. "Oh, fine," she said, forcing her voice to sound carefree.

"The customer from the bank called and wants to know when we're getting there with the flowers. They're right in the middle of the birthday party."

"They're next." They were now. Bobbi looked at the card envelopes in her hand. One of these belonged on flowers destined for the bank. But which one?

"Okay," Hope said. "I'll tell her that Linda will have her lavender roses in what, ten minutes?"

Bobbi sighed inwardly with relief. Good old Linda of the lavender roses. "Absolutely."

She snapped the cell phone shut and hurried back to the flowers. The little fork that held the card was history, so Bobbi propped the card in among the flowers. That took care of Linda.

Now, what about the two remaining mystery arrangements? Neither one of them were orders that Bobbi had taken. One was a gigantic wicker basket of plants. The other was an arrangement of yellow roses, one of which now lay discarded off on the side of the road. She chewed her lip as she studied the clipboard. Who did we have to choose from here? Millie Baldwin and Altheus Hornby. So, which of these looked like a Millie and which one looked like an Altheus?

And then she remembered. Hope had met Millie at the community garden. So, of course, the plants had to go to Millie the gardener. Whew, that was a close one. She took a deep, calming breath, propped the cards back in the arrangements as best she could and shut the door.

Now, the next challenge was to get the Cruiser safely backed up. She slipped in behind the wheel, restarted the car, and then, holding her breath, backed up very slowly. The wheels started searching for ground to bite.

"Come on!" Bobbi yelled.

The wheels tried harder, and, just when she thought she was going to have a complete nervous breakdown, they grabbed onto dirt. She backed up and stopped as soon as all four wheels were safely on the road again, leaned her head back against the seat, and let out her breath. Okay, she would be fine. Everything would be fine.

At the gas station, she gave the flowers a drink and cleaned up her scary face before she went into the bank. There wasn't anything she could do about her sopped hair, but oh well.

No one noticed anyway. Everyone was too busy raving over Linda and the flowers. Bobbi slipped out of the bank and fled back to the Cruiser. Before she made any more deliveries, she went by the apartment and exchanged her sopped hoodie and jeans for dry clothes. There. Now everything was right again.

The rest of her deliveries went just fine. Hope would never have to know.

Except then, right as Bobbi was pulling away from the last house, Hope called, and one second after Bobbi said hello she knew that Hope knew.

"I just had a call from Amber. Millie called her to thank her for the plants. But Millie was supposed to get yellow roses. Is there something you need to tell me?"

The jig was up. She was fingered. Like a criminal in one of those ugly rooms at the police station getting grilled by the cops, Bobbi broke down and confessed. "I had an accident. I almost hit a dog."

"Oh, no."

"Thank God, I stopped just in time. And the car's fine," she added. "Not to worry. I got everything put back together and everything's fine." Except Hope was calling, which meant everything wasn't fine.

"Then how did you wind up delivering Altheus Hornby's plants to Millie Baldwin?"

Hope's tone of voice reminded Bobbi of Miss Whangle, her eighth-grade English teacher. Miss Whangle had never liked her. "It was the dog. I had to stop suddenly. The flowers just got a little, um . . ." *Crap.*

"A little what?" Hope prompted.

"Mixed up."

Hope expelled a breath. "Oh, no. What did they look like?"

"Don't worry. I got them all fixed back up, good as new."

"And delivered two to the wrong place."

There was that. "I'll go back and redeliver the mess-ups right now," Bobbi assured her.

"No. It's okay. It's taken care of."

Hope was trying to sound forgiving, but Bobbi could hear frustration deep down at the bottom of her voice. "You're mad."

"No. Well, sort of."

"I'm sorry," Bobbi said. She felt like a worm, no a caterpillar; Bobbi the plant-killing, business-wrecking caterpillar. "I should have told you. I was just so afraid you'd be mad at me. I thought I could fix it." But she hadn't. She'd only made things worse. "You should fire me now and get it over with." She thought of their customer from the morning. "You're going to end up really mad at me, like that sister, the one we did the flowers for."

"No. We're there for each other. But Bobs, I really need you to tell me when something is going wrong. Then we can fix it together."

Bobbi felt her eyes tearing up. "I don't want us to ever end up like those sisters."

"We won't," Hope assured her. "We'll always be there for each other."

"And we'll always tell each other the truth, no matter what," Bobbi vowed.

"No matter what," Hope agreed.

Hope hung up the phone and mentally added, but only if one of us asks. No way was she telling her sister that she wanted her man. Plant mix-ups could be fixed. Wanting your sister's boyfriend was another matter altogether.

EIGHTEEN

Millie Baldwin settled the basket of plants on the backseat of her car. Hope had been terribly embarrassed when she called to apologize for the delivery mix-up, but Millie assured her that it was not a problem. It was also not a problem for Millie to take the flowers to their rightful recipient and make an exchange. In fact, she insisted.

She didn't tell Hope, but she wanted to get out. She'd done her morning crossword puzzle, tidied up the kitchen, and finished her book, and then found herself at loose ends. The children wouldn't be home for another hour, and she had just been wondering what to do next. Now she had something.

It had taken a great deal of persuading to convince Hope to give her an address and some directions and let her play delivery girl, but at last Hope had relented. So, now Millie was climbing into her car and ready to take a little drive.

It was drizzly, and Millie was bound for a side of the lake where she hadn't gone much yet, so she drove carefully, paying attention to street signs as she went. This house was off North Lake Drive, which meant it was right on the lake. She was to look for Loveland Lane and a big camellia hedge, then, past that, a set of mailboxes. Just beyond those, she would see the driveway.

This is lovely, she thought as she took in the still undeveloped lots, brimming with fir and alder trees. In between the wooded lots, big yards with houses gave her glimpses of the lake, gently pocked with raindrops. Some of the yards hid behind laurel hedges, but many of them simply spread out like a green carpet to the lake, showing off rhododendrons, ceanothuses, and old fruit trees, and, down by the lake, made-over summer cabins or old Victorians tucked in by azaleas and rosebushes. This was what she'd envisioned when her daughter had first told her she'd moved to some place called Heart Lake.

Millie hit another stretch of wooded lots and the lake disappeared from view. Oh, there was Loveland Lane. And the camellias. And there were the mailboxes. She turned down the graveled drive, a jumble of trees, ferns, and brambles rising on each side of her.

And then the road widened and she saw lawn and

a pond, and beyond that an old yellow Victorian with a wraparound porch, its trim painted white. Fat azaleas spread across the flower beds. In back of it, she caught sight of a dock slipping out into the lake. Oh, and what was this? A little dab of sunlight and a rainbow. She smiled. Whoever owned this house was one lucky woman.

Not the world's best gardener, though, judging from the weeds popping up amongst the shrubs.

Millie stopped the car and took the plants out of the back. She had just shut the car door when she looked to the house and saw that a man had opened the front door. He was a tall, squarely built man with a thick mane of gray hair and a big, square jaw. Looking at this man managed to stir up flutterings Millie hadn't felt in years. Oh, my!

She put a hand to her chest to settle her heart, then took a deep breath. At this time of day, she'd expected to find a woman, not a man, and a handsome retired man at that. It's of no consequence, she told herself. *You're only here to drop off flowers.* Even so, she put a hand to her hair for a quick touch-up before starting toward the house.

She didn't get very many steps before he reached her and took the basket. "Here, let me. You must be Millie. The flower shop called and told me you were on your way. I'd have been happy to come to you."

"Oh, nonsense," said Millie. "It's a nice day for a drive." Well, not really. What nonsense was she talking?

He nodded to the lake. "It is with the rainbow."

The rainbow was enough to make them both stop.

"There must be a pot of gold somewhere in that lake," he said, and held out a hand. "Altheus Hornby. I'm new here."

"So am I," said Millie as they shook hands. "How do you like it so far?"

"This place is the best-kept secret in Washington," he said.

"And your wife, is she enjoying it here?" It would be nice to make a friend her own age.

His smile got smaller. "I'm afraid my wife's no longer alive. I lost her three years ago."

"Oh, I'm sorry," said Millie. "It's hard to lose a mate."

"I miss her a lot, but I know she's in a better place."

Millie nodded. "That is a comfort."

He motioned her toward the house and they began walking again. "This is a lovely house," Millie said as they reached the porch.

"I like it," he said. "I have your flowers inside. Would you like to come in?"

Into a strange man's house? When was the last time she'd done that? Hmm. Never. She suddenly felt thirteen. Ridiculous. "Oh." She looked at her watch. She should get home.

"Your husband is probably expecting you back," he said.

"I'm a widow."

"Oh. I'm sorry," he said, but he looked more than sorry. He looked . . . interested.

She was being silly. She'd been watching too many movies. "I'm living with my daughter. My grandchildren will be home pretty soon."

He nodded, polite resignation on his face.

She had a few minutes. She didn't really need to rush off. "But I'd love to see some of the house before I go."

That made him smile like a boy who had just gotten his first date. "Great. Come on in."

And so she did.

The house had a reverse floor plan, with the living room at the back to take advantage of the view of the lake. She took in the furniture, Sheraton style with delicate straight lines and contrasting veneers. The dining set was especially lovely—old and well worn, like it had gone through life with this man and his family. She did notice a new leather recliner chair in one corner, set to face the TV. He'd probably gotten that since he moved.

She stood in front of the window. "My, isn't this a lovely view!"

Altheus came to stand next to her. "It's what sold me on the house."

"And your neighbors, are they nice?" Millie asked.

He gave a half shrug. "Haven't really gotten to

know them yet. They're both young families, gone working a lot."

Millie thought of that lone recliner. She looked at the flower beds, full of promise and in need of care. "A wonderful place for a gardener," she mused.

"My wife was the gardener," said Altheus. "I don't know what to do with all this."

"I'm sure you'll figure out something."

"Maybe you'll help me," he said, with a twinkle in his eye.

"Oh." She was blushing. She could feel it. This was silly.

No, this was fun.

No, this was silly. "You know, I should probably be going," she said.

"Oh, sure, the grandkids. Well, let me carry your flowers for you."

"My, they are lovely," Millie said when she saw them.

"Someone here cares a lot about you," said Altheus. "I imagine you have lots of admirers."

He was flirting with her. At her age, a man was flirting with her. She was too old for girlish romance, she tried to tell herself. But the part of her that still loved sunsets and rainbows, English gardens and movies with happy endings simply couldn't agree.

He escorted her to her car and carefully installed the box containing the vase on the back floor. It looked like he'd actually put the flower box inside a bigger cardboard box and carefully packed it with newspaper to ensure a safe journey home.

"Thank you so much," she told him.

"No, thank you for driving all the way over here. Say, I was just thinking."

"Yes?" Did she sound eager? Too encouraging?

"How about letting me really thank you for your trouble? Would you like to have lunch with me tomorrow?"

"Oh, well." Why not? It would be nice to have lunch with someone her own age, with someone who had a voice lower than hers. "I'd love to."

So then, before she knew it, Altheus Hornby had her phone number and address, and they had plans for him to come pick her up at eleven thirty. "I'll take you to the Two Turtledoves. It has a great view of the lake."

"That sounds wonderful," said Millie. Lunch with a handsome man—Alice would be green with envy. Millie almost giggled like a schoolgirl at the thought.

As she drove home, she found herself singing Tony Bennett's "Because of You." You're a silly, old woman, Millie, she scolded herself, but it didn't wipe the smile off her face.

She got home and carefully carried her flowers into the house, settling them on the dining room table. The card she'd put in her scrapbook. Amber had written, "You've so been there for me, and I just wanted you to know it."

You've so been there for me. Her own daughter hadn't even told her that. Millie sighed. Life took the oddest turns.

She had just tucked away Amber's card when the kids came home, each bringing a friend. Millie shifted gears from Queen for a Day to Grandmother of the Year and got busy making cookies, which they devoured with much gusto and minimal thanks. The large amount of cookie consumption was, in itself, high praise, she reminded herself.

"Who sent flowers?" Debra asked when she got home.

"A friend of mine."

"Oh." Debra sounded disappointed.

For a moment, Millie almost wished she'd lied and said they were for Debra. But, no, Debra was going to have to get out and start planting more good things in her life and start seeing the sunshine as well as the rain. Then maybe she, too, would have flowers.

They watched a movie together that night, a romantic comedy that did little to make Debra laugh. Mostly she slumped on the couch with a martyred expression on her face. Millie decided not to share with her daughter about her lunch date.

But it was no fun keeping such delicious news to herself, so the next morning she called Alice.

"Are you ready to come home yet?" Alice greeted her.

"Oh, no. I'm having too much fun out here."

Alice gave a snort. "Since when?"

"Since yesterday. Alice, I met someone."

"Met someone?" Alice echoed. "You mean, a man?"

"Yes. We have a date for lunch today."

"Oh, my God. How did you manage to find a single man our age?"

"By accident," Millie said, and proceeded to explain how she met Altheus Hornby.

"That is simply amazing," Alice said. "And I'm jealous. Ask him if he's got a brother. And, Millie."

"Yes?"

"Don't play too hard to get. At our age there's no point wasting time."

Millie chuckled and rang off, then went to make the all-important decision of what to wear. She settled on her navy blue slacks and a white turtleneck, covered with her favorite thick red blazer, accessorized by the red glass bead necklace Duncan Jr. had given her for Mother's Day. Her hair wasn't as easy. She wished she'd had time to go to the beauty salon to get it done. The curl from her last perm was nearly gone. She styled it as best she could, then made up for the fact that her hair was less than perfect by applying some lipstick. There. That would do.

Altheus arrived promptly at eleven thirty. He looked her up and down and grinned, then made her blush by observing, "Millie, you're quite a dish."

"Oh, don't be silly," she said, with a little wave of her hand.

"I've got to tell you," he said after he'd helped her into the car, "I've been looking forward to this since yesterday. I was beginning to think I'd made a mistake moving up here." He gunned the motor and squealed them backward out of the driveway and onto the street.

Millie surreptitiously grabbed for the door handle. "What did bring you here?"

"I needed something new," he said as he sped down the road. "I'd been in a rut since my wife died. So, I let the kids have the other house, bought a new car, and got in and headed north. The gang at the senior center thought I was nuts, but I told them that at seventy I've still got lots of miles left. I'm not ready to park this chassis and die."

"You're seventy," Millie said. Oh, dear. She was turning seventy-seven soon. She was out with a younger man.

"Seventy's not old."

"Oh, no," she agreed, and hoped he didn't ask her age.

The restaurant looked expensive. Millie took in the linen tablecloths and crystal, the jacket-clad waiters, the soft cello music discreetly piped in, and felt immediately concerned for Altheus's budget. But she didn't say anything. That would only insult him. She did vow to find something inexpensive on the menu.

That was going to be impossible. Even ordering appetizers wouldn't be kind to the budget of a senior citizen on a limited income. They ran the gamut, from a Dungeness crab and prawn martini to a morel and goat cheese tart, and prices started at fourteen dollars. Everything was à la carte.

"The mahi mahi is very good here," Altheus said.

He'd eaten here before?

He grinned. "Please, order anything you want. I'd like this to be special."

"Simply being out with a new friend is special," Millie told him.

"I hope it's going to be the first of many times," he said, "so let's make it memorable."

Being here in this fancy restaurant was memorable enough for Millie. She ordered vegetables in puff pastry, the most inexpensive thing she could find.

And she was going to settle for a cup of tea, but Altheus ordered wine for them. Wine with lunch, it was so extravagant. She hadn't drunk wine in years.

"Now," he said, once the waiter had left, "tell me all about yourself."

"Well, I'm afraid there's not much to tell," Millie said with a shrug.

But that didn't quite turn out to be true. By the time they'd finished their salad, Altheus had heard all about her gardening addiction, her love of books, and her penchant for crossword puzzles.

"I do them, too," he said. "Keeps the mind sharp."

Millie wondered how sharp her mind would stay if that waiter kept filling her wineglass. The second glass loosened her lips the rest of the way, and, before she knew it, Altheus had heard about her children, her concerns over Debra, and even worse, had learned that she was almost seventy-seven.

"I'd never have guessed," he said gallantly. "You don't look a day over seventy."

She blushed. "Oh, what nonsense."

"No matter. I like older women," he said with a wink, and saluted her with his wineglass.

By the time they finished with coffee and dessert, two hours had slipped by. "How about a drive around the lake?" Altheus suggested.

The way he drove, he should have offered her a race around the lake. But Millie wasn't ready to go home to that big, quiet house yet, so she said yes. Since they were looky-looing their way around, Altheus drove at a more sensible speed. The sun came out, turning the lake a dark spring blue.

"Here," Altheus said and pulled the car off the road. "I'm thinking of buying this piece of land as an investment. What do you think?"

"It's like a wooded fairyland," Millie said, taking it all in.

"It's money in the bank," added Altheus. "Waterfront, too."

"My," said Millie, thinking of her tiny nest egg. "I certainly admire you for being so daring."

"Not daring, just business. I'm a working stiff, Millie. Retirement's for old guys."

"Well, I like your attitude," she said. "What kind of work do you do?"

"I buy and sell real estate. I'm no Donald Trump, but I've turned a buck or two. And," he continued with a puckish grin, "I can even manage to foot the bill for a nice meal. So, next time I take you out to eat, you don't have to worry about finding the cheapest thing on the menu."

"Next time?"

The look he gave her made her think of John Wayne and Maureen O'Hara in *The Quiet Man*. Oh, how the sparks had flown in that movie! And how they were flying here in this car right now. "There will be a next time, Millie, and soon."

And, to prove it, he called her the next night. Debra got to the phone before Millie. The surprised look on her daughter's face told Millie who it was. "It's for you," she said as if she couldn't quite believe it, and handed over the phone.

"Thank you," Millie murmured. And, as she said hello, she walked out to the kitchen where she didn't have to see her daughter watching her with that unnerving expression of curiosity and wariness.

"How about dinner with me tomorrow night?" Altheus suggested. "And a movie after. It's classics night at the Edgewood, and they're playing *Harvey*."

How sweet. He remembered that she'd said she loved Jimmy Stewart. "That sounds wonderful," she decided.

"Then I'll pick you up at five thirty."

"I'll be looking forward to it," she said.

"Looking forward to what?" Debra asked from behind her as Millie placed the phone receiver back on its stand.

Debra's unexpected presence gave Millie an unpleasant start, making her jump. "I'm going out with a friend tomorrow night," she said, willing her heart to stop racing.

Debra regarded Millie like she was up to something. "A friend?"

"Yes, a friend."

"I don't even have a life yet," Debra protested. "How could you? And where did you meet a man?"

Debra's question sounded more like a scold. "Quite by accident."

"I wish I was accident prone," Debra muttered. "Just be careful," she added. "You don't know anything about this man."

"He's perfectly nice," Millie said. Really, how silly Debra was being!

"Yeah, well, that's what I thought about Ben. I don't want to have to worry about you," she added.

"Don't worry about me. I think you have your

240

hands full worrying about yourself," Millie said crisply. Honestly, what did Debra think she was going to do at this age?

One thing she knew she was going to do. She was going to enjoy this little bit of excitement that had come into her life. She dressed carefully for her date, putting on her favorite black skirt and pink rayon blouse. Pantyhose were a struggle to get on, but she managed, then slipped into her favorite, easy-walking black pumps—heels were a thing of the past—and put on her pink pearl necklace. Her hair was still a mess, but she did the best she could and vowed to get to the beauty salon the following week. Looking at it, she wished she still had long, brunette tresses instead of this short, gray cotton wool. And her skin— she used to have such perfect skin. "Just like peaches and cream," Duncan used to say.

Her body had aged in such a sneaky way, each year slipping in some new bit of decay. First it was that lone wrinkle at the top of her lip. Next thing she knew, she had crow's-feet around her eyes, and her muscles were protesting after a day of working in the garden. Sagging breasts, aging skin, gray hair—it was all such a cruel trick when she didn't feel old inside. She certainly didn't feel old tonight.

"You're only as old as you feel," she reminded herself, and gathered up her purse and coat and went downstairs to wait for her date.

Eric was busy with his video game. "Gram, wanna play?" he offered.

"I can't tonight, dear," Millie said.

Emily looked up from where she lay sprawled out in an easy chair, with a schoolbook open in her lap. "Are you going out?"

"Yes, I'm going out to dinner with a friend," Millie told her.

Emily cocked her head, studying Millie. "You look nice."

"Well, thank you," Millie said. This was high praise, indeed, coming from a teenage girl. More than she was going to get from her daughter, she was sure.

The doorbell rang, and that brought Debra out from the kitchen where she was working on dinner, something she hadn't done much of since Millie moved in. But Millie beat her to the door.

There stood Altheus, looking distinguished in slacks, a shirt and tie, and a navy sports coat. He smiled at the sight of her. "Well, well. You look good enough to eat."

Millie felt herself blushing. "Oh, really. Come in," she added, and stepped aside. "This is my daughter, Debra."

He crossed the threshold and shook Debra's hand. "You're just as lovely as your mother."

Debra was underwhelmed by his gallantry. "Thanks."

Millie felt like saying, "She's much lovelier

when she's smiling." Really, she'd taught her daughter better manners than this.

Altheus looked over at the grandchildren. Eric was involved with his video game and present only in body. Emily, however, was regarding Altheus with unbridled curiosity. Altheus nodded at her. "Hi there."

She smiled. "Hi."

"And these are my grandchildren," Millie said, and made proper introductions, as proper as one could make when the children were still in their seats. "Eric, can you say hello to Mr. Hornby?" she prompted.

If she'd been hoping for a handshake, she didn't get it. He gave Altheus a quick wave and a hi, and then was back in Video-Game Land.

It didn't seem to bother Altheus. "Well, shall we go?" he said to Millie. Without waiting for an answer, he took her coat and helped her into it. "Nice to meet you," he said to Debra, who was now gawking suspiciously. He opened the door and whisked Millie out, saying, "I don't know about you, but I'm hungry." Once they were in the car, he said, "I have a feeling your daughter wants to know my intentions."

"Or mine," Millie said. "I'm not sure she's excited that I've found a friend."

A corner of his mouth lifted. "You said she's divorced?"

Millie nodded.

"Crabs in the pot," he said cryptically.

"I beg your pardon?"

"Ever go crabbing?" he asked.

Millie shook her head.

"Well, you catch a bunch of crabs, there's always one who wants to get away. But if he gets too far, the others pull him right back down. They want him to stay with them, miserable and doomed."

"Debra's not like that," Millie protested.

He shrugged. "With kids, who knows? One thing I've learned. They sure don't like their parents to get a life."

"Oh?" Millie prompted.

"I started going out with a woman, oh, six months after my wife died. I was so lonely, you know. Let me tell you, my girls ripped into me good. How could I dishonor their mother like that? What was I thinking? This woman would come in and take all Ruthie's things. On and on it went."

"What did you do?"

His chin jutted out at a pugnacious angle. "I didn't stop dating the woman, that's for sure. I told the girls in no uncertain terms that what I did with my life was none of their damned business. Pardon my French."

Millie couldn't help smiling. "I guess I'll have to tell my daughter the same thing. Without the French."

That made him chuckle. "Hear, hear. Let her

sulk. At our age, we've earned the right to do as we please."

And, after an enjoyable evening of fine food, fine conversation, and a walk down Movie Memory Lane, when he'd returned her to her doorstep, it appeared he wanted to keep on doing as he pleased. "I hope you'll let me take you out again," he said as she took her key out of her purse.

She smiled at him. "I would love that."

"And I hope you'll let me kiss you good night," he added. He took her by the arms and turned her to face him.

Millie's heart began to race. If she were to be honest, she'd have to admit she'd entertained this very thing as a secret fantasy. But really, it was rather preposterous to be kissing a man on her front porch at her age, and a man who was seven years younger than she was at that.

"Oh, Altheus, I don't know," she began.

"I do," he said, and pulled her to him and kissed her.

She felt a jolt as if someone had applied those emergency-room paddles to her chest. *Oh, my.* She pulled away, completely frazzled. "Really, Altheus, I'm seven years older than you." *And I haven't kissed a man other than Duncan in fifty-four years.* What was she thinking?

That it felt awfully good. And yet, she felt so silly, like she'd just been caught trying on her granddaughter's clothes.

"It doesn't matter to me," Altheus countered. "You're an attractive woman, Millie, and I enjoy being with you. And I certainly enjoyed kissing you just now." He put a finger under her chin and raised her face, forcing her to look at him. "Don't you miss this?"

With her husband gone, one of the things she missed most were those little moments of closeness—the hugs in the kitchen in the morning, the soft kiss good night before they turned out the lights. She had to nod and murmur, "Yes, I do."

He gave her a hug and another kiss, this time on her forehead. "I think we've got something good going. Let's enjoy it."

She smiled up at him. "I think you're right, Altheus."

Who would have thought it? So many people at her age were starting to live in the past. But here, in this new place, Millie was now living in the future.

Buds

TIPS FOR MAKING YOUR GARDEN LOOK GREAT

Regularly pinching off (or deadheading) spent blooms on reblooming plants will often hasten the development of new blooms, as well as improve the appearance of your plant.

Taking a stroll through the garden with your morning coffee on a regular basis will help you become more familiar with your plants and their particular growth habits. This will allow you to spot any developing problems or unusual growth and determine whether it's something that needs further attention.

To gauge bloom times, make note of when plants flower in gardens in your neighborhood. Nursery plants are often shipped from warmer regions, so they're not always reliable indicators of when your plants will bloom.

Vinegar makes a great organic weed killer. Pour a little directly on weeds. But pour carefully or it will also take out your flowers.

Make a treasure map of your garden by taking pictures and marking the location of your spring and fall bulbs with rocks or pretty stones. That way, you won't accidentally dig them up when planting or turning mulch into the soil.

NINETEEN

*I*t was Saturday, and Slugfest, Heart Lake's annual spring festival named after the Northwest's famous pest, was in full swing in spite of intermittent May showers. The downtown section of Lake Way had been cordoned off and packed with everything from bounce houses and climbing walls to sidewalk chalk art, with chalk provided by the local merchants. Every restaurant, local church, and service club had set up some sort of a food booth along the edges of the street, which was packed with revelers. Amber and her family walked along the street, bundled in raincoats, taking it all in.

Amber had saved up her cookie money so she could spring for eats, and now they were sampling hamburgers from the Family Inn.

Ty frowned at his. "This is a case of *E. coli* waiting to happen." He gathered their burgers and handed them back to the cashier. "You wanna cook these a little longer?"

She looked at him like he had a problem, but nodded and took the gut-rot burgers.

"If all their food is this bad, they're in trouble," said Amber.

Had Ty checked with this restaurant? They could sure use help. Should she even bring up the subject, or would she risk ruining a perfectly good day? They'd had so few, especially since her big blow-up. Well, what the heck. "Did you ever drop off an app there?"

He shook his head. The woman handed him back the burgers. He took another bite of his. "This was a waste of money. And probably even going there would be a waste of time. If their food's this bad, they don't know anything."

She wanted to push him to at least check it out. WWMD? (What would Millie do?) Millie would probably drop the subject, saying something like, "Whatever you think, dear."

Except these days, Ty needed help thinking. His brain was in a TV-numbed depression fog and the family money tree was shriveling. She didn't want to spend the rest of her life doing price comparisons at thrift stores and scrounging day-old bread from the bakery and having barely enough money to pay the rent.

It was as if Millie was standing next to her whispering in her ear, "Well, then, give him some armor."

"They'd be lucky to get you," she said, working hard to keep her words casual. "And who knows? You may save them from going out of business." That hadn't been so hard. And it was certainly true. *There, try that on for size.*

He gave a thoughtful nod. "Maybe I'll check it out next week."

It was such a small thing. A maybe. Not a for sure

that he'd follow through, certainly not a guarantee he'd even get an interview, let alone a job. But it was progress. Progress of any kind was good. She smiled at him and gave his arm a squeeze as they started walking toward the bounce house.

Halfway there, she spied Millie on the opposite sidewalk, strolling along next to a big man with gray hair, each of them eating a cotton candy. Old friends, maybe, a brother in town visiting? No. The way they were looking at each other, it was plain to see they weren't related.

"There's my friend, Millie. Let's go say hi," she said, giving Ty's arm a tug.

"You say hi," he said. "Seth wants to get to the bounce house."

"Come on," she wheedled. "It'll only take a minute."

He heaved a long-suffering sigh and let her tow him through the crowd, calling to Millie as they went.

"Well, Amber, hello," said Millie, lighting up at the sight of them. "Isn't this fun?"

It sure beat staying home watching her husband mope around the house. "It is," Amber agreed and introduced Ty.

"I've heard so many nice things about you. It's nice to finally get to meet you in person," Millie told him.

Ty looked questioningly at Amber. *What nice things?*

She ignored it. "I don't think we've met," she said to Millie's companion.

"No, we haven't," he agreed, "but I'll bet you're one of the garden girls. Millie talks about you a lot."

Millie made the introductions, referring to Mr. Tall, Gray, and Handsome as "my friend" Altheus.

Yeah, well, those weren't platonic looks Amber had been seeing these two giving each other. Friends with benefits? At Millie's age? Amber thought of her grandparents, still going dancing together at the Eagle's Club every Friday night. She guessed love could blossom at any age.

It could die at any age, too. Your love's not dead, she told herself. It was sick, wilted, but not dead. All they needed was to get just a little bit of sunshine back in their life.

"Have you eaten?" Millie asked. "Altheus and I were talking about stopping by that Family Inn booth. We could grab a bite. My treat."

"Was that going to be your next course, after the cotton candy?" Amber teased.

"Oh, you know what they say about life being uncertain," Millie said with a smile. "Eat dessert first."

Ty spoke up. "I wouldn't waste your money. We just tried the burgers. They're bad."

Millie's eyebrows shot up. "Really?" She turned to Altheus. "I guess that's not surprising, is it?"

He shook his head. "I met Charlie Thomas, the

owner, at Rotary. He's having a hard time finding a decent chef."

"Really?" Ty said, his voice speculative.

"It is hard to find good chefs," Millie said with a shrug. "I'm trying to remember. Didn't your wife tell me you're a chef? Mr. Thomas might want to steal you from your current employer."

As if Millie didn't know Ty was unemployed. Amber could almost feel the warmth from her husband's red cheeks. "He is a great chef," she said.

"Can we bounce?" Seth asked, pulling on Amber's arm.

"I guess we'll take a rain check on the food," Amber said to Millie.

"That's fine. You enjoy yourselves," she said.

"So, what *did* you tell her about me?" Ty asked Amber as Millie and Altheus strolled off.

"Not much," Amber lied. "Just that you're a good cook. And a good man."

There. Husband armored up. And, who knew, maybe next week, Ty would actually feel equipped to enter the job-hunting battle again. Right here in their own backyard—if he got the job it would be a win-win situation.

And, speaking of jobs, why had Millie suddenly wanted to get something to eat when she and Altheus were already snarfing down cotton candy? Had she known the owner of the Family Inn was in need of a chef? If so, Amber had to hand it to Millie. She was smooth.

TWENTY

$\mathcal{B}$obbi was insistent that Hope come to Slugfest. "You need to get out and have fun."

Like it would be fun to follow her sister and Jason around. "A threesome?" How desperate did Bobbi think she was, anyway?

"Just come for a while," Bobbi pushed. "When you've had enough, you can take my car home and I'll have Jason bring me back."

Hope knew Bobbi would push and push until she gave in. *Might as well give in now and get it over with.* "Okay. But just for a while."

"Great!" Bobbi picked up her cell phone and punched in a number. Not hard to figure out who. "Okay, Hope's coming with."

The little beast! "You already had this planned," Hope accused.

Bobbi ignored her. "We'll meet you by the beer garden."

"*You* can meet him at the beer garden."

Bobbi stuck a finger in her ear. "What?" Now she was grinning. Hope knew from experience that this didn't bode well for her. "Great. Thanks. See ya later."

"What's great?" Hope demanded as her sister hung up.

"You have to stick around, at least for part of the dance."

"No, I don't," Hope said stubbornly. What was the point of going to the street dance if she didn't have anyone to dance with?

"Duke's coming. We're double-dating."

A million thoughts swarmed Hope like angry bees. How dare Bobbi set her up on a date without asking! This had all been a trick. "I don't want to date Jason's friend. I don't want to date anyone. And, most of all, I don't want to be manipulated." She slammed the dryer door shut on her laundry and gave the setting control knob an angry twist.

"Oh, come on," Bobbi pleaded. "It will be fun."

"No, it won't. I'll be too mad at you to have any fun at all. I don't even like Duke."

"He's hot," Bobbi protested.

"He's not my type." He looked like the kind of man who would unthinkingly trample flower beds, eat cake with his fingers, and move in on his best friend's girl in a heartbeat. Hope remembered the looks she'd caught shooting between him and Bobbi. This man wasn't coming along because he wanted her. He was coming because he wanted to poach.

"Just for a while," Bobbi pleaded. "Come on. When was the last time you did something fun?"

"I went to Megan's just last month for a chick flick."

Bobbi rolled her eyes. "Wow, a social life one night a month. How do you stand it?"

"Maybe I don't need as much of a social life as you," Hope snapped.

"I know you don't. But you need to have some fun, especially after all the hard stuff you've gone through." Bobbi wrapped an arm around Hope's shoulder and squeezed. "Come on. Pleeease?"

Hope gave up. "Okay. But I'm not staying for long. I have plans." *To come home and water my plants.*

It was enough for Bobbi. She grinned. "Great. Now, let's get gorgeous and get out the door. I'm starving."

Getting dressed turned out to be a production. Bobbi took one look at Hope's jeans and her favorite figure-hiding top and shuddered. "Oh, no. I'm not going to be seen with you in that." She grabbed Hope's arm and hauled her to Bobbi's bedroom, still full of unpacked boxes of kitchen things and knickknacks.

But the clothes had all been carefully stowed away. Before Hope knew it, she was in a soft pink sweater with a white camisole under it.

Too clingy. She shook her head vehemently. "No, that won't work."

"Your boobs look fine," Bobbi assured her.

Not to her they didn't. The difference wasn't that noticeable in most clothes and not to most people, but to Hope, clinging sweaters were like neon signs. *Fake boob, fake boob, fake boob.* "I can't wear this."

She started to take it off, but Bobbi stopped her. "We're not done yet. Here, put this on." She handed over a denim jacket. "Wear it open."

Hope slipped it on and looked in the mirror Bobbi had hung on her door. The vertical lines drew the eye up and down, not to the chest. She looked normal, cute even. Behind her Bobbi was indulging in a knowing smirk. "Told you. Now here, put on these earrings."

Hope slipped on Bobbi's favorite garnet drop earrings. They looked great. Next, the tennis shoes she'd been about to wear got traded for pink pumps Bobbi declared were too big for her.

"Those look great," Bobbi approved.

"And they fit. I can never fit in your shoes." Hope took one off and checked the size. "Size eight?"

"They're a little big for me," Bobbi admitted.

"Why did you buy shoes a size too big?"

Bobbi shrugged. "They were on sale."

Hope just shook her head.

"Hey, don't be giving me grief. That was a psychic buy. I knew, somehow, those shoes would come in handy." Bobbi stepped back and admired her handiwork. "Now you look ready to go out. Good thing you've got me or you could end up on *What Not to Wear* with the whole world watching."

Hope couldn't help smiling as she put the shoe back on. "You're absolutely right."

Bobbi acknowledged the compliment with a

brief grin, and then got back to business. "Now, let's do something about your makeup. You have got to quit walking around looking like a fashion fugitive."

Makeup, too? She hadn't worn makeup since she was first diagnosed with cancer. It was a habit long dead. And Hope wasn't sure it was worth reviving. What was the point? She waved away the suggestion. "Let's not bother."

"Oh, come on," Bobbi said, digging in her makeup bag. "You can't stop now."

"I'm fine like this. Anyway, there's no point. I'm not going to . . ." It shouldn't be hard to complete that sentence, but it was.

"Not going to what?" Bobbi asked, studying her. Then sudden understanding dawned in Bobbi's eyes, followed by concern. "Don't go there. Of course you're going to find someone. You don't want to go through your life alone."

"Yes, actually, I do. That way I don't have to worry about the toilet seat getting left up."

Bobbi threw up both hands. "You have got to stop doing this to yourself. So, you've got some scars. So, you're not perfect and you've got an implant. Half of Hollywood has implants."

"They had better surgeons." Or better genes. Or better . . . something. If any member of the Hollywood Big-Boob Club had experienced capsular contracture—that dreaded complication that demanded more surgery and rewarded with more scarring—or had problems with the new addition not matching up or feeling normal, they weren't announcing it.

Stop acting like such a thistle. It's one date, and a group date at that. No one's asking you to peel off your top and do show-and-tell. Anyway, it was easier to let Bobbi have her way than argue, especially when Hope knew she'd only lose the argument anyway.

"Ha! I'm amazing," Bobbi crowed when she'd finally finished. She pulled Hope off her bed and planted her in front of the mirror. "There. Do you look great or what?"

Hope looked in the mirror. Her face had changed. Had her lips always been that full or had she simply forgotten? And her eyes, she couldn't stop looking at them. They were big and her lashes were thick and sexy. She looked . . . alive. And healthy. "Wow," she breathed.

"Now you look the way you used to," Bobbi approved.

Well, almost, but Hope wasn't about to belabor the point. She couldn't fix what was wrong, but thanks to Bobbi, she was sure playing up what was right. She did a little turn in front of the mirror. "I can't believe it's me."

"I can," said Bobbi. "Now, we so have to go or I'm going to collapse. I'm so hungry I'm about ready to gnaw my arm off."

Ten minutes later, Bobbi had created a parking

space out of half a No Parking zone and a bunch of sticker bushes. "I'm going to come back and find your car towed away," Hope predicted.

"Then Duke will have to drive you home," Bobbi said, and waggled her eyebrows.

What a terrifying thought.

Bobbi must have seen the fear in Hope's eyes because she quickly said, "Don't worry. It'll all work out." And without giving Hope any further chance to protest, she slid out of the car, taking the keys with her.

"Maybe you should give me those now," Hope said as they started walking toward the surging crowd.

Bobbi stuffed the keys in her pants pocket. "Not yet. You might just turn and run." She gave her sister a taunting grin. "You gotta eat something and dance at least three dances before you get to go home."

"Boy, are you bossy," Hope muttered.

"I'm pretending I'm the big sister," Bobbi cracked, and gave her a hug. "Oh, the band is already playing. Let's move it."

Hope could hear a guitar screaming, and under it, the pounding of drums and the thumping of a bass. Like a heartbeat. The smell of grilling onions and cotton candy drifted on the air, making her taste buds water. She took a deep breath, picked up her pace, and followed her sister to the party.

TWENTY-ONE

*I*t wasn't hard for Jason to spot Bobbi Walker in the crowd, not in that red leather jacket. Under it she was wearing a black top and tight jeans. Her blond hair gently caressed her shoulders as she walked. She looked like a model.

But she wasn't the only one.

"Check it out," said Duke, standing next to him. "The sister took a hot pill since the last time I saw her."

No joke. Dressed in pink, Hope looked soft and feminine, and made him think of cupcakes. As they got closer, he saw she was wearing makeup. It made her whole face come alive and moved her up the babe meter from an eight to a nine and a half.

"Not bad at all," said Duke.

Jason wasn't sure he liked the way his friend was checking out Bobbi's sister. Duke was a connoisseur of women, a no-commitment gypsy. This hadn't bothered Jason before. But now, watching him checking out Hope, and knowing he was doing the S-Man X-ray vision thing and seeing what was behind those clothes, Jason wasn't feeling so laid-back. It had seemed like a good idea at the time when Bobbi suggested a double date, but now he realized he'd just served up a dove on a platter to a wolf.

Bobbi caught sight of them and waved, pushing

her way past a clump of noisy women. "We're here," she announced. "The party is on."

"I'm down with that," said Duke.

The wolf had a big appetite. Duke was doing the S-Man thing with Bobbi now and not trying to hide it. That was going to earn him a fist in the nose.

Then Jason caught the way Bobbi looked back and felt like he was the one who just got punched. Sucker punched.

But when she curled her arms through his and smiled up at him, showing off those dimples in her cheeks, he decided he was imagining things.

"Let's get something to eat," she said. "I'm starving."

"We can't have that," said Duke. He put an arm around Hope. "Whaddya say to something . . . hot?"

She slipped out of his easy embrace. "Maybe we'd better start with something cold."

That made Jason snicker. Okay, this woman could take care of herself. He didn't need to worry about her.

They filled up on barbecued ribs and corn on the cob, washed down by beer from Brewsters, the local brew pub. Then Bobbi led them to the big, inflatable bounce house, which was filled with trampolining kids, and insisted they go in.

They were the only grown-ups in there and the noise level was enough to turn Jason deaf, but he couldn't help laughing as he bounced around like a human spring. And then everything went downhill. Hope lost her balance and fell into him. He tried to keep her upright and wound up with a handful of soft, female ass. She had too much momentum going, so down they went, Jason's hand still on her butt. She landed on top of him. The groin-to-groin contact was a double whammy, but she turned it into a triple when she wriggled to get off of him, muttering, "Sorry."

He wasn't, and that, naturally, made him feel guilty as an altar boy at a porn site. He got to his feet just as Bobbi moon-jumped over to him and threw herself into his arms, taking him over backward again. And now, she was on him and he felt like he was in some kinky movie, doing foreplay for a threesome. This was wrong. What was going on in his head, anyway?

By the time they left that big bubble of trouble, Jason was sweating, and it wasn't from exercise. He wished it was just him and Bobbi here tonight. Including Duke and Hope had been a bad idea. It was like mixing your liquor when you drank. It screwed you up.

It'll be okay now, he reassured himself as he draped an arm over Bobbi's shoulder. Everything would be fine. Bobbi was everything he wanted in a woman. He didn't have to go confusing the issue by checking out her sister. He had another beer to wash away the confusion. Duke had two.

Then it got dark and the dancing began in

earnest. And suddenly, Duke and Bobbi were dancing together in a way that should have burned off their clothes. The other dancers cleared a space for them and started cheering like they were at *Dancing with the Stars.*

And Jason started imagining his hands around Duke's throat. "I'm gonna kill him."

"Oh, I don't think you need to go that far," said a soft voice at his elbow. "Just cut off his feet."

He turned to find Hope standing next to him, hands in her pants pockets, watching her sister. She didn't look ready to commit murder, but judging by her disapproving frown, she probably wasn't above some foot cutting herself. "Bobbi loves to dance," she explained.

"I've figured that out," he said sourly. Well, it was caveman manners to stand there like a lump and not ask the woman next to you to dance. "I could use a lesson," he said to Hope. "Wanna teach me?"

"I'm not the dancing queen my sister is," she said, and took a step back.

"I'll bet you've got some moves." He shouldn't have said that. It made him remember their aborted horizontal bop in the bounce house. *Never mind that. You're just being nice to your girlfriend's sister.* As he took her hand and led her to a corner of the crowd where a few determined couples were putting on their own exhibition, he couldn't help asking himself if "girlfriend" was an accurate label for Bobbi since they still hadn't had sex. Girlfriend in the making, maybe? Did she want to be his girlfriend? Tonight he felt like he was getting mixed messages.

He and Hope had barely started moving—stumbling in Jason's case—when the band stopped. She smiled at him and shrugged a shoulder, indicating he was off the hook.

But now the band was going into a slow song, and Duke had already whirled Bobbi into some kind of showy slow dance. Jason really was going to kill the guy.

He forced himself to put murder on the back burner and said to Hope, "I think my feet will do better at this speed, anyway."

"Oh, that's okay. You don't have to."

She looked flustered, almost frightened. Did he make her nervous? "I promise I won't bite," he teased.

Even though she looked like she wanted to run, she let him take her hand. It was trembling, and she had sweaty palms. He was making her nervous, which was weird. There was no need to be nervous around him. It was Duke she had to watch.

Jason put a hand to her back and drew her to him. She had longer legs than her sister and it made her just about the right height to fit him perfectly. What did those long legs look like without the pants covering them? What did they feel like? He could almost imagine skating his hand over one of them and feeling silky skin beneath his fingers.

Where the hell had that thought come from? The bounce house, of course. He reminded himself that this woman could wind up his sister-in-law and put a brotherly distance between them.

"After this, we should find Bobbi," Hope said, searching the crowd.

"Good luck with that," Jason grumbled. *Duke should be arrested for kidnapping.*

"I know she looks like a flirt, but she's not really. She's just bubbly, full of energy," Hope explained.

"Duke's being a shit," Jason said. "If I had a two-by-four handy, I'd hit him with it. He's supposed to be your date."

And Bobbi was supposed to be his. It wasn't fair of either Bobbi or Duke to ignore them like this. No wonder he was getting into mental trouble here with Hope, with Bobbi ignoring him the way she was.

Out of sight, out of mind? What kind of a shit did that make him? He decided he didn't want to think about it. Easier to be pissed at Bobbi and Duke.

"That's okay. Duke and I aren't a match," Hope said. "He's not my type."

Somehow, he'd known it. He should never have listened when Bobbi suggested he bring Duke along. The guy liked his women with an edge.

"So, what is your type?" Jason asked, making conversation.

She cocked her head, considering. "Oh. I like

men who think about more than the next party. Who think, period," she added with a smile.

"What? Guys don't think?" he teased.

"Some do. I get the impression you do."

"I try," he said, flattered. "So, what else?" The music was still playing. They had to fill the time somehow.

"I like a man who enjoys nature."

"Hiking?"

Her cheeks turned pink as soon as he'd said that, and Jason remembered their trail encounter when she'd landed on her back. "Sorry. I didn't mean to embarrass you," he said.

"I'm really not a klutz like that."

"Everybody has klutzy moments," he said. The music ended and, as he turned to see what had become of Duke and Bobbi, he felt something soft under his right foot. Hope's toe.

He quickly removed his foot as she said, "Yeah, I guess everybody does."

She was grinning. He found himself grinning, too. Then chuckling. Then they were both laughing.

"Well, you two are having fun," said Bobbi, now back at his side again.

They were. Hope would make a great sister-in-law.

If he and Bobbi got together. Right now, looking at her all flushed and happy from dancing with his friend—make that former friend, former dead friend—he wasn't so sure. She'd seemed so right, so perfect. But a perfect woman didn't leave a guy to go off dancing with his friend.

"Let's get something to drink," Bobbi suggested. "I'm dying of thirst."

"I think I'm going to go home," Hope said. She turned to her sister and held out a hand. "Keys?"

Bobbi made a face. "Oh, come on. Not yet. We're just getting started. And you've only danced two dances."

"Yeah, the best is still coming—dancing with me," added Duke.

Hope shook her head. "I really need to get going. Sorry."

"That's okay," Duke told her. "Good hangin' with ya."

Bobbi gave up the keys and Hope said her good-byes. "Thanks for the dance," she said to Jason.

"I enjoyed it," he told her. And he had. Now, maybe, before the night was over, he'd get to enjoy a dance with Bobbi.

Hope left and the trio went to the beer garden for more beer. And then Bobbi went to the bathroom, leaving Jason and Duke together for a little talk.

"Okay, you shithead," Jason growled as soon as she'd left their table. "What's the idea of dancing off with my woman?"

Duke looked surprised. "Hey, we were just dancing."

"You had someone to dance with."

"She wasn't into me."

"Well, neither is Bobbi."

Duke leveled him a get-real stare. "Yeah? I hate to say it, man, but I don't think she's that into you."

"The hell she's not," Jason growled and shot up, ready to seize the moment and Duke's throat.

But Duke held up two hands and scooted his chair back. "I'm not fighting with you over a chick, not when I didn't even put the moves on her."

"The hell you didn't," snarled Jason. "I saw you out there."

"Hey." Duke stabbed a finger at him. "She asked me. You got a problem with that, maybe you need to talk to her."

TWENTY-TWO

*B*efore Jason could rip his head off, Duke left the table, calling over his shoulder, "I'm out of here."

Jason fell back onto his chair. Bobbi asked Duke to dance. Why was she asking Duke to dance? Well, duh. The guy was friggin' Patrick Swayze. Still, Bobbi was his date, not Duke's.

She returned to the table, all smiles. She was so damned cute, so fun. Jason was ready to forgive her.

Until she opened her mouth. "Where's Duke?"

"Missing him already?"

271

She slid into her seat and her smile ran out of energy. "Just curious. Are you okay?"

"Yeah. Just wondering how my date wound up dancing with another guy."

Her face turned as red as her jacket. She lowered her eyes, unable to meet his gaze. Or was she simply showing off that thick curtain of eyelashes? "That was tacky. I just love dancing with really good dancers. So, when he made some crack about giving the women a treat on the dance floor, I had to ask if he knew how to dance and he said he did and I said, 'Yeah? Show me,' and then . . . he did." Bobbi looked at him earnestly, leaned across the table, and put a hand on his arm. "I'm sorry. Let me make it up to you."

"I can't dance like Duke," Jason said grumpily.

She grinned at that, all dimples. "No, you can't. But you can be taught."

Okay, she'd said she was sorry. She wanted to make up. He'd be a bastard to sulk. He stood up, managed a smile, and held out his hand to her. "Let's dance."

And they did. Mostly slow dances and some shaking around to the fast numbers. She tried to show him a couple of steps, but even though he had the moves on the softball field, even though he could untangle the most confusing architect's drawings, here, on this asphalt dance floor, he felt like a dumb clod. His brain and feet refused to cooperate.

"You'll get the hang of it eventually," Bobbi promised.

Jason wasn't sure he wanted to get the hang of it, but he kept his mouth shut. As the evening wore on, he realized he was not having fun. Bobbi didn't seem to notice his gritted teeth as he struggled with the steps, and that dropped the fun factor even lower. Finally, he said, "How about taking a break?"

She looked wistfully at the other dancers, but said, "Okay. Let's bag it for the night. Want to come back to the apartment and watch a movie? It's still early."

Actually, what he really wanted was to go home and feel grumpy. But that was dumb, so he said, "Sure."

They were halfway to the truck when fat rain droplets began to pelt them.

"Oooh, my hair," wailed Bobbi, and pulled her red jacket up over her head. She huddled in close and hugged Jason, as if for warmth.

That female softness next to him swept away the sudden question of how she survived activities in the great outdoors if she hated getting her hair wet.

Hope was at the apartment when they arrived. She'd changed into sweats and was curled up on the loveseat with a book.

"We thought we'd watch a movie," Bobbi said to Hope. "Want to join us?"

The idea of hanging with them seemed to make

her uncomfortable. "No. I think I'm just going to go to bed and read."

"It's only nine," Bobbi protested.

"Don't let us chase you off," Jason added.

"I'll be fine," Hope said quietly.

Jason suspected she was leaving to give them privacy. Well, he sure wasn't going to do her sister with her in the same apartment. "Stay," he urged.

She bit her lower lip, considering.

"I just got the latest James Bond from Netflix. We can watch that," Bobbi said, pulling a package of Oreos from a cupboard. "Come on," she urged her sister. "You can read anytime."

Hope surrendered, positioning herself in an old, overstuffed chair and leaving the loveseat for Jason and Bobbi. Bobbi set cookies on the coffee table, and then moved to the TV to put in the DVD. Jason took a cookie and idly picked up the Jane Austen book sitting on the coffee table.

Hmm. The bookmark hadn't moved since the last time he was here. It was still on page two. It seemed like slow progress for a smart woman who loved to read.

"You guys are going to love this movie," Bobbi said, and snuggled in next to Jason.

Maybe he would have loved the movie, if he'd been able to concentrate. But he kept thinking about that bookmark. And his and Bobbi's dance incompatibility. And, after the movie, after she'd walked him to the door and given him a kiss that should have fried his memory chip completely, he walked to his truck thinking about something else: the look he'd seen flash between her and Duke.

Bobbi flopped on the loveseat and helped herself to another cookie. "I swear, I could have eaten this whole package, but I didn't want to look like a pig in front of Jason."

Hope was looking at her in disapproving shock. "*Now* you think about what you look like in front of Jason?"

"What's that supposed to mean?" Deep down she knew, but the last thing she wanted to do was admit it to her big sister, who was acting very much like a big sister.

"Do you want this man or not?" Hope scolded.

"Of course I do."

"Then maybe you shouldn't be looking at his friend like you're on a diet and he's Boston cream pie."

"I was not looking at him like that," Bobbi protested. She could feel her cheeks flushing.

"Jason saw it, too," Hope said. "And I don't think he was very happy that you left him to dance with Duke."

"We got that all straightened out. I said I was sorry."

Hope shrugged and picked up the package of cookies, returning it to the kitchen.

275

"He was fine with it," Bobbi insisted, clinging to the arm of the loveseat.

She could feel panic starting to rise in her. She couldn't afford to lose the perfect man. Damn that Duke anyway. Why did he have to come along and make her mess up? "What am I going to do?" She realized she was wringing her hands. She forced herself to stop. This was silly. Things were fine with Jason. Hope was making her panic for nothing.

Still, insurance would be good. "A card," she decided. "I'll get him a card tomorrow and put it in his truck." But she didn't want to wait till tomorrow. "I'll write him a letter and go leave it on his doorstep."

"Or better yet, pretend his friend is invisible."

That could prove hard to do, but she'd make an effort. Meanwhile, though, she'd inputted her problem into her internal computer and the answer had come up loud and clear: do damage control now.

Okay, damage control. "Have we got any paper?"

"Printer paper." Hope pointed to where her laptop and printer sat in the corner.

"Perfect." Bobbi snagged a piece and sat down at the Formica table with paper and pen. She chewed on the pen. "What can I say?"

"That you're sorry," Hope suggested.

She picked up her book and started for her room,

and that made Bobbi panic all the more. "Don't leave me," she begged. "I already said I was sorry. This has to be something more, you know, poetical."

"Poetic." Hope slumped in the loveseat and closed her eyes.

Hopefully she was thinking and not falling asleep. Bobbi held her breath, waiting for magic to happen.

And then her sister, the good fairy of love, spoke. "What about this? Rhythm and music and feet aren't the real dance. The real dance is when two hearts move together."

Her sister was amazing. "How do you do that?"

Hope opened her eyes and looked at Bobbi. "What?"

"Just close your eyes and be so brilliant. I couldn't do that in a million years. I wish I was smart like you."

Hope was looking at her earnestly now. "You are smart."

"Not like you." Bobbi rested her elbows on the table and buried her face in her hands. "This is like cheating on a test. I shouldn't be doing this."

"Well, then, you come up with the last part," Hope suggested.

"Okay." Bobbi sat and gnawed on her lip. *Come on, brain. Think of something.*

It was like her inner computer had gotten fried. It just sat there, doing nothing. "I can't," she moaned.

"Yes, you can. Think about your heart."

Bobbi heaved a sigh and stared at the paper. Heart, she should write something about her heart. And then it came. "My heart wants to dance with you!"

Hope nodded approvingly. "Only maybe change the *you* to *yours*."

Bobbi nodded eagerly and scrawled out the sentence. There. She'd done it. She wasn't a fraud. She folded the paper and jumped up from the table. "I'm going to go put this under his windshield wiper so he'll find it first thing tomorrow."

"You'd better put it in a plastic bag then," said Hope. "It's still raining out."

"Oh, good idea."

Bobbi bagged up her letter and drove to the duplex Jason was renting. She braved the pouring rain and slipped her offering under his windshield. There. Now everything would be fine again.

TWENTY-THREE

*O*n Sunday, Bobbi was a basket case and the sisters' usual Sunday lunch together was more torture than fun for Hope. Bobbi kept up a constant stream of fretting. "Do you think he got the letter yet?" . . . "Does it sound like I wrote it?" . . . "Should I be doing this?" . . . "I'm a fake" . . . "I need retail therapy. Let's go to the mall."

Bobbi wasn't the only one who needed therapy.

If Hope had to keep talking her sister down from the ledge, she was going to end up in a padded cell before the day was over. Forget the mall. She needed garden therapy.

"I should really run over to the garden for a while. Why don't you see if Anna wants to go?"

Bobbi looked disappointed. "You don't want to go to the mall with me?"

The clouds from the day before had gone and the sun was shining. The air at the garden would smell fresh and clean. "You know I'd love to," Hope lied, "but I really need to get over there and check on my cilantro." Like her cilantro really needed her. It was going gangbusters.

Bobbi slumped in her seat. "Okay." She sat bolt upright. "I should just go over to Jason's."

"Good idea," Hope said. Bobbi would go over and fall into Jason's arms, and then they'd fall into bed. And then they'd live happily ever after. Her little sister would be with the perfect man and everyone would be happy.

Hope shot out of the apartment as soon as Bobbi left and drove ten miles over the speed limit all the way to Grandview Park. *Garden therapy, garden therapy, garden therapy.*

Millie and Amber were both already there by the time she arrived, and busy putting chicken wire around Amber's veggies.

"Welcome to the Bunny Produce Mart," Amber greeted her grumpily. "That stupid rabbit broke into my garden and ate down my lettuce. I should have listened to you earlier, Millie."

"Better late than never," comforted Millie.

Amber looked to where Seth sat by the bunny's favorite camping spot, inching a carrot under the bushes. "I doubt he needs that as well fed as he is. I swear, if I ever catch that animal, we're going to be eating rabbit stew."

"You couldn't really kill that cute little animal," said Millie.

"Probably not. I can't even kill spiders, and I hate them almost as much as I hate that rabbit."

"And the animals have to live, too," Millie reminded her.

"I don't know why they can't learn to live on things we don't want to grow, like dandelions," said Amber.

"It's the Murphy's law of gardening," said Millie.

That made Hope chuckle. Just being here with these women sloughed off her bad mood. The sun was warm and the air smelled of earth and growing things.

"We were just talking about how much fun the Slugfest was," Millie said to Hope. "It looked like you were having fun. I saw you dancing as my friend and I were leaving."

Hope felt her stomach clench. Oh, no. No talking about Jason here. That would be pathetically un-Zen.

"Millie's *male* friend," added Amber, her voice teasing. "He's a hottie, Millie."

Millie's cheeks suddenly looked sunburned.

Relieved to have the topic turned away from herself, Hope asked, "Who's the friend?"

"Actually, it's the man I met when the flower deliveries got mixed up," said Millie.

"Is this someone special?" Hope asked. As if they couldn't tell simply by Millie's smile. She looked like a fourteen-year-old with her first boyfriend.

"He is," Millie admitted. "He's a widower, new to Heart Lake."

"Millie's the welcoming committee," Amber teased, then quickly added, "Seriously, I think it's great that you've got a boyfriend."

Millie suddenly got very busy weeding around her sweet peas. "Well, I am enjoying his company. Life is short, girls. It's foolish not to take advantage of every good thing that comes along."

Amber grinned wickedly. "Have you taken advantage of Altheus yet?"

Millie shook a gloved finger at her. "You are a naughty thing." She sat back on her heels, admiring her handiwork, and took in a deep breath of spring. "A garden is such an amazing thing, isn't it? There it is, the whole cycle of life played out for us every year—death, then resurrection, new buds, new life, new beginnings." She returned her attention to Hope. "And speaking of new beginnings, dear, tell us about that handsome man you were dancing with at the street dance."

How did they get back to her? "There's nothing to tell, really. I was just having a dance with my sister's boyfriend."

"Your sister's boyfriend," Millie said in surprise. "Why wasn't your sister dancing with him?"

Good question. "She was dancing with someone else."

"You young people do things differently than we did," Millie said. "In my day, when a girl was trying to hook a man, she didn't send him off to dance with someone else."

"Bobbi shares," Hope quipped.

"Maybe if she shares so well, she should keep right on sharing," Millie suggested. "You two looked like you were meant to be partners."

Hope shook her head. "Jason wants Bobbi. And that's just as well."

"Why is that?" asked Amber.

Hope gave a one-shouldered shrug and smoothed out the dirt around her basil. "She's the pretty one. Men love her."

"You're not exactly an aarf-aarf," said Amber.

"I am naked." Hope regretted the words the second they slipped out of her mouth.

"Oh, let's not be going there," Amber said with a snort. "We can't have sixteen-year-old boobs forever. Mine left after Sethie was born." She shook her head. "There's nothing like childbirth to mess with your body image."

"I can think of a few things," said Millie. "Is it the fallout from the cancer, dear?"

Suddenly, Hope was a watering can. She watched in horror as her tears seeped into the soil.

"But that's gone," protested Amber.

What it left behind wasn't. "No man wants a woman who's scarred."

Amber left her garden patch and came into Hope's, sitting next to her and putting an arm around her. "Hey, come on. That's not true. A real man cares more about what's inside than what's outside. And it can't be that bad."

Hope shook her head and swiped at the corners of her eyes. "It is. Trust me." She ran a hand through her hair. It was getting longer all the time, the curl slowly loosening its hold as her hair remembered it had once been straight. "This is so embarrassing. I don't know what's wrong with me today." But, of course, she did. It was the same thing that had been wrong with her since Jason Wells first walked into her shop. She had to get a grip.

Millie joined them now and sat on the other side of Hope, giving her arm a gentle pat.

"You had reconstructive surgery, right?" Amber pressed.

Hope nodded, unable to speak. She supposed if she had it to do over, she'd do it again, in spite of the complications, the second surgery, the scarring. An imperfect fake boob was better than no boob.

But not good enough to parade in front of someone. "It's not the same." She could barely speak. The words came out as a croak.

"Trust me," Amber said, giving her a squeeze, "guys don't care if the girls are real or not. They get turned on either way."

"Think of how many women are walking around with implants and leading perfectly normal lives," Millie added.

"I am leading a perfectly normal life," Hope insisted.

"A life where you turn your back on love is not perfectly normal," Millie gently chided.

"It's better than trying to build a future with someone when I don't even know how much of a future I'll have," Hope said, her voice barely above a whisper. She'd been trying so hard to look and act normal, and now here she sat, showing her friends her biggest scar of all, the one on her heart. "Getting cancer this young, my chances are so much higher that . . ." She couldn't show any more. Her voice broke, failing her.

"None of us has any guarantee," Amber said, hugging her fiercely. "You can't just give up and sit on the sidelines."

"Listen to an old woman and live your life to the fullest," Millie added. "Take advantage of every good thing that comes into it."

"Like Millie's taking advantage of Altheus," cracked Amber, easing them into a lighter mood. "So, when *are* you going to take advantage of Altheus?" she added, waggling her eyebrows.

Millie blushed. "Now, don't be asking nosy questions. Anyway, he's seven years younger than me."

"Sweet. A boy toy," said Amber, clapping her hands.

"We're just friends," Millie said firmly.

Amber cocked an eyebrow. "I hope you're going to practice what you preach. After that lecture you just gave Hope, we don't want to hear you didn't go for it because of a little thing like age."

"A little thing like age is why I don't have to be in a hurry to go for it," Millie replied crisply. She gave Hope's shoulder a pat and then used it for balance as she got stiffly to her feet. "I think that's enough serious conversation for one afternoon. But let's take a lesson from our flowers. They seek out the sun. How can we do less than these sweet flowers?"

"I'm going to remember you said that," Amber warned her.

Bobbi arrived at Jason's place to find his truck gone. Darn! Now what was she going to do? Leave, of course. She wouldn't stalk him, wouldn't call him on his cell. Sometimes a woman had to back off. This was one of those times. She went back to Plan A: mall therapy.

But the mall wasn't much fun, not without a purse full of tip money to spend, and especially not when, everywhere she looked, she saw women with their boyfriends. By the time she'd wandered through Macy's, Nordstrom, and Anthropologie, she'd had enough. She drove back to the apartment. Still no Hope. She turned on the TV and flipped through the channels. Nothing. With cable TV and a million channels to choose from, you'd think there'd be something.

She called Anna and they met for coffee. But then Anna had to leave. Her boyfriend was coming over for dinner. That really depressed Bobbi, so she went to Crazy Eric's and had a bacon cheeseburger, fries, and a Diet Coke. Like the Diet Coke could save her from the burger and fries? She sat in her car and scowled at the giant wooden cartoon Viking perched on the roof as if her misery were all his fault. Okay, now she had to go work this off. Line dancing at the Grange. Perfect.

But it wasn't. Bobbi normally enjoyed joking with the kids and their parents, commiserating with the single women who wound up here because dancing alone was better than not dancing at all, flirting with old Joe Burns who took her money at the door every week, showing off how quickly she learned the steps to new dances.

Not tonight. Line dancing couldn't do it for her—not when all she could think about was how much fun she'd had dancing with Duke and wondering if she'd ever be able to bring Jason up to speed or if Jason would even want to keep dancing with her. Or doing anything with her.

"You must have gone to the Grange," Hope greeted her when she walked into the apartment.

"Yeah," Bobbi said listlessly.

"I take it you didn't see Jason?"

"No." Bobbi frowned. "But, you know, I don't need a man around all the time. I can be perfectly happy on my own."

With all Hope's plants and her cool, vintage furnishings, it was such a cozy apartment. Hope herself looked cozy, curled up on the loveseat with a book. She was living proof that a woman could be just fine without a man. Bobbi joined her sister, settling in with her Jane Austen book and a glass of wine. She could be cozy, too.

She lasted an hour. She was too stressed for all this coziness. "Want to watch a movie?"

"Sure," said Hope, and set aside her book.

The movie didn't really help, either, even though it was a good one with lots of funny scenes. Bobbi kept thinking about Jason. He had to have read her letter by now. Why hadn't he called?

Hope was at the shop early on Monday so she'd be there for her flower deliveries from the wholesaler. Once the flowers arrived she had roses to prep and a cooler case to stock. By nine the phone was ringing. She should have had plenty to keep her mind busy, but the sawing and hammering, which got closer to her end of the building every day, kept luring her thoughts in the direction of Jason Wells.

"You have to stop this," she scolded herself.

And she almost had when, out of the blue, he wandered into the shop. His pants were dusty and he had sawdust in his hair. He looked like he'd stopped mid-project. "Hi."

"Hi," she said, and tried out a new mantra. *It's only Jason, my sister's boyfriend. It's only Jason, only Jason.*

He rubbed his chin as if he were trying to remember what he was doing in her flower shop. "Is your sister in yet?"

Hope shook her head. "Not yet. She should be any minute though."

He nodded. And then he stood there in the middle of the shop, deep in thought.

He needed to get the message and leave since her mantra wasn't working. "I'll tell her you came by," Hope promised, hoping to shoo him out the door.

"You don't have to do that," he said quickly. "Look, can I ask you a question?"

"Sure."

"About Bobbi?"

Okay, now he was going to ask what kind of flowers she preferred. He probably wanted Hope to whip up a bouquet and have it waiting for

Bobbi when she came in. Or maybe he wanted advice on rings.

"Does your sister like to read?"

What? "Excuse me?"

He shook his head. "Never mind. See you later." And, with that, he turned and left.

What on earth was that all about? He'd filled a bookcase full of books for Bobbi. Never mind that they were Hope's. He didn't know that. She sighed. There was a lot Jason Wells didn't know, and never would.

TWENTY-FOUR

*T*y dropped off an application at the Family Inn on Tuesday. On Wednesday, Charlie Thomas, the owner, called him in for an interview that afternoon. Amber played Cootie with Seth and bit off every fingernail as she waited for Ty to come home. She even did something she hadn't done in a long time. She prayed. *Come on, God, please come through for us. Pleeeaassee.* It wasn't the most spiritual prayer on the planet, but she figured God got the idea.

Now if God would just hurry up and answer. Ty had been gone forever. What was taking so long?

She heard the crunch of tires on gravel and tensed.

"My Cootie's done," crowed Seth. "I beat you again, Mommy."

"That's good," she said absently.

The door opened. Seth hopped up and ran to greet his dad. She stayed rooted at the kitchen table. She was afraid to even look Ty's direction. What would she do if she saw failure on his face again? How could she handle it? She was out of words and Millie wasn't here to coach her.

She heard Ty say, "Hey, buddy." Was there a new energy in his voice or was she imagining it? Now Seth was laughing.

She forced her head to turn and look her husband's direction.

He'd picked Seth up and was twirling him in a circle. And then she saw his face.

Oh, God. A smile. She looked at her husband hopefully. "How'd it go?"

He set Seth back on his feet. "You're looking at the Family Inn's new chef."

She jumped up with a squeal and ran to Ty and threw her arms around him, and now he was twirling her in the air and Seth was clapping and giggling. It was like they had just stepped out of a big, dark cocoon. God had been listening, and maybe there was hope for their future.

"This calls for a celebration," she said. There wasn't anything much to celebrate with other than popcorn, but she put a scented candle on the table and presented the treat with much fanfare. And the guys were pleased.

"The place is a disaster," Ty said, digging into

his bowl. "Their chef quit two weeks ago and the owner has been trying to do it all. He says the cooking isn't really his thing."

"Then why on earth did he open a restaurant?" It was such a tough business. Who in their right mind would do that if he didn't love to cook?

"He did it for his kids. His daughter had just finished cooking school; his son needed work. He bought the business from some family who had been here forever and thought he could do like they did and make it a family business. But then his daughter got pregnant and decided on a career change and his son moved to L.A. The guy's heart's just not in it now. He doesn't know what he's doing and he's losing money."

Her husband had just gotten hired by a man who didn't know what he was doing to work in a restaurant that was going down. This was not what Amber had in mind when she asked God for help.

"But here's the cool part," Ty went on.

There was a cool part?

"Thomas might be willing to sell down the road."

Leave it to Ty to find that out. Amber stared at him. He couldn't really be thinking about throwing them from the frying pan into the fire.

Of course he could. She felt suddenly sick. "Why don't you just feed me poison now and be done with it."

Ty's smile reversed direction. "Hey, hear me out."

No. No hearing out, no talking. She blew out the

candle. "Sethie, you want to watch *SpongeBob SquarePants*?" She picked up his bowl of popcorn.

"My popcorn!" he protested.

"You can eat it while you watch cartoons. Okay?" She settled Seth in front of the TV with his plastic bowl of popcorn, then went to the bedroom to put a pillow over her head and scream.

Ty followed her in, shutting the door after him. "You didn't let me finish."

She spun around. "I don't want you to finish! I don't want to own another restaurant. We don't have anything left to lose."

And she didn't have anything left to give. No more trying to be encouraging, no more armor. She was done.

"We wouldn't own it right away," Ty explained. "I'd be the head chef, run the kitchen for the next five years, and Thomas would stay in. I'd get a percentage of the profits and that would go toward buying the place. That would give me time to turn it around."

Turn it around? Turn it around? Was he crazy? They hadn't been able to get their first restaurant going, and now he was an expert on turning around one that was in trouble.

She threw up her hands. "Why can't you be happy to just be the head chef?"

"You can lose a job." His voice wasn't hysterical like hers, but his anger hit her like he was talking through a bullhorn.

"You can lose a business, too. Or have you for-gotten?"

He stiffened. "No. You won't let me."

"Why is everything my fault?" she cried. "Why? Why is it always about you and what you want and never about me? When does it matter if I'm hurting?" She'd said her share of angry things when the restaurant went under, and since, but she was well beyond that now. This was new territory. Thoughts that had been backing up in her brain for months spilled out. "God, Ty, what have I done to deserve the sulking and the moping and the emo-tional disconnect? Where did it say in our wedding vows that I have to be your emotional punching bag? Where does it say I get to carry everyone in this family on my back?" She was waving her arms around like a mad woman, and Ty was staring at her in horror. And that made her all the more berserk. "When does it start mattering at all what I need? When do you start remembering that there are two other people in this family?"

He had no answer, of course.

She turned her back on him, buried her hands in her face, and burst into bitter tears.

He didn't try to comfort her. Instead he left her. Big surprise there.

A moment later she heard the front door slam. Well, screw him, and screw his stupid armor. She fell on the bed and kept on crying. What was she going to do?

She was going to go see Millie. Millie would probably give her all kinds of advice she didn't want to hear, but Millie would also give her a cup of tea and a listening ear. Even though things would never be better, Millie would make her feel better.

Except Ty had probably taken the car, and that thought made Amber angry all over again. He was wasting gas to burn off his mad, and she was trapped here at home, stewing in bitterness.

She went back out into the living room. Seth, fortunately, had gotten sucked into cartoons and was oblivious to everything else. She looked out the window and saw the car still parked outside. Wonder of wonders, Ty had taken off on foot. Well, good. Then she'd waste some gas herself. Except going to see a friend was hardly a waste of gas.

She called Millie and didn't bother with small talk. "I need help. Can I come over?"

"Of course," said Millie. "I'll make tea."

Amber hung up and joined Seth on the couch.

He was now mesmerized by a commercial for a sugary power drink. "Can we get that, Mommy?" he asked.

"Would you like to go get a drink right now?" That commercial had come at the right time. The promise of a treat was the only thing that would have pulled Seth away from *SpongeBob SquarePants*.

"Yes, yes, yes!" He started jumping up and down on the couch like he had springs on his bottom.

"Well, okay then, let's go."

She loaded Seth in the car and took off. They hadn't gone far when they passed Ty, storming down the road, still in the clothes he'd worn to his interview. Amber stepped on the gas and floored it past him.

"There's Daddy!" cried Seth.

"Yes, Daddy's taking a walk." She should have told Daddy to take a jump, right into the lake. She hoped he got blisters.

Millie's house, which had been quiet the last time Amber was there, was now a hotbed of noise and action. A boy sat on the couch, playing a noisy video game on TV, and a young teen or tweeny, Amber wasn't sure which, was on her cell phone, talking. Seth took it all in, wide-eyed.

"Hi, Seth," Millie said. "I've got some apple slices for you. Would you like to eat them out here with Eric?"

Seth nodded, staring at the TV.

Millie set the plate she'd been carrying on the coffee table and settled Seth on the couch next to Eric, then she led Amber into the kitchen.

Here it was like another world, filled with the smell of something baking, and the sound of a simmering kettle gently whistling on the stove. Kabams and booms so loud in the living room were muted here, like a wind howling outside that wasn't allowed in.

"Sit down," said Millie. "I'll have tea in a minute."

Amber fell onto a chair and slumped over the kitchen table. "Have you got anything stronger, like arsenic?"

"Oh, dear. This doesn't sound good," said Millie.

"It's not. Ty got a job."

"But that's wonderful," Millie protested.

"He and the owner really hit it off."

Millie poured hot water into a china teapot. "I guess there's a downside here, but I'm not seeing it."

"The man is already talking about selling the restaurant to Ty."

Millie stopped pouring. "Oh."

"Yeah, oh. The food is bad news, this guy's got a lemon on his hands he wants to unload and in walks Ty, with sucker written on his forehead."

Millie brought the teapot to the table. "I assume you and Ty discussed this."

She set a cup and saucer in front of Amber and one in front of the chair opposite and sat down.

"I'm not sure 'discussed' is exactly the word. Oh, God, Millie, what am I going to do?" The tear level in her eyes was dangerously high now. Any minute they were going to spill and she didn't dare let them. Not when Seth could walk into the kitchen and see her crying.

Millie poured tea in each of their cups. "Surely the owner didn't expect Ty to come in and buy him out immediately, not when he only came in looking for a job."

Amber shook her head, trying to get herself under control. "No. Ty said something about doing this over the next five years. I don't even know how the subject came up. He was there for a long time."

"They probably got to talking, swapping war stories." Millie added some honey to her tea and stirred it thoughtfully.

"Millie, I don't want to own another restaurant. I don't want to lose everything I have."

Millie leaned back in her chair. "You've already lost a business and a house. What more could you lose? Except your family?"

Amber's fingers clenched around her cup. "Ty's the one who's going to lose the family. I can't do this again, but he doesn't care. He only cares about himself."

"What if he sees this as a second chance, an opportunity to save his family?"

"What if he sees this as a chance to save his pride?" Amber countered. Really, Millie was not helping at all.

"Well, dear, I certainly can't tell you how to live your life, but if I were in your shoes . . ."

Amber made a face. "You'd be perfect." Why had she come over here, anyway? What had she thought she was going to hear? Millie would, of course, tell her to support her husband. Millie was from a different generation.

Millie shook her head. "I was far from perfect,

both as a wife and a mother. And there were probably times when I should have put my foot down. Maybe if I'd been a little more assertive, especially in financial matters, my life would be different now." She paused for a sip of tea.

"Then I shouldn't just go along with this?"

"I didn't say that. I do think you need to look beyond the immediate future."

"I am," Amber said. "Long term, we'll never own a house."

"But if he does well and this restaurant succeeds, if you're able to buy it, you'll have built up both your husband and a valuable asset, and in the process made your family stronger. And this is still in the thinking stage, anyway. Isn't that correct?"

She guessed it was. She had been listening to Ty through her filter of fear, so it had been hard to hear the details very clearly. "I don't know." Amber stared miserably into her cup. "I just feel like no matter what I choose, I lose. If I get behind Ty and say, 'Go for it with the restaurant,' then we'll probably lose our shirts. If I don't, then we'll probably lose our marriage."

Millie gave a deep sigh. "That is a hard choice. I guess you have to ask yourself which is more important."

If she were to be honest, Amber would have to admit that right now security and peace of mind were what she wanted more than anything. "I'm just so sick of struggling. I want to be past this."

"I felt like that when Duncan was ill," said Millie. And now she was the one staring into her mug. "In fact, I felt like that so many times."

"Yeah? When?" It was hard to imagine Millie having problems in her marriage.

"Oh, when the boys were little, Duncan lost his job. He developed a . . . problem."

"What kind of problem?"

"He drank." Millie looked embarrassed, like her husband's flaw was hers. "But he got over it."

"Just like that?"

"Not quite. He was a member of AA for years."

"So, how'd you manage that?"

"I didn't manage it, although God knows I tried," Millie said with a shake of her head.

"Okay, then, what happened?"

"It was Christmas Eve. He was still out of work and he'd been out job hunting. He stopped off for a beer and didn't come home. I took the children to my mother's and spent the night."

"That sounds good to me," Amber said. Talking to her mom on the phone was good, but what she'd give for a hug and a chance to fall into her old childhood bed and just sleep off this nightmare. Maybe she should move back to California.

"Being separated from my husband wasn't what I really wanted," said Millie. "I was prepared to do it if I had to, though."

"I guess it worked."

"You could say that. But it wasn't as if I had a

plan. It was more a case of Duncan finally coming to his senses. He came to the house Christmas morning with a note he'd written on a piece of my stationery, promising no imbibing in the new year. He never touched another drop of liquor."

"And, obviously, he got a job."

"In Little Haven. It turned out to be the best thing that ever happened to us."

"Because you held his feet to the fire."

"Oh, on the drinking, yes," Millie agreed. "But I wasn't thrilled when he got that job, I can tell you. I didn't want to leave my family and move to Little Haven. I wanted to stay right where we were. They were my security, you see. The job he took—the pay was pitiful and I couldn't see any future in it. I was terrified."

"So, what happened?"

Millie smiled. "I went with him. In my mind, I suppose I always hoped he'd give up and we'd move back home. But he didn't. And, in the end, things worked out. The pay got better, and Duncan eventually became vice president of the company. We had a very nice life."

"But," Amber began.

"Yes, I know. Now here I am living with my daughter. We made some mistakes and paid for it. It happens. Life doesn't always go smoothly. What Duncan and I grew together in those early hard years was how we survived all the bumps that came after. That was what worked for us."

"I could survive the bumps better if my husband wasn't the one making them," Amber muttered. "I can't take much more of this."

Millie took a sip of her tea. "You're a strong girl. I know you'll sort everything out."

Amber lifted her cup. "I wish this was a magic potion that would just fix everything."

"I wish I had such a thing for you," Millie said with a wistful smile.

Seth's laughter drifted in from the living room. "Seth likes it here. Too bad this isn't your house. Maybe we'd stay until Ty showed up with a 'no new restaurants in the new year' card," Amber joked. She looked at the wall clock. Five thirty. "I'd better get going so you guys can have your dinner," she said, and stood.

"Oh, don't worry. Debra won't be home for another hour."

Now Seth let out a high-pitched squeal.

"If I don't get my son out of here pretty soon, he's going to start spinning around the room like a flying saucer."

They went into the living room and found Seth madly pushing video-game control buttons right along with Eric.

"Awww, you got me," Eric moaned and fell over on the couch, pretending to be dead.

That made Seth laugh all the louder.

"Come on, Sethie," Amber said. "We need to go see if Daddy's back from his walk yet."

"I don't want to go," Seth whined.

"We can come back another time," Amber promised.

"No." Now he started to whimper.

The front door opened and in walked a woman in her late thirties. She was slender like her mother and had the same blue eyes, but there the resemblance ended. Her face was thinner than Millie's, almost gaunt, and instead of laugh lines, this woman was carving angry furrows between her brows and beside her lips. She was like a psychic porcupine, sending out sharp, angry vibes.

"Debra, you're home early," Millie said.

"I've got a migraine starting." Seth, who was squeezing in one last bit of video play, let out a high-pitched screech, and the woman put a hand to her forehead.

"You should probably go right to bed," Millie told her. "I can take care of dinner."

"Thanks," the woman murmured. "Sorry to be rude," she added to Amber, but she didn't look all that sorry. Of course, she was in pain. Hard to be nice when you were in pain.

"This is my friend, Amber," Millie said, "but you girls can get better acquainted another time."

"We were just leaving," Amber explained. She gave Millie a hug. "Thanks for the shrink session." To Debra she said, "Your mom's the greatest."

"Yes, she is," agreed Debra, and managed a smile at her mother.

"Come on, Sethie," Amber said. "Let's go."

"Noooo."

"Yes." She picked him up from the couch, and now, naturally, in front of the porcupine chick who clearly didn't want them there, Seth decided to make a scene, crying and protesting. "Sorry," Amber muttered. "He's tired." And, with that, she carried her wailing child out of the house. An unhappy kid, an unhappy husband—*Are we having fun yet?*

Ty was nowhere to be seen when Amber got home. That was just as well, she decided as she made burritos for her and Seth. She didn't want to talk to her husband anyway, not if they were going to talk about starting another restaurant.

"I want to get a Halo game," Seth announced as they ate dinner.

In his dreams, but she said, "We'll see."

They finished eating and she put Seth in the tub to play with his soap chalk. She was cleaning up the kitchen when Ty finally showed up. And what was this? Flowers? "I walked into town," he said. "I thought you might like these."

Who are you and what have you done with my husband? "What are these for?"

He shrugged and leaned against the kitchen counter. "I'm a rat's ass."

"I'm . . . not following."

"I'm sorry I got so pissed. I was mad because . . ." He stopped.

"Because why?" she prompted.

He didn't look her in the eye. Instead, he shifted

his gaze out the kitchen window to the lake, slowly darkening in the twilight. "I want you to believe in me." His jaw clenched tighter with each word. "But I haven't given you any reason to, so I guess I can't blame you. Anyway, you were trying to make a celebration and I ruined it. You've been trying hard. I've been nothing but a loser."

She felt her throat tightening. "Oh, Ty." She didn't want to not believe in him, but she supposed the bottom line was, she didn't. She came closer and slipped her arms around his waist. "I'm so scared. I have been for so long. We lost everything. And then, I lost you. I just . . . want to feel safe."

He didn't say anything, but his arms came around her.

"Oh, God," she whimpered, and began to cry. "I don't want to lose anything more."

He was rubbing her back now. "I know. I'm sorry."

She hated herself for not being a Millie, not being willing to gamble everything for her man, but she couldn't. She just couldn't. She craved time to simply savor the stability of a steady paycheck. "Can we just wait for a while and see how this place does? Do we have to make a big decision like this right now? I need to be able to stop holding my breath." As soon as the words were out, she realized what she'd done. She'd opened the door to the dangerous possibility that they'd risk it all again.

He hugged her close. "We can wait."

"And what if I don't want to buy the restaurant, what if I never want to?" She looked up into his face, searching for the one answer that would truly allow her to breathe easy.

He looked like a man bracing to face the gas chamber, but he nodded. "We have to both want it or I won't do it."

"You mean it?" Could he really do this?

He nodded. "I want my own place, but I'm not going to throw us under the bus again. For now, I can be happy to be working."

"What are you going to tell Charlie Thomas?"

"Just that."

"Thank you," she whispered. Maybe they hadn't lost everything. Maybe they still had each other. To see, she kissed him.

He kissed her back. Really kissed her. And, next thing she knew, she was on the kitchen counter with her legs wrapped around his waist and they were going at it hot and heavy, like a couple celebrating the end of a long war.

"Mommy, I'm done," Seth called from the bathroom.

They broke off the kiss. "I guess we are, too," said Amber.

Ty was smiling, and she hadn't seen that glint in his eye in months. "No, we're not. We'll finish this later."

And later Amber realized they weren't going to be finished for a long time.

Blooms

TIPS FOR THE BEST BLOOMS

To keep your early spring bloomers per-forming at their best year after year, give them a good trim and fertilize them about two weeks after they quit blooming. This sets them up to do their job optimally next spring.

Summer-blooming perennials will look their best if you give them a shape-up trim in early spring. Their bloom will only be delayed by a couple of weeks, and you will enjoy a much more attractive and vigorous bloomer the whole season long.

To ensure healthy plants and lots of blooms, make sure you give your plants enough mois-ture over the hot summer months so they don't suffer from heat stress. Applying a layer of mulch will help plants retain moisture.

For the best blooms on your roses, feed them every two months from March through October. Avoid watering at night because it encourages disease.

You can pinch out the tips of any perennial for more blooms. Start in late spring or early summer. Using your forefinger and thumb, pinch the tips of the stems. For each pinched stem, two branches will grow. Don't pinch a flower stem after the buds are set though, or you'll cut off flower growth rather than encourage it.

SHOWING OFF YOUR BLOOMS
IN THE HOUSE

To make your flowers last in the vase, add a plant-food packet (which you can purchase at your local florist's). Also trim the stems. You don't want any leaves or debris under the water level. This produces bacteria that shortens the life of the flower. Change the water regularly. The cleaner the water, the less bacteria to shorten the life of the flower. Trim off 1 to 3 inches of the stems when you change the water. Keep an eye on your vase and make sure you don't run out of water.

TWENTY-FIVE

*A*mber called Millie the morning after her visit. "I can't talk long," she said, "but I just wanted to tell you that we have had a major breakthrough over here. It's like a miracle."

"I'm so happy for you," said Millie, and Amber could hear the smile in her voice.

"Thanks for being there. You're better than a shrink. I'm working tomorrow. Come on in and have a thank-you latte on me. Oh, Ty's out of the shower. Gotta go."

Better than a shrink. Amber certainly had a way of exaggerating, Millie thought as she hung up the phone. But she couldn't help feeling glad, both that her young friend was doing well now and that she'd been able to help. It was good to be needed, good to have someone want to hear what you had to say.

"Who was that?" Debra asked, coming into the kitchen. She was still in her bathrobe and her hair was going every which way, but she looked better than she had the day before. Her features weren't as pinched.

"Just a friend," Millie said. "Are you feeling better?"

Debra sighed and nodded. "I'm glad I called in sick though. I need some downtime."

Maybe she needed some mother-daughter time.

"Since you're home, would you like to do something fun today?"

Debra nodded thoughtfully. "Why not?"

By eleven thirty, Millie and her daughter sat with the early-lunch crowd, sampling the quiche at Sweet Somethings. "My, this place does a brisk business," Millie observed.

"They should. No one bakes like Sarah Goodwin. Except you," Debra added with a quick smile. She took a sip of her tea, closed her eyes, and sighed. "It feels good to take the day off."

"You've been going awfully hard," Millie said.

Debra set down her mug and looked around mournfully. "I hate my job."

"Maybe you should look for a new one," suggested Millie.

Debra looked at her like she'd suggested her daughter run away to Tahiti. "Mom, I can't just quit. I've got bills."

"Well, I know, but . . ."

"It's not like it was for you. I can't just say, 'Oh, I want to stay home and play in the garden.'"

She didn't have a garden, so if you asked Millie, that was a moot point. And Millie wasn't sure she liked the implication that her life as a wife and mother had been one long garden party. Gardening was very satisfying, but it was still work.

"Life is all about choices, Debra," she said firmly. "If you don't like your life, make it different."

312

Debra blinked in surprise. Then her features soured. "I didn't choose to be divorced, Mom."

"Yes, you did," Millie said with a sigh. "You probably made a million little choices that brought you to this point. But that's water under the bridge. If you want to go somewhere better, you're going to have to start picking some new paths."

Millie realized she should have given her daughter this kind of a tough-love pep talk years ago. She and Duncan had treated their baby like a hothouse flower. They hadn't done that with the boys and, even though Millie tried not to see it, the difference showed.

Whenever Debra got in trouble at school, Millie and Duncan took her part, something they'd never done with the boys. When she overspent her allowance in college, they bailed her out. And when her wedding had gone several thousand dollars over what they'd budgeted, they hadn't reined her in. Instead they'd emptied their savings. When Debra and her husband fought, Millie always took Debra's side. If she'd been able to be as impartial as she'd been when giving advice to Amber, would Debra still be married? Who knew? But it hadn't helped that she'd never built in her daughter the endurance for weathering hard times. What a painful thing to have to admit!

"Well," Millie said as their waitress approached. "Let's make today the first day of the beginning of some new choices, shall we? Let's have fun and not dwell on the things in life that are unpleasant."

Debra wasn't saying much of anything, so to get her started, Millie picked up the tab for lunch. Old habits died hard.

But Millie began to take hope that maybe her pep talk had done Debra some good. On Sunday, she announced she was going to check out line dancing at the Grange. "You don't need a partner to dance," she told Millie. "They have a beginner class at five. You don't mind feeding the kids, do you?"

"They don't want to go with you?" Millie asked. She'd actually planned to go out with Altheus.

"They wouldn't be interested. Anyway, I need to get out on my own."

"I'll make something," Millie promised. She also promised herself that next time she had plans with Altheus, she wouldn't cancel them.

So, when Debra called on Tuesday asking if Millie could run Eric to his five-thirty dental appointment, Millie informed her she'd have to work late some other day.

"Come on, Mom, help me out here," Debra begged.

"I'd love to, dear, but I have plans," Millie said.

"With Altheus?" Debra made it sound like plans with Altheus couldn't compare with the importance of chauffeuring a grandson to a dental appointment. How far they had come from Debra not wanting her mother to even drive, let alone have a car.

"Yes," Millie said, determinedly pleasant.

Debra gave a disgusted snort. "I thought you moved out here to help me."

"I did," Millie said, her voice less pleasant. She could feel her blood pressure rising, right along with her ire. "I also moved out here so we could enjoy spending more time together, something which we've done very little of. I didn't move out here to become your au pair. Things like dental appointments and Little League games are your department, Debra, and I wouldn't dream of depriving you of the satisfaction of being able to do those motherly duties. If you leave work now, you should get home just in time."

Debra was still sputtering when she hung up, and that made Millie feel a little guilty. But not guilty enough to break her plans with Altheus. Debra wasn't the only one who needed to choose her way to a new life.

TWENTY-SIX

*J*une had followed a soppy Memorial Day weekend. Other than meeting for coffee, Bobbi hadn't seen much of Jason. She could have. Her note had worked wonders and he was securely in her back pocket now. So securely that he'd invited her to go camping over the weekend. She'd invented a big wedding and claimed she couldn't possibly leave Hope to fill the order single-handed, so Jason had gone off alone to shiver in the cold and wet and pretend he was having fun. Except he hadn't gone alone. His brother went with him to eastern Washington, where the sun had shone and everything was beautiful.

There were still spiders, though, she was sure. And snakes. And bees. Much as she would like to have started meeting his family, she didn't regret her decision one bit. Anyway, she wanted them to see her at her best. It would be hard to be her best with no bathtub and no way to do her hair.

And now he was back, it was Friday, and they were going dancing. Everything was going according to plan.

Until someone new wandered into the flower shop: Mr. Not Perfect, all dressed up in jeans and a biker's black leather jacket. Bobbi stared at Duke and swallowed hard in a feeble attempt to water her dry mouth. Hope was in the back room working on an arrangement for a bridal shower, so here was Bobbi, all by herself, unprotected with Mr. Bad Boy.

"What are you doing here?" she blurted.

He frowned. "I came to order some flowers."

"You've got a girlfriend," she accused. She should have known.

"No, they're just for someone I wish was my girlfriend."

Ouch. After all that chemistry when they were dancing at Slugfest, this felt about as good as a sticker in the butt. What did she care, though? She wasn't interested. She didn't want Duke. She wanted perfect, stable, sweet, boring Jason. Boring? Where had that come from? Jason wasn't boring. He was smart. And he liked to read and hike and camp and, oh, dear, she was listing all the wrong things. He was gorgeous and he was a good kisser and he was responsible. There. Perfect.

"What kind of flowers do you want?" Bobbi asked.

He sauntered over and leaned on the counter. He smelled like leather and man. "I'm not sure."

"It's a little hard to help you if you don't know what you want."

"Oh, I know what *I* want."

The way he was looking at her was not good. Neither was the way she was feeling. Well, actually, it was very good. Every happy hormone in her body was now on red alert. But this wasn't supposed to be happening with Duke.

Bobbi bit her lip. "I'm dating Jason."

"Lame."

"Shouldn't you be working?"

"I had the morning off. Tooth cleaning." He flashed her a smile, showing off his newly cleaned pearly whites, and leaned in close. "You can still taste the cleaning stuff. Know what flavor they used?"

Bobbi stood staring at his lips like a deer caught in the headlights of a Mack truck. "No."

"Chocolate."

"Ummm."

He leaned closer. "So, Jace tells me you guys know what flowers mean. Secret messages and stuff like that. What flower says you belong with me?"

"I don't know." The words came out as a squeak.

"Well, find out and then send yourself some. And let my boy off the hook. You guys don't belong together."

"Yes, we do," she called as Duke left the shop, giving her a mouth-watering view of his hind end. "Yes, we do," she whimpered.

Jason returned from a mess on the new house they were building on the lake to discover one of his workers at the downtown project was in the process of demoing the wrong wall. "Borg, what the hell are you doing?" he demanded.

His new hire, covered in drywall dust, let his maul drop and turned to stare at Jason. "Whaddya mean?"

"You're demoing the wrong damned wall, dick-head. That's a weight-bearing wall. You want to bring the whole side of the building down?"

"Damn," growled Borg.

"Damn is right," Jason growled back. "Get your head out of your ass, shore that up, and be glad I don't saw you in half."

The whole day went downhill from there. Why

318

did he ever go into construction, anyway? He should have listened to his mom and his old man and gotten a teaching degree. Except then he'd have had to try to educate guys like Borg who had no brains and less ambition. And, if he'd threatened to saw them in half, he'd have gotten fired. No, much as this job made him nuts sometimes, this was where he belonged. Construction was the last frontier in the work field, the one place where a man could still be a man.

But being a man could be tiring. By the time he'd put out half a dozen more small fires, Jason was fried. He was seeing Bobbi that night, and he'd promised he'd take her dancing in the city. All he wanted to do was crash in front of the TV. Would Bobbi want to crash?

He called her on his cell as he drove home to shower.

"Hi, Jason," she said, chipper as always. No, not as always. Today she seemed even more manic.

He felt even more tired. "Hey, do you mind if we just watch the tube or something tonight?"

"I thought we were going dancing," she said. The disappointment wasn't exactly hiding in her voice.

"I've had a hell of a day. Could we postpone the dancing?"

"Okay," she said. He could almost hear the gears grinding as she reluctantly shifted from Plan A to Plan B. "Come on over and I'll order a pizza."

He didn't even want to drive. "How about you come over here and I'll order the pizza?" The privacy would do them good.

"Okay," she agreed. Her enthusiasm was underwhelming.

Even though he was shot, he did a quick detour by the Safeway to pick up some Ben and Jerry's chocolate fudge brownie ice cream, her favorite. Hopefully, the chocolate offering would appease her.

But she was only mildly appeased when she arrived at his place at seven and he showed her what he'd gotten her. "What happened at work?" she asked, dumping her purse on his kitchen counter. "Did somebody drop a hammer on your foot?"

"Somebody damn near dropped a whole building on my head. And that was just for starters." He pulled her to him and said, "I'll make it up to you, I promise. I just needed some peace and quiet to get centered again." So, what he probably should have done was canceled the whole night. Bobbi went with peace and quiet about as well as oil mixed with water. Never mind, he told himself. She liked movies. They'd put in a DVD, flop on the couch, and eat pizza and ice cream.

She did settle in and enjoyed the action flick he'd rented. And she really enjoyed the ice cream. Watching her lick her spoon, Jason realized he wasn't so pooped anymore. "Come here," he murmured, and pulled her in close for a kiss. And another, and another. And . . .

Then, suddenly, she was pulling away. "I know we've been dating awhile now."

"Yeah?" he prompted. What was she getting at, and why was she getting at it now? He put an arm around her and leaned in to nibble on her neck, but she slipped out of his embrace and left the couch, saying, "This is wrong. I can't do this." She snatched her purse from his kitchen counter and started for the door.

"What? Where are you going?" he protested.

"I have to go home and think."

He was off the couch now, and following her. "What?" What the hell was going on? He felt like the only player on the team who didn't know the playbook.

Instead of clueing him in, she shook her head. "I have to go."

And, just like Cinderella, Miss Right went running off. But she didn't leave behind a shoe. Instead she left Jason with something much more uncomfortable. He swore and marched off to the bathroom for a cold shower. This relationship was completely screwed up.

What was she doing? There she'd been, kissing Jason and thinking of Duke. How sick and wrong was that? If she hadn't remembered Mom's favorite saying, she'd have really made a mess of things. Mom was right. When in doubt, keep your legs crossed.

Now she didn't have any doubt at all. She knew for sure she couldn't keep Jason. They weren't right for each other. She had to tell him they were through. Right now.

Her inner computer calculated the chances of him being mad when she did. One hundred percent. Then it calculated how messed up both their lives would be if she didn't. One hundred and fifty percent. She whipped the car around and squealed back down the street. She was going to set this poor man free. It was past time. He needed to go find the woman who really was perfect for him.

In less than four minutes, she was back on his porch, banging on the door. He yanked the door open and greeted her wearing nothing but a towel around his waist and a look of shock on his face.

"Oh." Dear Lord, but he was gorgeous. Why was she here again?

TWENTY-SEVEN

*N*ever mind that this man is gorgeous, Bobbi told herself, he's not the gorgeous for you. And all she had to do to prove it to herself was remember Duke in the flower shop and the way he'd made her feel even with all his clothes on.

"I can't see you anymore," she blurted.

Jason looked at her like she was nuts. "What? Here, come on in."

"Only if you get dressed," she said, stepping through the door.

He didn't say anything, just padded away, the muscles in his back rippling as he went. What did Duke look like in a towel? Suddenly, she was dying to know.

Jason returned wearing jeans and pulling on a T-shirt. He joined her in the living room where she was now on the couch, nervously fiddling with the empty ice cream container. Boy, she could have used some more chocolate right now. She'd broken up with men before, but never Mr. Right. And she'd never had to explain to Mr. Right that he was wrong because she was a fake. Ugh.

"Bobbi, what's going on? If it's about not going dancing tonight . . ."

"No." She put the empty pint carton back on the coffee table next to the half-eaten pizza. "It's about us not being a fit."

"What?"

"We don't have anything in common."

His brows knit. "We don't?"

"I think you'd better sit down."

He sat on the other end of the couch and slung one arm over the back and looked at her expectantly. "Okay."

"I'm a fake."

His eyes rolled heavenward as if praying for supernatural help. "I'm not following."

"I hate hiking. Totally. And I'm not that into books."

"But all those books," he protested.

"Belong to my sister. Well, except the Jane Austen one. I like to read magazines and romance novels with lots of action. I don't like long, boring books or long, boring movies. And I don't own half the flower shop. I just work there. My sister gave me the job when I got fired."

"What about the cards, the letters?"

He looked like he wished she could at least offer him that. She couldn't. She hung her head. "My sister wrote them for me. I just couldn't think of what to say."

The silence coming from Jason's end of the couch was unnerving.

"I know it was wrong," Bobbi rushed on. "I wanted to impress you. I thought you were the perfect man. But the problem is, you're not the perfect man for me. And I'm sure not the perfect woman for you."

"I can't believe this."

She ventured a look at him and then was sorry she did. He was staring at her like half her face had fallen off. "I'm sorry." The words came out almost as a whisper. "I never meant to hurt you."

He shook his head. "God, what a dumbass I am. And your sister went along with this?"

"Don't blame Hope," Bobbi begged. "I made her do it. Anyway, she only wanted to help me. She wanted me to be happy."

He gave a disgusted snort that reminded her of a bull about to charge. Okay, it was so time to go. Bobbi stood and managed one more "I'm sorry," then fled, crying.

She was still crying when she stumbled into the apartment. Hope shot up from the loveseat where she'd been reading a book. "What's wrong? What happened?"

"I broke up with Jason," Bobbi wailed.

Hope looked at her like she'd just confessed to vehicular manslaughter. "No. Why?"

"Because I couldn't do it anymore. I'm a phony." She went to the refrigerator and started rooting around in the freezer. "I'm a mess. I need more chocolate."

She pulled out a pint of the same flavor Ben and Jerry's she'd devoured at Jason's, got a spoon, and plopped down at the yellow Formica table and dug in. "He hates me. It was terrible. But I couldn't keep pretending. I had to get everything off my chest."

Hope sat down opposite her. "Everything? What do you mean by everything?"

Bobbi spooned a mountain of ice cream into her mouth. "He even knows I don't own the shop. He even knows about the cards. I told him you wrote them."

Hope reached over and took Bobbi's spoon and the ice cream and shoveled herself a big mountain of it. "We'll never see him again."

"Like I want to?" Bobbi said.

"Oh, Bobs," Hope said with a sob. She dropped the spoon and left the table.

"Hope," Bobbi cried after her, but she shook her head and kept on walking down the hall. She went into her bedroom and shut the door after her.

Bobbi scowled and pulled the ice cream back. She dredged out the last of it and stuffed it in her mouth. "Everybody hates me. Even I hate me," she decided, looking at the empty ice cream carton.

All Saturday morning, Hope kept watching the door, hoping Jason would come into the shop, maybe want to hear her side of the story. But he never did. She supposed it was just as well since she wasn't sure she even had a side. She'd started out simply trying to help her sister, and then gotten caught in a sticky web of deceit. So, what was there to tell, really?

She was doing some bookwork in between customers when the phone rang.

"Those flowers are incredible," gushed her friend Megan Wales.

"You can thank Mr. Boston Legal for them, not me."

"I already thanked him properly," Megan said, sounding smug.

Things had been heating up between Megan and the man who had been her business mentor, and Hope was beginning to smell orange blossoms in the air. Every time Megan called she expected to hear she'd be coming in to pick out wedding flowers.

"Anyway, Turner wouldn't know a tulip from a turnip," she continued. "I know who's behind all that gorgeousness. The arrangement really is spectacular."

"I figured you deserved a special tribute for running a race in the rain."

"I've got to tell you, I never thought I'd see the day when I'd be out doing a Memorial Day Five K in the rain. But it felt so good to cross that finish line."

"You've got a lot to be proud of," Hope said. "Losing so much weight, starting your own legal firm. And now you're out running marathons. I could never run that far."

"Oh, I bet you could," Megan said. "If I can do this, anybody can. Anyway, I'm glad I did. Next year, I want to run the Boston Marathon."

"Wow."

"Sometimes you've just got to go for it. In fact, all the time you've got to go for it. And speaking of going, I've got to run. Turner's here."

As she hung up, Hope thought of the mess with Bobbi and Jason. Going for it sometimes landed you in a ditch.

She was barely off the phone with Megan when Amber stopped by the shop. "Don't forget you're sneaking out early today for Millie's birthday."

Hope had completely forgotten. "I'll start on her arrangement right away."

"And I'm bringing the birthday cake. She's going to love it. It's a lavender cake from Sweet Somethings and it's now my all-time favorite. And look what I found." She opened a pink paper bag from Something You Need, Heart Lake's favorite gift shop, and pulled out a little plaque proclaiming, "Friends Are Forever."

"She'll love it," said Hope. She reread the words. This was what mattered, her friends. As long as she had them, she'd be fine.

She finished Millie's bouquet, then left Bobbi in charge of the shop and went to the community garden. Amber had been waiting on the side of the road and now followed her into the park. As usual, Millie was already there, wearing her favorite purple outfit and tending her flowers.

Amber pulled a picnic basket out of the backseat of her car and gave it to Seth, then got out a Tupperware carrier with her cake. "Okay, let's go make her day."

"We're gonna have a party," Seth informed Hope.

"Yes, we are," Hope said, smiling with determination.

"What's this?" Millie said as their little parade approached.

"It's a garden party," said Amber, "for your birthday."

Next to her, grumpy Henry leaned on his hoe and eyed the Tupperware container. "You got cake in there?"

"It wouldn't be a birthday party if we didn't." Amber started singing "Happy Birthday," and Hope and Seth and even Henry joined in.

"Oh, girls, you shouldn't have," Millie protested when they'd finished.

"Of course we should have," Hope said, presenting her with the birthday bouquet. "We just want you to know we love you."

Millie put a hand to her chest. "I'm overwhelmed."

"You better not be too overwhelmed to eat this lavender cake," said Amber.

"Lavender? Oh, how lovely!"

Amber cut pieces of cake and they sat in Millie's garden plot among the flowers, eating cake and drinking bottled juice.

"This cake is wonderful," said Millie.

"It's okay. Carrot cake is better," said Henry.

The women ignored him. "You saved my marriage," Amber said to Millie. "I owe you cake for life."

Millie brushed away her gratitude with a wave of her hand, but she did want to hear more about how things were going on Amber's home front.

"We just had the most romantic anniversary,"

Amber said with a sigh. "Ty came home from the restaurant with chicken curry sandwiches and champagne. That old rowboat behind the house, we took it out on the lake and just went at it like it was our wedding night."

"Oh, brother," muttered Henry.

"It was awesome," Amber said. "At least until the boat leaked," she added.

"Now, that's romantic," Hope teased.

Amber sobered. "I'm falling in love all over again. You saved me, Millie."

"I'll have another piece of that cake," Henry said, ending the emotion-packed moment. "No sense letting it go to waste."

"What are you doing for your birthday?" Amber asked, cutting Henry's second serving.

"Well, let's see. Debra's coming home from work early Monday and making birthday dinner, and on Tuesday, Altheus is taking me to the Family Inn."

"I thought he'd take you someplace really nice, like the Two Turtledoves," said Amber.

"Oh, he offered. But I told him I wanted to go to the Family Inn. I hear they have a wonderful new chef there."

Amber beamed. "Yes, they do."

"Let's open the present," said Seth, tired of grown-up conversation.

Amber dug their gift out of the picnic basket. "It's from Hope and me."

"And me," piped Seth.

Millie lifted the plaque out of its tissue paper bed, and her eyes filled with tears as she read it. "You girls, you shouldn't have."

"We mean it," said Hope, and Amber nodded.

Just then a butterfly swooped down and landed on one of Millie's cosmos. "Look, a butterfly!" cried Seth.

Millie smiled. "We always used to say butterflies mean good luck."

"He must be here for one of you guys," Amber said. "I've already got mine."

"Then it must be you, Millie," Hope said. It sure as heck wasn't her.

Bobbi sat at the order desk, leaning on her elbows and looking out the window at the shoppers browsing up and down the sidewalk in the afternoon sunshine. She wished someone would come into the shop. She'd finished her latest issue of *People* and now she was totally bored. They should start doing deliveries on Saturdays. There was no reason not to with two of them here. She drummed her fingers on the counter. What to do?

The order counter was kind of a mess. She'd tidy up. She went into the workroom and wet a paper towel, then came back out and started to wipe down the counter, moving things around. Spring cleaning. Hope would be so impressed. Bobbi even moved the computer so she could clean behind it.

And what was this? A little piece of paper with Hope's writing. Hmmm. How long had this been back there? Bobbi picked it up and read it.

I teach the steps. She dances. I wish I could dance. With him.

Even though it didn't rhyme, Bobbi got that it was a poem, and not a happy one. But who was the she? Hope? And what him? Who was her sister talking about? *Okay, Bobbi. You can do this.*

She sat at the counter and stared at the poem, but after half an hour she hadn't gotten any closer to figuring it out than she was when she first started.

The bell over the door jingled and in walked Duke. Bobbi's heart started doing the happy dance at the sight of him. So did other parts of her.

"When do you close?" he asked.

"In about an hour. Why?"

"Because in an hour, you're getting on my bike and we're going to this place I know on the lake to celebrate." He held up two wine coolers.

"Celebrate what?" Like she cared.

"Your freedom. It's about time," he added.

She slumped down at the counter, feeling bad all over. "I hurt him."

"He'll get over it. Anyway, you guys weren't a match. Trust me, I know."

She couldn't resist asking, "How do you know?"

" 'Cause you're right for me." He leaned over the

counter and gave her a kiss that had so much heat, it should have wilted every flower in the place.

"I think you could be right," she murmured.

"I know I am."

She sighed. "I still feel bad though. And not just for Jason. Look what I found."

She held out the paper.

Duke took it, read it, and frowned. "It's a poem."

She made a face and snatched it out of his hands. "I know that. I just don't know what it means."

"It means that whoever wrote this ain't happy."

"I figured that much. But who's the she in it, and who's the him?"

"Hmmm. Set it down here on the counter," Duke said, and leaned over to study it. She leaned, too, but this close to that strong jaw and sexy mouth it was hard to concentrate. "Do you know who wrote this?" he asked.

"My sister. It's her handwriting."

"Hmmm."

He studied the poem some more and Bobbi studied him. Boy, was he a hot beefcake. And he could dance. Wearing his black leather jacket, he had bad boy written all over him. But something told her this bad boy was a good man. He'd helped her move when he didn't even know her. And, now, here he was helping her figure out this poem. Smart, too. What more did a girl need?

He thumped the paper. "You're the she. Your sister's jealous of you."

"What?" Bobbi picked up the paper. "That's impossible. She doesn't have a jealous bone in her body."

He shrugged. "She did when she wrote this."

"Oh, it's got to be something else. How could she be jealous when she thought Jason was perfect for me?"

Duke gave a snort. "How well does your sister know you, anyway?"

"No, you don't understand. I tend to pick losers."

"Used to pick losers," Duke corrected her.

Bobbi rewarded him with a smile, then returned to the subject of Hope. "She thinks I blew it and she's not happy that we'll never see him again."

"We?"

"That's what she said." Bobbi remembered it clearly. The lightbulb suddenly clicked on and she gasped. "Oh, my gosh. All this time Hope's been helping me and she's been in love with Jason." Bobbi ran around the corner, grabbed Duke's hand, and started running for the door. "Come on." Once there, she flipped the sign to Closed and shut and locked the door.

"I thought you had to stay open," he said.

"Not now," she said. "We've got an emergency."

TWENTY-EIGHT

he Sticks and Balls was a rundown tavern
that camped on the outskirts of town like an
unwanted relative. The barn-red paint on its old,
wood siding had faded to mud. It needed a new
roof and the *t* in the sign had come down, so it read
"Sicks and Balls." The regulars didn't care. They
knew what the place was about. It was man haven,
a hangout where guys could have a beer, shoot
some pool, and shoot the bull. Once in a while
someone brought his woman for a game of pool,
but for the most part, it wasn't really a woman-
friendly place. No hip décor, no girly drinks. Ollie,
the owner, had been married three times and he
was done catering to women, so it was fine with
him if most of the women in Heart Lake preferred
to hang out at the Last Resort. And anybody who
wanted to chase skirts and pay through the nose for
their booze was welcome to go there with his
blessing. Women were tolerated but not necessarily welcomed. As far as Ollie was concerned,
they were trouble.

The one walking in today certainly was. Jason
watched warily from the murky corner where he
was playing a solitary game of eight ball as Bobbi
hurried toward him with his so-called friend right
behind her. Duke hadn't wasted any time moving
in on Bobbi. Jason had only told him about the

breakup that morning when Duke came by to return his band saw.

Jason tightened his grip on his cue stick. Right now, he'd like nothing more than to bring it down over Duke's head, even though, deep down he knew none of this was Duke's fault.

"You need to know something," Bobbi greeted him.

Her perfume was a strong totem, eating up the room's comforting smell of beer and male sweat. "I think I know all I want to know." Jason took aim and launched the cue ball at the two. It hit its target with a resounding clack and the two jumped into the corner pocket.

"About my sister."

He didn't want to hear anything about either one of them. Jason lined up his next shot.

"I think she's in love with you."

He missed the cue ball entirely and skidded the tip of the cue stick along the felt surface. Damn, now he owed Ollie for a patch job on the table. He straightened and frowned at Bobbi. "That's nuts."

"No," she corrected him, "that's Hope. She'd never take you for herself if she thought I wanted you. In fact," Bobbi added sadly, "she'd never take you for herself at all."

He shook his head and turned his attention back to the balls. All these mind games. He preferred pool. At least you saw everything that was on the table.

"I know I messed up," Bobbi said. "But I didn't mean to. I was so sure you were perfect for me. That's how everything started with Hope. She's the smart one, and I thought if I got her to help me, then I could really impress you."

Jason focused on his next shot. Maybe if he ignored her long enough, Bobbi would give up and leave. She could take Duke with her.

A small hand slipped within his field of vision, setting a piece of paper on the green felt. "I just found this. Hope wrote it."

Jason brushed it away. "I've read enough of your sister's writing."

The paper came insistently back. "You need to see it. She's been in love with you all along."

"Right. That's why she's putting words in your mouth." Jason sent another ball tumbling into a corner pocket. "How about you two beat it and leave me alone?"

Duke scowled and took Bobbi's arm. "Come on. You tried."

"Please, just read it," Bobbi begged as Duke led her away.

Jason turned his back on them and sat on the edge of the pool table, chalking the tip of his cue stick.

After he was sure they were gone, he turned back around to continue his game. Now it was just him and Ollie in here manning the place, him playing pool, Ollie hunkered down at the far end of the bar, doing paperwork—two guys with nobody in their lives, two guys with some paper in front of them. What did that little slip Bobbi brought in say?

Like he cared. He lined up another shot. Out of the corner of his eye the paper lay there and taunted him. *Wouldn't you like to know? Pick me up? What's the matter? Chicken?*

He snatched it, perched his butt on the side of the pool table, and read the hastily scrawled words. This was bullshit. He tossed the paper aside.

Then he picked it up and reread it. Bullshit. This was all bullshit.

He folded the piece of paper and stuffed it in the pocket of his denim shirt, where it rode around for the rest of the afternoon. It kept him company through two more pool games, then accompanied him to the Safeway for beer, and it kept him company that evening while he worked on a wood carving and wondered what Bobbi and Duke were up to. Probably mud wrestling. They weren't reading, that was for sure.

Hope Walker obviously had a brain, a damned Machiavellian one. Someone read all those books in the apartment. Hope, of course. If he wasn't such a dumb shit he would have realized it when she was talking about how she shelved her books. And all those books on gardens and flowers—Hope's of course.

He cut deeper into the wood than he'd intended and swore. Now the cowboy he was trying to bring to life would have a deformed arm. He gave up on his wood carving, went inside, and flipped the TV on to the fight, then sprawled on the couch and glared at the boxers.

He didn't care how smart Hope Walker was. She was a sneak, just like her sister. Duke could have 'em both. Jason wasn't going to give either one another thought.

So then, why, on Monday, did he find himself wandering into the damned flower shop?

Hope was standing at the counter, taking an order over the phone. She saw him and her face suddenly looked like she'd gotten a three-alarm sunburn. "We'll get that out today," she said weakly. "No problem. Thanks for calling." Then she hung up and stood there, looking at him like he was a giant Venus flytrap about to swallow her whole. She cleared her throat. "I'm sorry things didn't work out with you and Bobbi."

"Did you think they would? Everything about her was a facade, and you built it."

Hope got busy straightening the counter. "Bobbi isn't good with words. She wanted to impress you. It got out of hand."

Jason gave a disgusted snort. "Do ya think?"

"Nobody meant to hurt you. And you can hardly blame my sister for realizing you two weren't a fit and stopping it before it went any farther. She felt like a fake."

"She also felt like taking up with my best friend."

Hope sighed. "There is that." She looked at him with regret in her eyes. "I can't help that my sister started falling for someone else. A heart's not like a car. You don't drive it. It drives you."

"Nicely put," he conceded sourly.

She has a way with words, whispered the little paper in his pocket. *Maybe you should ask her about me. And ask nicely. Can't you see she's upset?*

"Look," Jason said, softening his voice. "I just want some clarification." He pulled out the paper. "Did you write this?"

She looked confused, so he handed it over. She read it and the blood drained from her face. "Where did you get this?"

"I found it."

She closed her hand around the paper, crumpling it, and took a step back. "It's just a poem."

"A poem you wrote?"

"I was doodling one day."

"Who's it about?"

She took another step. "I don't remember."

Like hell.

"I've got an order to fill and I'm sure you've got to get back to work." Another step. "I'm sorry you got hurt. I'm sorry for everything. Next time you want to send flowers, it's on the house." She whirled around, nearly tripping herself. Then she disappeared behind the velvet curtains, taking the little piece of paper with her.

But the words on it stayed with him. And they

invited company, a crowd of memories: Hope sorting through piles of books like they were treasure, Hope falling on him in the bounce house at Slugfest, Hope in her apartment, making oatmeal cookies. Hope in his arms at the street dance.

A heart's not like a car. You don't drive it. It drives you.

He rubbed his forehead. Right now, his was driving him crazy.

TWENTY-NINE

*O*n Monday night, Debra came home from work early and made birthday dinner. And she and Emily baked a chocolate cake. It wasn't from scratch like Millie would have made it, but she pretended it was wonderful because she was so thrilled that they'd gone to the trouble. She didn't have to pretend to appreciate the music box Debra gave her or the little pots of marigolds from Emily and Eric. After dinner, they even played a game of Crazy Eights before the children drifted off to do their homework, and that was the best present of all—time spent together.

Then it was just Millie and Debra at the kitchen table. "Thank you for a lovely birthday," Millie told her.

"I do appreciate you, Mom. I want you to know that. And we'll spend more time together, I promise."

Except on Tuesday, as Millie was getting ready to go out with Altheus, Debra called to say she'd be late getting home. Would Mom mind starting dinner?

"Well, I don't mind making some sandwiches," said Millie, "but that's about all I have time for. I'm going out to dinner."

"You are?" Debra sounded surprised and a little miffed.

"Altheus is taking me out for my birthday."

"Oh." This was followed by a moment of silence while Debra digested that information.

"And doesn't Eric have a Little League game tonight?"

A martyr's sigh drifted over the phone lines. "I'll find him a ride."

"Debra, he'd probably love it if you came to the game," Millie said, trying not to sound too accusative. "These years go so fast and then the children are gone." And have their own lives and no time for their parents.

"I know, Mom," Debra said in THAT tone of voice. "I'll make it back for the last half. I've got to go."

Millie hung up with a sigh. When it came to life lessons, her daughter was a difficult pupil.

Altheus could tell immediately that Millie was bothered. "Trouble on the home front?" he asked as they drove to the restaurant.

"I do worry about Debra," she confessed. "I'm

afraid she's very . . ." How to phrase it? It was hard to say words like spoiled and self-centered.

"Self-absorbed?" he guessed.

"That's probably as good a way as any to put it."

He shook his head. "That's this younger generation." He reached a hand across the seat and took hers. "But she'll sort things out. She'll hit a few more bumps and get her eyes opened in the process." He gave Millie's hand a squeeze. "She's your daughter, Millie girl. Sooner or later she'll figure that out and want to be more like you."

"Oh, Altheus," Millie said, tears springing to her eyes. "That's so sweet."

He gave her hand one last squeeze, then said, "And now we're going to focus on you, not her. Okay? You still have a life of your own to live. And we're going to live it up tonight!"

He made good on his promise, taking her to the Family Inn where they enjoyed salmon grilled in some exotic sauce and a salad of greens, blueberries, and feta cheese. The waitstaff all sang happy birthday to her and presented her with a little carrot soufflé, compliments of the chef. Embedded in the top, she found a ring with her birthstone, alexandrite, centered among a cluster of diamonds.

She plucked it out and gasped, "Oh, Altheus. I can't accept this."

He grinned. "Sure, you can. I'm hoping you'll wear it on your left hand."

She stared at him. "Altheus, what is this?"

"I guess you could say it's a proposal."

"But we've only been seeing each other a short time," she protested.

"Millie girl, I knew I wanted to spend the rest of my life with you from the first day we met," he said. He reached across the table and took her hand, making her heart flutter. "Didn't you?"

"Well, I just can't. I mean really," she sputtered.

"What's wrong with two people finding happiness? At our age, don't you think that's a good thing?"

He was smiling at her like she was the most beautiful woman in the world. Who would have thought? "Oh, Altheus."

"Does that mean yes?"

"I'm seven years older than you." Duncan had been five years her senior. She felt like she was robbing the cradle.

"Well, you don't look a day over sixty-nine," he assured her. "Say yes. I'd hate to unbook that cruise."

"Cruise?" she repeated.

"I've booked an Alaskan cruise. For next week."

"Oh, my." Millie's heart began to race. What would Debra say about this? She would surely think her mother had gone insane. "I don't know."

"Yes, you do."

"And a cruise. That's so much money."

He outright laughed at that. "Millie, my dear. I'm no millionaire, but I promise you I can afford a cruise. And I can afford to give you a comfortable life. You'll have your own garden," he added, sweetening the deal.

She had a sudden vision of herself as mistress of her own home again. She could see Altheus sitting with her on the porch of that charming house on the lake, could envision the flower beds all weeded and prettied up. "A ring, a cruise—I feel like a gold digger," she said.

He reached across the table and took her hand. "You feel free to dig in my pockets all you want." He sobered. "You know, I've been so lonely since my Ruthie died. You've given me a new lease on life."

He had done the same for her, but still. Marrying this man was a big step. All those years married to one man. "There's still so much we don't know about each other."

"We know we share the same politics, and we like church services where they sing hymns and not these modern songs. We know we both like to get up early. We know you like to garden and I like to golf. We both like Gin Rummy and an early dinner." He waggled his eyebrows. "And we like the taste of each other's lips."

That made her blush.

"I like to travel. You want to travel. And we both love it here. You can still be near your daughter, but you'll have your own house."

"You do make it hard to say no," she said.

"That's because I want you to say yes. Put on the ring, Millie girl. Let's enjoy our golden years together."

She slipped the ring onto her right hand, over the gold wedding band Duncan had given her so many years ago. When she moved that gold band to her right hand, she had thought she'd be a widow the rest of her life. She'd told herself she was fine with being a woman alone. But now, with a chance to find a friend and partner, she wasn't sure she was all that fine with keeping the status quo. The rest of her life could be really special with Altheus.

Still, it was a big decision. "Give me a couple of days to think about it," she said.

"I'll give you one to get used to the idea," he said, and raised her hand to his lips, making her heart flutter.

Oh, my!

Debra was in front of the TV, doing something on her laptop computer when Millie finally came home. "Did you have fun?"

"Yes, I did."

"Good." Debra continued looking at her computer screen. A bit of punishment for Millie's lack of cooperation earlier, Millie was sure.

Was this a good time to tell her daughter her news? There probably was no good time. "Altheus gave me a ring."

Debra looked up from her computer. "A birthstone?"

346

"It has my birthstone in it." Millie crossed the room and showed off her new jewelry.

Debra's eyes got big. "That's a lot of diamonds. This isn't just a birthstone, is it?" she asked, her voice laced with suspicion.

"Well, no," said Millie. "Altheus would like it to be an engagement ring."

Debra made a disgusted snort. "You're seventy-seven."

Of all the things she might have said! Millie frowned at her. "I didn't know there was an age limit on love."

"Love! You hardly know this man."

"I know him well enough to know he's a wonderful man."

"What would Daddy say?" Debra protested.

"I hope he'd say he was glad I'd found someone to love."

Debra's lips pulled down at the corners. "You have someone. Me."

"Yes, and your brothers. But I think there's room in my life for one more person."

"Mom, you can't just marry some person you hardly know," Debra said. "Go out with him, go to the movies, but, Mom, don't go crazy."

Now her daughter was patronizing her, talking to her as if she were Emily. "Getting married hardly qualifies as crazy," Millie said stiffly. "You're busy. I'll let you get back to work."

"Where are you going?" Debra demanded. She

might as well have added, "Don't walk away when I'm talking to you," something Millie had said to her many times during those turbulent teen years.

"I'm going to bed," snapped Millie.

"I'm calling Duncan," Debra threatened.

Debra always was a bit of a tattletale. Well, let her tattle to the boys. They'd probably tell her to mind her own business.

Wouldn't they? What if the boys didn't want their mother to get married?

She'd tell them the same thing she told Debra: there was no age limit on love. Why did grown children always think their parents shouldn't have a life? Debra obviously thought that Millie should be content to live out the rest of her life as a shadow, that because her skin had shriveled her soul had shriveled, too. Well, Debra was wrong.

By the time Millie had finished her nighttime routine and gotten into bed, she had indigestion and her head hurt and she just plain didn't feel well. It was upsetting to have a flare-up with her daughter. How could a woman love her child so much and feel disappointed so often? She remembered Duncan Jr.'s warning when she first decided to move out here. He was certainly right about one thing. Debra enjoyed telling people what to do. If their positions were reversed and Debra had moved out to live with Millie, would Debra still have told her what to do?

It was too late to wonder about that now. It was water under the bridge.

Millie frowned at the new ring, abiding on her right hand. She pulled it off and moved it to her left hand.

THIRTY

*I*t was prom week and the phone was ringing off the hook at Changing Seasons Floral. Hope loved doing corsages and boutonnieres for dances. She loved seeing the high schoolers come in to pick up their orders. The boys came in alone or by twos, venturing into the shop like nervous explorers checking out a foreign world. The girls always came in groups, giggling and excited, eyes shining with anticipation.

Hope still remembered her prom night. She'd never owned a dress as beautiful before or since. She'd wanted to go with Jonathan Edwards, the great love of her life who didn't know she was alive—was there a pattern here?—but she'd settled for going with her buddy Joe Green, and she'd had a great time. And Joe had treated her like a princess. Of course, it had been the prom dress. And the night. Prom night was always magical.

So, now, to help with the magic, Hope made each prom offering with special care and slipped a small Andes mint into the plastic container, along with a tiny slip of paper with "Dance with all your heart" printed in italics.

"I love that saying," Bobbi sighed as they worked side by side. "What a great way to live."

"Yep," Hope agreed.

"For both of us," Bobbi added, subtle as a boulder.

Hope leveled a scolding look at her. "I'm living just fine, don't worry. So, don't even think about *helping* me again or your life is going to be considerably shortened."

Bobbi's face reddened. "I just wanted you to be happy."

"Well, you completely mortified me by taking that poem to Jason. That was private." If ever two people needed to stop helping each other, it was them.

"Maybe he needed to know who's really right for him," said Bobbi, who was still having a hard time admitting she'd done something wrong.

"Now he thinks I'm like some dopey thirteen-year-old with a crush, so thanks a lot. I was so humiliated. I thought I'd die."

Bobbi kept her focus firmly on the carnations she was wiring together. "I made a mess of everything. I'm sorry. Why didn't you tell me you wanted him in the first place? I'd have backed off."

"He already wanted you, so what was the point?"

"He just thought he wanted me. But what he was getting wasn't really me, anyway. It was you."

"It doesn't matter anymore anyway," Hope said with a shrug.

"Doesn't it?"

Her sister's all-knowing stare made Hope squirm. The bell over the shop door jingled. "I'll get it," she said, glad to get away.

But then she emerged from behind the theater curtain and saw Jason Wells walking toward her and wanted to turn tail and run into the back room. Looking at him made her think of some labor negotiator coming to the table reluctantly. Why was he here? Her heart went into overdrive.

She smoothed her sweaty palms on the back of her pants and forced herself to look calm and polite. "Can I help you?"

He nodded. "I want to order some flowers."

Okay. He was taking advantage of her peace offering. Good. She nodded. "Who are they for?"

"My grandmother. It's her birthday tomorrow."

She opened up an order document on her computer. "What would you like to send?"

"She likes chrysanthemums. What do those stand for?"

Hope felt her face flaming. "Truth." She looked up to see him cocking an eyebrow at her and hurried on, "It's still just a little early for those. How about a pot with herbs—sage for wisdom, rosemary for long life, thyme for strength and courage."

He nodded, satisfied. "That'll do. Where'd you learn all this, anyway?"

351

"I found a book at a garage sale years ago."

"All those books I made the bookcase for were yours." He didn't necessarily say it accusingly— more like a discovery he wanted to share.

But Hope felt the weight of her deception. She bit her lip and nodded.

"Well, I'm glad it's getting used." He stood there for a moment, looking almost as awkward as she felt. Then he cleared his throat and said, "My grandmother's in Oregon. You can see she gets that by tomorrow, right?"

"Of course."

He pulled out his wallet. "Put it on my MasterCard."

"No. This one's on the house. Remember?"

"You can't stay in business that way," he said, pushing his charge card at her.

Hope kept her hands firmly on the computer keyboard. "My business is fine." *It's my life that's a mess.*

He set the charge card on the counter. "I insist."

"Take your card when you go. You don't want someone stealing it," she said as she walked into her back room.

She practically trampled Bobbi, who was jumping away from the curtain as fast as she could. "Were you spying on me?" she hissed.

"Spying is a strong word," Bobbi answered.

They'd gotten into this mess because Bobbi had insisted Hope take an interest in her love life. They weren't going to repeat that pattern in reverse. "Now, look," Hope began sternly.

The phone rang and Bobbi snagged the workroom extension. Saved by the bell. "It's for you."

"Were you with a customer?" asked Millie.

"No. This is a perfect time, especially for my sister. You just saved her from strangulation."

"Well, I'm glad I could be of service to your sister. I'm calling to ask a little favor."

"Sure. Name it."

"I'm hoping you'll keep an eye on my garden. I'll be gone for a few days."

"Oh? Where are you going?"

"On a cruise." Millie's voice trembled with excitement.

"A cruise? With who?" And then Hope knew. "Altheus, the boy toy."

"Not exactly," Millie corrected her. "Altheus the husband."

"You're getting married? Oh, my gosh. That's fabulous!"

"Who's getting married?" asked Bobbi.

"Millie, from the garden."

"Millie? That's the one who just turned seventy-five, isn't it?"

"Seventy-seven," Hope corrected her.

"Wow. Go, Millie."

"Does your daughter know?" Hope asked.

"No. We're eloping."

Eloping at seventy-seven. Hope couldn't help grinning. "It sounds really romantic."

"It is. He is. I'm so happy. I feel like a girl again."

"And I'm happy for you. When did this all happen?"

"Tuesday night. He gave me a ring for my birthday."

"And you're just now calling?" Hope teased.

"I've been so busy. We had announcements to send to our friends, and Altheus insisted on buying me a trousseau. I swear, I'm almost overwhelmed. I didn't get out of bed until an hour ago."

Millie in bed all morning? That wasn't like her. "Are you feeling okay?" Hope asked.

"I'm more than okay."

Being more than okay couldn't happen to a better person. "When are you leaving?"

"Tomorrow," Millie said breathlessly.

"You tell Altheus to come in this afternoon then. I'll have something for both of you."

"Thank you, dear, that's terribly sweet of you."

"My pleasure," Hope said. "And I really am happy for you." Not to mention inspired. If Hope ever reached that age, would she be a Millie, always reaching out for something new?

She probably shouldn't wait to find out. "I think I'll take a cruise this summer," she decided as she hung up.

"By yourself?" Bobbi sounded totally disgusted.

"I'm sure not going to wait for the perfect man to come along. And speaking of men."

"You know, I think we need a frap," Bobbi said, edging for the curtain. "Want a caramel frappuccino, caffeine free? Okay, I'll be right back."

"You owe me fraps for life," Hope called after her. "And maybe we'll be even," she muttered. "Maybe, but probably not." It was a good thing they were related, otherwise Bobbi would be dead.

Millie called Debra at work on Friday morning from the deck of the ms *Amsterdam,* using the new Jitterbug Altheus had given her. "Hello, dear. I'm sorry to bother you at work, but I thought I should let you know I won't be home for a few days, so you and the children are on your own."

"What do you mean you won't be home?" Debra demanded. "Mom, where are you?"

"Well, right now, I'm on a cruise ship, and we're about to depart for Alaska."

"Alaska!" Debra shrieked. "We who?"

"Altheus and I. The captain of the ship is marrying us this afternoon."

"Mom, you can't just run off and marry this man. Get off that boat. I'll come get you."

"No, you won't, and yes, I can," Millie said, and smiled at Altheus, who hugged her. "Don't worry about my things. I'll come pack them and take them to the new house when we get back. You'll love Altheus's house, by the way. It's right on the lake. We'll have you all over for dinner."

"Mom!"

"I have to go now," Millie said, and hung up on her daughter.

THIRTY-ONE

*O*n Monday, the shop bell jingled. Hope looked up from where she and Bobbi were stocking the cooler case to see Jason making his way past the arrangements of sunflower miniatures, the red and pink gerberas, and dancing balloons.

She wasn't surprised to see him. Unnerved, but not surprised. Even before she looked up, she'd felt his presence. It was as if the shop suddenly was flooded with testosterone. He was wearing his usual work wear: boots, jeans, a shirt thrown carelessly over a T-shirt. The only thing missing was the tool belt. He'd probably shed that back at the work site. She suddenly had a vision of a male stripper at a party. The tool belt's gone. What's coming off next? The shirt, of course. Jason Wells without a shirt, that had to be an amazing sight.

Oh, bad line of thought. Here came those nervous tremors. She ran a hand through her hair. What was he doing here, anyway?

"Hi, Jason," Bobbi managed.

He nodded at her and offered a polite hello, then said to Hope, "I need some flowers."

"You just bought flowers last week," she informed him. *Way to be a good businesswoman.*

"I know. I need some more, for my secretary. Secretary's Day," he added.

"That's in April," Hope informed him.

"I forgot. I have to make it up to her." He grabbed a beribboned pot brimming with Gerber daisies. "I'll take these."

"Okay," Hope said, moving toward the cash register.

"So, what do these mean?" he asked, setting the pot on the counter.

"They can symbolize several things," Hope said, double-checking the price on the pot. "Innocence, purity."

"Scratch that. She's gone through two husbands."

"They also symbolize loyalty and cheer."

"I guess they'll work," he said.

"They should. Everyone needs cheer," Hope said. She wished she could think of something else to say. Why couldn't she think of anything?

He had his charge card out now. "I'm paying this time."

"I probably owe you flowers for life."

He half-smiled and shook his head. "Somebody does," he said, looking in Bobbi's direction.

Bobbi, who had been shamelessly eavesdropping, turned as red as the gerberas and got back to work stocking the cooler case.

Hope felt her face warming, too. Guilty by association.

He scooped up the flowers. "Thanks. I guess I'm done here."

"I guess so," Hope agreed.

"Come back anytime," Bobbi called after him as he left the shop.

Hope leaned on the counter and watched, mentally drooling, as he walked past the window.

"He's interested in you," said Bobbi.

"That's ridiculous. He couldn't be. He was just interested in you."

"So? Men are like dogs. They're easily distracted."

"Look who's talking," said Hope.

Bobbi made a face at her. "Anyway, he only thought he was interested in me." She shrugged. "All we'd have had in common was sex. He'd have figured that out eventually and moved on."

"How do you know Duke won't do that?"

"Because he'll never find a better dance partner than me." Bobbi's eyes turned dreamy. "Duke's amazing."

"You said that about Jason," Hope reminded her.

"I know I made a mistake with Jason," Bobbi said. "I got confused because he looked right. But Duke, he feels right. I could spend my whole life with that man and never get tired of him. And I

358

don't have to worry about being what he wants. I just am."

"That's as good a description of love as I've ever heard," Hope admitted. "But is he a commitment kind of guy?"

Bobbi's smile was smug. "He is now." She pulled one of the flower-tipped pens from the cup by the cash register and began to idly fiddle with the petals. "How long do you think a person should wait to get married?"

"You barely know the guy," Hope protested.

"I know, but I think he's the one."

"You thought that about Jason." She also thought that about her first husband and several men after him. The last thing Bobbi needed was to end up with the wrong man again.

"I told you. I was thinking with my head and not my heart. You know, Mom and Dad are coming back in August."

"To look for a summer home on the lake, not to plan a wedding."

"There's nothing wrong with killing two birds with one stone."

Hope pointed a stern finger at her. "Don't even think it."

Bobbi looked highly offended. "I didn't say I was going to."

"You didn't have to. I can read your mind."

"Well, it's a quick read," Bobbi quipped and stuffed the pen back in the mug.

What a strange flower love was, Hope thought. In the heat of passion it could grow like a weed. But no weed was as easily killed. Maybe finding the right person was more like looking through a flower shop and trying to decide what to purchase. Which scent did you prefer? What plant could you keep alive? What would look nice in a vase on your dining room table or living room coffee table? What went with your colors? It was easy to be attracted to many different arrangements, but in the end you purchased one. Sometimes she worried that Bobbi was fickle when it came to men, but maybe Bobbi wasn't so much fickle as simply shopping, making sure she got what she really wanted.

Maybe Jason was shopping, too. But interested in her? No. Couldn't be.

Yet, the next day, there he was again. "My secretary wanted to know what kind of flower that was. I forgot."

"Gerbera daisy," Hope said. She grabbed a piece of scratch paper and wrote it down. "Here, so you can remember."

He slipped it in the pocket of his jean shirt. "Thanks." He casually looked at his watch. "It's almost lunchtime. Are you hungry?"

Her? Suddenly, she could barely breathe, let alone think about eating.

"You do eat, don't you?"

"Only mealtime and in between."

He smiled. "Well, then. Come on."

He wasn't interested in her. Why would he want to go to lunch with her? "Why do you want to go out to lunch?" she blurted.

He cocked an eyebrow. "Because I'm hungry?"

Just then, Duke walked into the shop. "Bobbi here?" he asked Hope.

As if drawn by radar, Bobbi came out of the back room. Hope watched as a huge smile blossomed on her sister's face. It was a different expression than Bobbi had worn when Jason showed up. That smile had been all about the thrill of the chase and had sparkled with excitement and speculation. This one held something more, something deeper, something rather like contentment. How had she gotten there so fast?

"Hi," she purred.

"Want lunch?" Duke asked her.

"Sorry, man, you're out of luck," Jason informed him in a voice that held not even a hint of sorry. "Somebody's got to hold down the shop and Hope's already leaving."

Duke bristled, but before he could say anything, Bobbi said, "You guys go ahead. We'll stay here and order takeout. In fact, Duke can help me in the back room."

Duke's hackles went down instantly and he grinned at Bobbi. "Okay."

"Come on," Jason said to Hope as if that settled everything.

He escorted her out of the shop and down the street to the bakery. The smell of freshly baked bread and chocolate chip cookies ushered them in. The espresso maker was getting a good workout, and the gurgle and whoosh as Amber made lattes served as background for the crowd of people visiting at tole-painted tables scattered around the room. They ordered sandwiches made with Sarah Goodwin's popular herbed bread, then moved on to order their drinks. Hope felt her cheeks warming under Amber's speculative look as she set them on the pickup counter.

They snagged the last vacant table. Jason slung an arm over the back of his chair and regarded her. "So, are you ever going to tell me what that poem was about?"

He said it teasingly, so she forced her voice to be light. "Just thoughts about love and life."

"Whose love and whose life?" he countered.

"Who knows?" she said, and became engrossed with her coffee.

"You're an interesting woman. You and your sister are polar opposites."

"I guess we are," she mused. "I wish I were more like her." Had she just said that out loud? Sheesh.

"Yeah? How?"

So many ways. "Oh, her looks, her charm, her energy."

He shrugged. "You're not so bad yourself, you know."

Which is why the minute you saw Bobbi I became invisible? Hope kept her mouth clamped shut.

He leaned forward. "Okay, I'll admit, when I saw your sister, all my brains fell out," he said, as if he'd just read her thoughts. "But you want to know something?"

Not if it was going to be more about how smitten he'd been with Bobbi. Perversely, she said, "What?"

"I'm not sorry things ended with us."

Hope raised an eyebrow.

"That's for real. And no hard feelings. Even though you two did a number on me, I think I get why you did it."

He did? Hope forced herself to close her dropping jaw.

"I helped my brother cheat on a test once."

He was comparing her helping Bobbi write clever poems and cards to him aiding and abetting his brother in cheating? "I don't think—" she began.

"Civics. He was flunking it. And he was getting D's in everything else. Never turned in his homework—had senioritis real bad. All of a sudden, it dawned on him what a dumb shit he'd been. He wanted to graduate. This one teacher was the only one who wasn't going to cut him any slack, even if he turned in all the assignments he'd missed. It all hinged on this one test." Jason shook his head. "Old man Meyers wasn't the sharpest pencil in the school drawer. He gave the same test every year. It never occurred to him that kids would figure that out."

"So, you fed your brother the answers."

Jason nodded. "I'd just graduated the year before, still had a folder full of tests and papers stuffed in my closet. We found the test and Joe wrote the answers on his leg. Meyers never got the connection between Joe's itchy leg and all those correct answers on the test." Jason shrugged. "He aced the test and squeaked by with a D. Went to junior college and brought up his grades. Then he transferred to a four-year college and graduated cum laude."

"The ends justify the means?"

"Only when you want to help somebody you care about," Jason countered. "It was wrong. I shouldn't have done it. At the time though, it seemed like the right thing to do. Good thing our parents didn't find out," he added. "I don't think they'd have agreed."

"Probably not," said Hope. "And I'm not sure that you can equate helping your brother cheat on a test with me helping my sister write some poems."

"Did you help her or write them for her?" he countered, cocking an eyebrow.

Hope's cheeks began to sizzle. "She just didn't want you to think she was dumb."

"I don't. She's pretty smart, really. She should have gone into advertising."

"Where people lie for a living?" Hope translated.

"Where people are good at creating an illusion, so other people will buy what they're selling," Jason amended.

"I guess we all do that," Hope said, running a finger around the rim of her mug. "Men buy fancy cars they can't really afford and women wear makeup and buy push-up bras." *Or get implants.*

Jason hoisted his coffee mug in salute. "Well, then, here's to false advertising."

Which was what she was doing right now. She was out with this man, pretending they could advance from a truce to a relationship. They couldn't. At least not the kind he'd want. No man was ever going to see her naked.

Amber called out that their sandwiches were ready and Jason went to pick them up, but Hope no longer had much of an appetite.

"Speaking of advertising," he said as he set her plate in front of her.

Let's not, she thought.

"You don't advertise at all. What's with that?"

She shrugged.

"Many a flower is born to blush unseen?"

"And waste its sweetness on the desert air," she finished. "I'd forgotten that poem."

"Me, too, until just now." He studied her. "So, is that you?"

She shook her head, trying to ignore the sudden heat in her cheeks. "I don't think my life is wasted."

"Maybe not so much wasted as not finished," he suggested. He pointed at her with his coffee mug. "You seem to spend a lot of time worrying about other people. What about you?"

"I'm fine. I'm happy just the way I am."

He let the subject drop with a nod and a bite of his sandwich.

After that, they stuck to small talk, chatting about great places to hike in the area, favorite food, and favorite books. And that was fine, until Jason said, "You know, my folks would love you. You're the real deal," and she knew it was time to end lunch.

She pushed her chair back. "I've got to get . . ." *Away*. "Back to work."

"Yeah, me, too," he said, reaching for his wallet.

"You know, I'm running out of people to buy flowers for," he said as they walked back to the shop.

"You'll have to switch to chocolates."

"So, I'm thinking maybe you should just go out with me this weekend. Not dancing," he quickly added.

"Bobbi's the dancer, not me." There had been no need to tell him that, really. They weren't going to go out. "I'm busy," she added. She had to garden sit for Millie.

"Your sister could watch the shop on Saturday," he suggested. "We could go for a hike."

"Thanks, but no. I think we're better off not starting anything."

"I wasn't asking you to marry me."

"I know."

"I just thought you might like to hang out," he persisted.

Men weren't into being friends. They always wanted to be friends with benefits. "I don't think that would be a good idea." Before he could press her further, she added, "I don't have time in my life for someone."

He frowned, but he said, "Okay."

Good. That settled it.

THIRTY-TWO

*J*ason didn't seem to get the concept of taking no for an answer. He came into the shop every day that week, each time with some new flimsy excuse that led to him hanging around to talk. The company's bookkeeper was having a bad day and needed flowers so she could get payroll done. He wanted to buy some of those red daisies to plant at his duplex. He'd killed the daisies—overnight— and needed more.

"You can't afford this," Hope informed him as he set an iced coffee on the counter for her. If only Bobbi hadn't gone to lunch with Duke, then she could have hidden in the back room and let her sister shoo him away. It was a very interesting coincidence that Jason had taken to waiting until she was alone in the shop and couldn't escape his visits.

"I think I can manage an iced coffee."

"You know what I mean," she said. "All these flowers?"

"So I like flowers," he countered. "Anyway, how do you know what I can afford?"

"I'm psychic."

"You're confusing. Were we connecting when we went out to lunch or not?"

"Yes," she admitted. "But I told you . . ."

"Bullshit. What you told me was bullshit. Why don't you want to go out with me? Give me one good reason."

"My reason is none of your business, okay?" Her unhappiness made her voice sharp.

He stood there for a moment, frowning. Then he shook his head and said, "I don't get you."

"You're right, you don't," she said. And he never would because she couldn't bring herself to share the intimate details that made up this new and far from improved Hope Walker. So, she stood there silently, sending off enough chilly vibes to turn him into a snowman.

He threw up his hands. "Okay, if that's the way you want it, I give up."

Still, she didn't say anything.

Instead, she watched him leave, tears in her eyes. All the flowers seemed to wilt. Even Audrey looked droopy. "Hey, guys, I'm sorry," she said after the door closed after him. "It was for his own good." Then she went into the back room and had herself a big pity party.

Which she was enjoying immensely until Bobbi crashed it. "What's wrong?" she cried, rushing to Hope's side.

"Nothing," Hope insisted, brushing at the corners of her eyes.

"Did you and Jason have a fight?"

"No." Hope knew her voice sounded snotty, but snotty was probably the only way she would keep Bobbi out of her business. "And will you please quit trying to matchmake?"

"But he's perfect for you," Bobbi protested.

"Well, I'm not perfect for him," Hope said bitterly.

Bobbi studied her a moment, then said, "That again. Are you going to let cancer take away your life?"

This was totally crossing the line. Bobbi didn't know what it was like to wonder if you'd be around to see another Christmas. She had no idea what it felt like to hold your breath when you went to the doctor, to look at your body and want to cry, to know that you'd go through your life alone.

She stabbed a finger at her sister. "Don't you tell me how to run my life. You haven't been where I've been and you have no way of knowing how I feel." She grabbed her purse from under the work counter and brushed past her sister.

"Wait. Where are you going?"

"Away. You can close up."

Swiping at bitter tears, Hope walked to the downtown lakefront park, marched to the end of the dock, and sat down, dangling her feet over the water. On a weekday, no one was renting paddleboats. No one was even around. She looked across the lake at the Cascade Mountains in the distance, stretching in rugged grandeur toward an endless blue sky, and considered the vastness of her setting. She was just a tiny speck in this great painting. What did it matter what one tiny speck felt or did?

She sighed. She'd been happy as a tiny speck, content to pour herself into making the picture pretty for everyone else, until Jason Wells had walked into her shop. Now she wanted to jump to a different spot in the picture. But it didn't work that way. She had to learn to be happy where she was.

On Sunday afternoon, working next to Amber at the community garden, tending her herbs and flowers while the sun massaged her back, she could almost convince herself that, deep down, when she wasn't getting distracted by handsome men who could quote poetry, she was perfectly content.

"I love it here," Amber said with a sigh. "I don't know what I'm going to do when winter comes and we can't be out here."

"We'll plan our gardens for next spring, of course," Hope told her.

"And wrangle more recipes out of Millie," Amber added. "Hey, and speaking of Millie." She pointed to the white Prius pulling up at the edge of the garden path.

Inside sat a beaming Millie, cuddling up to a good-looking older man with gray hair. They shared a kiss and she slipped out of the car and gave him a little good-bye wave that made Hope think of Betty Boop. He grinned, then waved up at Amber and Hope, who were shamelessly spying, and the car purred off.

"Welcome back, world traveler," Amber greeted her. "You look like married life agrees with you."

"What was your first clue?" Hope joked. "The ear-to-ear grin?"

Millie shook a playful finger at them. "All right, you two."

"Except you're moving kind of slow," Amber added.

"I'm a little tired," Millie admitted, stepping into her plot and caressing her flowers.

"I wonder why you're so tired," Amber teased, making Millie blush.

"I've been so busy. I got all my things from Debra's yesterday."

"I bet that was fun," Amber said.

"Well, Debra is a little unhappy about the suddenness of everything," Millie admitted.

"She'll come around," Hope predicted.

"So, I suppose you worked yourself to death trying to get everything organized at the new house," said Amber.

"Altheus won't let me work too hard," said Millie. "Although, a little hard work never hurt anyone."

But as they weeded, Hope noticed that Millie was becoming increasingly quiet. The late June weather was warm, but not warm enough to justify the profuse sweat on her face as she straightened and massaged her temples.

"Are you okay?" asked Amber.

Millie frowned. "I have such a headache."

Amber left her garden and came around to rub Millie's shoulders. "Does that help?"

"Thank you, but no."

"Maybe you should quit for the day," Hope suggested.

"Maybe," Millie agreed. "I just feel so . . . I don't feel well," she finished weakly and sank down on the ground, crushing her pansies. She barely seemed to notice. She put a hand to her chest and took a deep breath.

"Millie," Hope said, fear making her voice sharp.

Amber sat down next to Millie and put an arm around her shoulder, but Millie hardly seemed to notice that either. She sat breathing as if it was the only thing she could focus on.

"Tell us exactly what you're feeling." Now Amber sounded as scared as Hope felt.

"I don't know," Millie fretted. "I just don't feel right. I feel like I'm going to faint."

Hope began to add up the symptoms. Sweating, light-headedness, anxiety. She pulled her cell phone out of her jeans pocket and dialed 911. "I'm calling from Grandview Park," she said as soon as someone came on the line. "I think we've got a woman here having a heart attack."

"No," Millie whimpered, and Amber hugged her, stroking her hair and chanting, "It'll be okay, it'll be okay."

Oh, God, would it?

They hung in limbo, waiting for time to start again. The whole garden had gone quiet. At the far end, they could hear someone's hoe scratching behind a wall of cornstalks. A bumble bee buzzed slowly by. And Millie sat, concentrating on breathing as both women watched her in concern.

At last the ambulance arrived, sirens wailing, lights flashing. Seeing it, Millie became agitated. "Oh, dear."

She clutched at Amber, who was nearly hysterical and pleading, "Stay calm, Millie."

It only took a couple of minutes for the paramedics to decide Millie needed to go to the hospital, but it felt like hours to Hope as she watched them checking her and asking questions. Then they loaded her into the ambulance and carried her off.

Amber and Hope got into Amber's car and followed. As Amber squealed around Lake Way, following the ambulance to North Woods Hospital, Hope brought up Amber's home number on her cell so she could borrow it to talk to Ty.

"We think Millie's had a heart attack," Amber said. "I don't know what time I'll be home." It seemed to Hope she barely waited for an answer before ending the call and giving back the cell. Then she burst into tears.

"She'll be okay," Hope insisted. "She has too much to live for to even think of leaving us."

At the hospital, Amber told the nurse at the desk that she and Hope were Millie's granddaughters and the nurse promised to let them see Millie as soon as it was possible. "We're the closest thing she's got," Amber rationalized as they sat down to wait.

"Altheus doesn't know," Hope realized. "We've got to call him. And what's her daughter's name?"

"Debra."

"No, her last name. Do you know it?"

Amber shook her head.

"Well, let's hope Altheus does. And let's hope he's listed. I'll be right back."

Amber nodded grimly.

Hope hurried outside to call. She found Altheus. He answered the phone with such a hearty hello she wanted to cry. She nearly did as she broke the bad news to him.

"I'll be right there," he said, grimly. What a sad change from the happy man who had come into her shop to pick up a corsage for his bride.

Why did this have to happen to Millie just when she'd found real happiness? She couldn't just leave everything right when her life was getting good. It wasn't right. Hope leaned against a corner of the building and cried. The crying didn't change anything. It didn't even make her feel better. In fact, it left her with a headache. Giving a nearby shrub a vicious kick didn't help, either. It just made her feel like some kind of a traitor. "Sorry," she told it.

She returned to the waiting area where Amber sat ripping off her thumbnail with her teeth. "No news yet?"

Amber shook her head.

No news is good news, Hope told herself, and tried hard to believe it.

At last the doctor came out and informed them that Millie had, indeed, had a heart attack.

They were finally allowed to see her and found her in a typical hospital room, with walls in a non-descript green and a long counter containing a stainless steel sink and decorated jars of cotton swabs and tongue depressors and a box of plastic gloves. A blood-pressure cuff dangled from the wall. Millie lay propped up in a bed with the usual worn sheet and thin blanket. She looked old, frail, like someone else.

She smiled and held out a hand to each of them

and they took up positions on either side of the bed. "Thank you, girls, for taking such good care of me."

"We're just glad you're okay," Amber said, her voice unsteady.

Hope couldn't speak, so she squeezed Millie's hand.

"Had you been feeling sick?" Amber asked. "Were you sick on the cruise? How could this happen? Do you have high blood pressure?"

She was sounding more upset by the minute. "Amber," Hope said gently.

"Oh, I've always had little health issues," Millie replied vaguely. "It comes with the territory when you get old."

"But you're going to be fine," Amber insisted.

"Of course, I am," Millie assured her. "I'm just so sorry I caused you girls all this trouble."

"Yeah, you're a regular drama queen," Amber teased.

"But we love you anyway," Hope added.

Millie chuckled.

Hearing it, Hope felt comforted. They hadn't lost her. Hope had kicked that poor conifer for nothing.

Millie started to speak, but instead her features contorted into a look of pain and confusion. She opened her mouth but nothing came out.

"Millie," cried Hope, as if simply speaking her friend's name could make her snap out of it and get her body working right again.

But nothing was working right. Now Millie's mouth was opening and shutting, like a dying fish at the bottom of a boat, begging for water.

Amber rushed to the door and called, "We need a doctor!"

Hope stayed next to Millie, holding her hand tightly.

Altheus arrived at the hospital in time to learn that his wife had had a heart attack and followed it up with a stroke. "I'm very sorry. This happens sometimes," the doctor said.

"Not to Millie," Amber protested, and Altheus put an arm around her as if they'd known each other for years.

"I'm so sorry," Hope said to him.

"She was feeling tired by the end of the cruise, but then we'd been going pretty hard. I wanted her to take a day and rest when we got back, but she insisted on going to her daughter's." That made him frown. "I offered to help her pack, load up the car, but she wanted to do it all herself."

"And I can guess why," Amber said as she and Hope set up headquarters in the little waiting room of the critical-care unit. "She was probably afraid to let him near her daughter."

Just then Debra marched in. Hope and Amber had ringside seats, right near the nurses' station, and it was easy to hear every angry word spilling out of her mouth.

"Why didn't someone from the hospital call me?" she demanded. "Where is my mother now?"

"She's in room 204. They're getting her settled," the nurse said. "You can see her in just a minute."

"I'll see her now," Debra snapped, and marched into the room, ignoring the nurse's attempt to call her back. And then they heard Debra's anguished cry, "Mom! Oh, Mom."

"I want my mom to live forever," Amber said in a low voice.

Altheus returned with coffee for them. At the sound of the commotion, he set down the cups and started for Millie's room. Hope and Amber exchanged looks and followed him.

"This is all your fault," Debra accused Altheus as they entered the room. "What were you thinking, hauling her all over the place like she was thirty?" She scowled at Hope and Amber. "This is a private room."

"These are my wife's closest friends," Altheus said calmly. "She would want them here."

Debra looked at all three of them like they were ganging up on her, then covered her face and burst into tears.

"It's all right, girls," Altheus said. "Everything's going to be fine."

, Was it?

THIRTY-THREE

On Monday, Hope left Bobbi to man the shop during lunch hour and went to the hospital.

As she entered Millie's bedroom, it struck Hope that her friend was beginning to disappear. Not just her body, which looked gaunt and small under those white covers, but her very soul. This wasn't the Millie Hope knew. Altheus sat slumped on one side of the bed holding Millie's hand. He, too, looked like he was shrinking.

She started for the other side of the bed, but Altheus motioned her over next to him. "Come over here where she can see you."

Hope fought down the panic and forced herself to smile as she took her place by Millie's side. "How are you doing?"

Millie's voice was softly slurred. Hope had to lean in close to hear her. It sounded like she said, "Fine."

"Don't worry about your garden," Hope told her. "We'll take care of it while you're busy getting better."

Millie mumbled something and shut her eyes.

"She'll be better tomorrow," Altheus said, giving Millie's hand a gentle squeeze.

The next day, Millie did look a little better, and, by mid-week, when Hope and Amber came to visit, she was eating. Her speech was still slurred, and she'd lost the sight in one eye and was paralyzed on one side, but Altheus was insisting that, with some physical therapy, she'd soon be right as rain.

"If you girls will excuse me, I have some places to check," he said to Hope and Amber. "The hospital is kicking her out soon."

"That's wonderful news," Amber said as he left. "By the way, your garden is doing great. You should see it. Everything's blooming."

Millie managed a smile with half of her face. "I think my . . . gardening days are over," she slurred, and Hope had to swallow down a lump in her throat.

"But you can recover," Amber insisted.

Millie shut her eyes. "I've had a full life."

"You're talking like people do in the movies when they're going to die," Amber protested.

"It . . . happens to all of us if we live long enough."

Amber reached out and caressed her drooping face. "Not you. Not yet."

Millie kept her eyes shut. It was as if the work of keeping them open was too hard. "You'll be fine now, dear. Hang on to that husband." She fell silent. Just when Hope had decided she was asleep and was about to suggest they leave, she spoke again. "Hope."

"I'm here," Hope said, squeezing her hand.

"Promise me . . ."

"Anything," said Hope.

"No Shasta daisies at my funeral. Those . . . smell awful."

"Millie, that's not funny," Hope scolded.

"And find . . . someone to love."

Where had that come from? "Oh, Millie."

"Don't let the past steal from the future. Life is . . . short. But it can be sweet." She sighed a rattling sigh and a moment later she was asleep.

Amber and Hope sat with her all afternoon, but she never woke up.

And, two days later, just before Altheus was going to move her to a nursing home, she suffered a second heart attack and died.

After getting the news, Hope drove to her favorite hiking spot in the Cascades and spent the day wandering along forest trails, looking for new growth. Once she spotted a lady's slipper. The delicate woodland flower was a rare sighting, and she knelt and took a picture of it. "You look like you belong in Millie's garden."

Life is short.

Hope stood and sighed. Yes, it was, and right now it wasn't very sweet. She brought up the picture of the lady's slipper and it danced onto the camera screen. Well, here was a little something sweet to savor. She'd enlarge this picture and frame it.

Millie's memorial service was set for Wednesday afternoon, July second. Hope supposed Altheus had picked that day because he feared that people would leave town over the holiday weekend. Few ever did. Most Heart Lake residents enjoyed hanging out for the festivities. Even with people still in town, Hope worried that the funeral wouldn't be well attended. Millie hardly knew anyone.

She was surprised when orders for flowers started coming in: from Altheus, of course, and Amber, but also from the Lakeside Congregational Church women's ministry, and the teller at the bank. And then the orders started flying in from out of town. Millie's friend, Alice, wanted a hydrangea that Altheus could plant in his wife's honor. Millie's old garden club sprang for a basketful of plants, also to go to the new husband. The parade of names continued, people ordering arrangements, potted plants, wanting help with just the right words to say to a new and grieving husband.

"The church is going to look like a garden," Bobbi said that morning as they finished the last of the orders.

"Millie will like that." Hope slipped orange gladiolus in behind a grouping of gerberas and roses. She could feel the tears coming. In another moment, she was going to be watering these flowers.

Bobbi slipped an arm around her shoulders. "I'm sorry. It probably feels like losing Grandma all over again."

"I hate losing cool people from my life," Hope grumbled.

"At least two of the coolest people we know are still here."

Hope knew exactly where she was going and couldn't help smiling. "Us?"

"Yep." Bobbi turned serious. "I'm glad you're still here."

"Me, too," said Hope. "Now, let's get these arrangements finished and over to the church."

Bobbi drove the little PT Cruiser very carefully—hey, she could be taught—to the church. All the way, she kept thinking about her sister. Hope so deserved to be happy. Why did she insist on working so hard to make other people's lives good, and then let her own go untended? All the way back from delivering the flowers, Bobbi chewed on how she could manage to get Hope a life. There was only one way to do it, really. Someone had to tell Jason what Hope's problem was.

"Oh, boy," Bobbi muttered. Someone—not Hope, who'd be too mad—would be doing flowers for Bobbi's funeral if Hope found out about this. Bobbi parked the little PT Cruiser in back of the shop and sneaked the few feet to where Jason and his crew were working.

Except Jason wasn't there. "Where is he?" she asked Duke. She had to find him fast, before Hope found out.

"He's over at the Smith job on the lake," said Duke. He frowned. "Whaddya need to see him for?"

"I have to tell him something important about Hope."

"Yeah? What?"

"Never mind. Just give me the address."

Duke was still frowning, but he rattled off an address.

She kissed him on the cheek and scampered back to the Cruiser. Hopefully, with all the banging and sawing, Hope had never heard her pull up. It would be hard to explain why she left with an empty delivery car.

She found Jason at the site, talking with a man who was holding a blueprint. When Jason saw Bobbi, he detached himself and walked over mounds of dirt and stacks of wood bits to where she stood. He didn't look all that excited to see her, but he asked politely, "Did you need something?"

"Not me," she said, "but my sister does."

That got him curious. "Oh?"

"She needs you."

Jason rolled his eyes and started to turn away.

Bobbi caught his arm. "Seriously. You have to know why she doesn't want anything to do with you."

Now she had his full attention. "I'm listening."

"She had cancer."

His features took on an oh-no look. "The book on cancer. It was hers. I should have figured that out. God," he added softly. "What kind?"

"Breast. She lost one."

He stood there staring at Bobbi like he didn't understand what she'd just said.

"Did you get that?" she asked, giving his arm a shake.

"Yeah. Yeah, I got it. Is she okay?"

"She's as okay as a woman can be who's had two surgeries: one to get a fake boob, the other to make it look good. It still doesn't as far as she's concerned and she's got scarring. It's why she doesn't want things to go any further with you, even though she's in love with you."

Jason clawed his fingers through his hair. "Why didn't you tell me this earlier?"

"You think she would have let me? You think she even knows I'm here now? Look, the only reason I'm telling you this is because I think you and my sister belong together. And you'd be lucky to get her," Bobbi added, in case he hadn't figured that out. "So, now you know. Don't tell her I told you. I want to live to see thirty."

"What am I supposed to tell her?" Jason held out his hands, the picture of male helplessness. Really, women had to do all their thinking for them.

"Tell her you put two and two together. Do something romantic with flowers. That'll help. Oh, and first hypnotize her and convince her she's pretty." With that, she left Jason to figure out where to go from there. She'd done all she could. It was up to him now.

The sanctuary wasn't packed, but it was respectably filled, probably with church members who wanted to rally around their newest member, Hope decided. Next to her, Amber was sniffing into a big ball of tissue. "I hope you're going to share," Hope whispered, and Amber peeled off a couple of sheets and passed them over.

Debra and her children and two men who were probably Millie's sons sat up front in a separate pew, leaving Altheus to grieve alone. "That woman will be lucky if anyone comes to her funeral," Amber hissed.

Hope had seen enough of Debra at the hospital to convince her that, after Millie gave birth, the baby must have gotten switched.

"They'll probably throw rocks at her from the other side of the pearly gates," Amber continued.

"All but Millie," Hope whispered back. "She'll be there with a plate of lavender cookies."

That made Amber burst into noisy sobs and set Hope's tears to flowing, too.

The minister commanded everyone to rise and sing Millie's favorite hymn, "Amazing Grace." How appropriate, thought Hope. She was all about extending grace.

The minister summed up Millie's life in ten minutes, finishing with, "And everyone here came to love her. We're all a little better for having known Millie."

Hope closed her eyes and saw Millie standing in her garden, wearing her purple outfit and her flowered garden gloves, waving. "Don't forget," she called. "Go and find someone to love." Hope's eyes popped open.

Now one of her sons came up to the podium. He ran a finger along his shirt collar and cleared his throat. "Reading from the book of Relevation."

Someone snickered.

He cleared his throat again. "That would be Revelation. 'Blessed are the dead who die in the Lord from now on. They will rest from their labor, for their deeds will follow them.' Rest in peace, Mom. You've done a lot of good. You deserve it."

That's for sure, thought Hope, as Amber blew her nose.

"At this time, the family would love it if some of you would share how much Millie meant to you," said the pastor.

Amber didn't hesitate to stand. "We just moved here this spring and I didn't know anyone. Millie adopted me. She was like a grandmother. She shared recipes and taught me how to garden. She was awesome," Amber finished on a sob and sat back down.

Another person stood up, an older woman. "I

still remember Millie bringing me chicken soup when I was sick."

"She came to my baby shower and brought me flowers from her garden," said a woman. "My baby had colic. She showed me how to carry him so he'd feel better. I wish I'd had a chance to know her better."

On and on the testimonials went. Hope had just worked up her courage to stand and say something when the pastor cut them off. "Let's close with Millie's other favorite song, 'Nearer, My God, to Thee.'"

"I should have said something," she told Amber as they stood.

"You did," Amber said, and pointed to the huge arrangement of flowers from Hope sitting by Millie's picture.

The churchwomen had put together a salad buffet, and so everyone trooped to the fellowship hall to sit on cold metal chairs and balance paper plates on their laps. Debra had positioned her brothers and herself near the doorway to accept condolences. Her children stood beside her, dressed in black. Both had red-rimmed eyes and looked like they wanted to be somewhere else. Poor Altheus hovered over by a table on the far side of the room, keeping the punch bowl company.

"I'm going to go give him a hug," said Amber. "You deal with the poop princess. You'll be nicer."

Hope started out nice. "Your mom was an amazing woman," she said to Debra.

Debra was a wreck. Her eyes were so red, she looked like a vampire. Her eyeliner had run, leaving ugly brown trails down her cheeks. She nodded and yanked back a sob.

"We're all going to miss her," Hope continued.

"I just can't believe she's gone," Debra said, her words coming out jerkily. "I feel so alone," she added, looking off at nothing.

This woman couldn't seem to sing more than one note: me, me, me. "Well, you don't have to be," Hope said with enough sharpness to make Debra blink in surprise. She took Debra by the arms and turned her so she could see Altheus on the far side of the room. "He loved her, too, and he's all alone. Just like you."

Debra's eyes widened, then narrowed, changing her from the mourning daughter to Dragon Lady. Now she was going to breathe fire and fry Hope to a crisp.

Let her try. Hope wasn't done. "Maybe if you start working at it now, you can be like her someday and make her proud. You could start by being nice to the man she loved."

Debra was staring at her in shock. Hope was a little shocked herself. Had all that just come out of her mouth? "Uh, sorry for your loss," she said, and made a hasty retreat to the safety of the punch bowl.

"What did you just say to Debra?" asked Amber as Hope hugged Altheus. "She looked like she was about to go into conniptions."

"I was just offering my condolences," said Hope. "Come on. Let's get out of here."

On the way home, they stopped by the community garden and had their own little ceremony, just the two of them. They picked some of Millie's pansies and sprinkled the petals over both their gardens, and they each cut a flower to take home and press and dry.

"We love you, Millie," Amber murmured. "We always will."

"Look," said Hope, pointing to the zinnias. There sat a swallowtail butterfly, gently fanning its wings. It left the flowers and swooped past them, then off and away.

"Good-bye, Millie," Hope whispered. "See you in heaven."

Back at their cars, Amber asked, "How about coming with me to the parade on the Fourth? I promised Seth we'd go and Ty has to man the Family Inn booth. I'd sure like the company."

Hope didn't feel like being by herself, either, but she wasn't exactly pumped about milling around at a big, noisy community event. WWMD? (What would Millie do?) She'd go, of course. "Okay."

Amber hugged her. "Thanks. We can do the craft booths before and even have a cotton candy in honor of Millie."

Hope got back to the apartment to find a flower on her doorstep. The little primrose wasn't from her shop—too plainly packaged to have come from Changing Seasons. She picked it up and the envelope that had been lying under it. What on earth?

Inside the apartment, she found a note on the table from Bobbi. *Out with Duke. See you later.* There was a surprise. Maybe that would just work out. And maybe there was nothing wrong with an August wedding. Like Millie said, life was short.

And speaking of notes. She opened the mystery envelope that had come with her flower and pulled out a small sheet of paper. The writing was blocky and careless, definitely male. She read, "It's from the competition, but it said what needs to be said. Since you know what flowers mean, you should get the message." It was signed with the letter *J. Jason.*

Primroses said, "I can't live without you."

So he thought. Still, she'd take this offering and treasure it, especially the note. She set the little pot on her kitchen windowsill to remind her that, even in desert times, a girl could always find flowers.

The next day at the shop was quiet, with only a couple of arrangements to make for Fourth of July parties. "Let's close up early," Bobbi suggested. "We can get drinks at Organix and go to the city park and sit on the dock."

Hope wasn't in much of a mood to work anyway. "Good idea."

They were just getting ready to leave when the phone rang. "Oh, for Pete's sake," grumbled Bobbi as Hope snagged it.

The female voice on the other end was subdued. "I'd like to order some flowers. Could you possibly send them today?"

"If it's local," Hope said, and slipped her purse off her shoulder.

"It is. I need something special and I hear you do flowers that have special messages."

"I can," said Hope. "What would you like to say?"

The woman's voice caught on a sob. "Sorry."

"That's okay. Take your time."

"No, that's what I want to say."

"Well, purple hyacinths say 'I'm sorry,' but they're not in season right now. All I have at the moment are silk ones."

"Oh." The woman didn't sound excited by artificial flowers. "I need it to be special. I haven't been very nice to someone," she added, her voice quavering.

"Maybe you want something that signifies a new start," Hope suggested. "Pink roses can stand for friendship."

"Do you have real ones?" the woman asked, her voice picking up.

"I do."

"That will work."

"Okay. What would you like the card to say?"

"Um."

"Maybe something like, 'Let's start again'?"

"Please."

"Okay."

"No, I mean add Please."

"No problem," said Hope.

"And you'll tell him what the flowers mean?"

"Of course. Who is this going to?"

"Altheus Hornby."

Altheus? "How would you like to sign it?"

"Just, I don't know. Sign it *Debra.*"

Hope nearly dropped the phone. Amber would never believe this. Millie had to be up in heaven, doing the happy dance. "Would you like to add *Your daughter-in-law*?" she asked.

"Oh. How did you know? Have we met?"

Maybe they didn't want to go there. "Briefly, at the funeral. Your mother was a friend of mine. She was quite a woman."

"Yes, she was. I miss her so much."

"She'd be glad to know you're letting new people into your life," Hope said. "I'll get those roses out right away."

She took Debra's charge-card information, then hung up.

Bobbi had been leaning on the counter, listening. "So, Millie's daughter is sending flowers to the guy she was mad at?"

"That about sums it up," Hope said with a smile. "I guess she can be taught. Life is short. What's the sense in wasting it?"

"Yeah. What's the sense?" Bobbi echoed, giving her a meaningful stare.

A picture of the primrose on the windowsill danced into her mind and echoed, "Yeah. What's the sense?"

THIRTY-FOUR

*T*he Fourth of July was a scorcher, but that didn't stop Heart Lake residents from celebrating. Downtown Lake Way was packed with throngs of people. Hope and Amber jostled the crowd, looking for the perfect curbside seat to view the parade. Hope was ready to sit. They'd spent the last hour walking around the booths in sizzling heat.

"Millie would have loved this," said Amber.

"Yes, she would," Hope said, not because she agreed that Millie would have loved this human zoo and the heat, but because it made them both feel better to talk about their friend. This is hot enough to fry my buns, she thought as she settled on the hot sidewalk and let her legs stretch out onto the street. She found herself wishing she'd gotten another drink before they moved to the parade route.

"Water?" asked a male voice.

She knew that voice. She turned to see Jason

squatting behind her. He was wearing flip-flops, shorts, and a red Hawaiian print shirt, which hung open over his bare chest. His well-muscled, tanned, bare chest. She grabbed the bottled water he held out. It was even hotter out here than she'd realized.

"Hi." Amber was all calculating stares. "Haven't I seen you at the bakery?"

Of course, she had, and she'd called Hope that very afternoon wanting the scoop on him. Hope had assured Amber he was just a friend, and then changed the subject quickly enough for Amber to get the message. But the way Amber was looking from Hope to Jason as Hope introduced them, it was clear she was getting a whole new message now.

"We're gonna see a parade," Seth informed him.

"Cool. Can I sit with you?" Jason asked him.

"Sure," said Seth, but before he could move to make space for Jason next to him, Amber scooted them both over, making room between her and Hope. Amber and Bobbi had to be twins separated at birth.

Jason plopped down on the curb, his leg grazing Hope's in the process and making her feel like someone had set off a sparkler inside her chest. "How're you doing? I hear you've had a rough time of it."

From whom? Bobbi, of course. "I'm okay," she said.

She'd gone to the community garden the night before and done some weeding in Millie's plot. Seeing all Millie's flowers blooming and healthy had been a comfort.

"I'm sorry about your friend," he added.

"Me, too. I already miss her."

He nodded and they sat in silence. She wanted to thank him for the primrose he'd left on her doorstep, but if she did, then they'd have to talk about what that flower symbolized, and things would really get awkward. So, she sat there like an ingrate while her buns burned and that sparkler inside her kept shooting sparks.

"You all going to watch the fireworks tonight?" Jason asked, including Amber in the conversation.

"After we go home and have a nap," Amber replied, ruffling her son's hair and making him giggle.

"How about you?" Jason asked Hope. "Hey, why don't you come with me? We can talk about flowers."

Hope took a long swallow from her water bottle.

He took her hesitation for a yes. "Good. I'll pick you up around eight."

And, if that wasn't bad enough, when the parade finished, Amber decided to play Cupid. "You know, I think Ty's going to need the car. Do you think you could find another ride home?"

"My truck's just around the corner," Jason offered. "I can take you home."

It was too far to walk. Hope resigned herself. "Okay."

Once in the truck, Jason started the air conditioning going and she fell back thankfully against the seat. "Better?" he asked softly. "You were starting to look a little wilted there."

"Yes, thanks," she murmured.

"You mind if I make a quick stop?" he asked as they drove by the Gas 'N' Go.

She shook her head, figuring he needed gas. But instead of getting gas, he pulled up in front of the little grocery store and ducked in. He came out carrying a pack of wine coolers and a big bag of chips.

He stowed them in back of the truck, then got in. "So," he said casually as they wound their way around the lake. "Want to talk about primroses?"

"Jason, I already told you," she began.

"I know what you told me, but you left out some details, like the little one about you having had cancer."

Her heart stopped for a moment. Then it began to run. Fast. She bit her lip and looked out the window at the fir and alder trees along the road. In between, she caught glimpses of the lake, winking at her like a gigantic blue eye. Everything was so lush and green out here. In a place like Heart Lake, you could almost forget about ugly things like death and cancer.

"That's why you don't want to go out with me. Right?"

"It wouldn't be fair."

"Maybe it's not fair to decide for someone whether or not you get to be together." Instead of going on toward the apartment, he turned and the truck began bumping down a private road edged with woodsy tangle.

"Where are you going?" No detours. She just wanted to get home, so she could shut herself inside her apartment.

"I need to check on something at this site. You don't mind, do you?"

Actually, she did. "Do I have a choice?"

"Not really," he said amiably.

They emerged from the woods to a view of the lake, sparkling in the afternoon sun and, off to the side, a framed-in house—a two-story monster with a huge deck. He turned off the engine, saying, "You look like you've got heat stroke. I think we should get in the lake and cool off."

This was all slipping sideways. "I thought you had to check on something," said Hope. Was she never going to get home?

"I can multitask."

She pointed to her shorts and top. "I'm not dressed for swimming."

"We can work around that," he said easily, and opened his door. "Stay put. I'll open the door for you."

She watched, heart racing, as he walked around the back of the truck and picked up the snacks he'd purchased, along with an old army blanket. She'd have to tell him everything. After a wine cooler, maybe she'd have the nerve.

"Is it okay to be here?" she asked, looking around them as they walked across the property.

"The owners won't care. They're in California. Won't be up here for another two months."

He spread out the blanket on the porch, saying, "Make yourself at home."

She sat down on it and tried to concentrate on the view instead of the man sitting on the blanket next to her. The other side of the lake was fringed with trees and dotted with houses, some with lawns running like green skirts to the lake's edge. Others sported rockeries and more natural landscaping. She wondered what the owners would do with this place. She hoped they wouldn't take out the water lilies. They were so lovely. Someone across the lake was playing Jordin Sparks. The words to "This Is My Now" drifted across the water to her.

"Beautiful here, isn't it?" he said. He sat down beside her, opened a strawberry daiquiri cooler, and passed it to her.

"Did my sister tell you this is my favorite drink?" she asked.

He shook his head and opened a bottle for himself. "Just a lucky guess." He clinked bottles with her, then leaned back on an elbow and took a deep drink.

Hope watched the muscles in his throat work as

he drank. Was there anything about this man that wasn't sexy?

He caught her watching him and smiled like he knew what she was thinking. "I don't know why I didn't see how perfect you were right from the start."

It was way too hot out here. Hope took a long drink of her wine cooler. "You don't know me that well."

"Yeah? I'd be willing to bet I know you better than you think. I've had a lot of chances to get to know you: when I was with you and your sister, when I've talked to you in the shop, when we went out to lunch, when I read what you wrote me in those cards and letters."

"I was writing for Bobbi," she insisted.

"Were you?"

His intense scrutiny felt like the sun's rays through a magnifying glass. She took another long drink from her bottle. "You know, you can't be in love with my sister one minute and chasing me the next."

"Who said anything about being in love with your sister? I never did."

"You were sure acting like it."

"Bobbi's fun, but I wasn't in love with her. And I never slept with her," he added as if reading Hope's mind. "Look. I'm sorry I didn't get more into you to begin with. I should have. You've got what I want."

"What do you want?" Why was she bothering to ask?

"I want a woman who likes to hike in the woods, who's happy to sit by the lake and drink wine coolers. I want you."

"I need another drink," Hope decided.

He opened another bottle for her and handed it over with a sly grin. Probably thinking he was going to get lucky. Well, there was luck and there was luck.

He reached up and began playing with the last of her chemo curls which swirled lazily over her neck. "Where'd you get these, from your mom or your dad?"

"From my oncologist. This is how it grew in after the chemo."

She didn't look at him, but she could feel the charming smile smothering under the heavy dose of stark reality. "God."

That about summed it up. "I said that a lot myself, mostly in prayers. 'God, please let me live through this. God, why did I have to get this?'" She turned and offered him a smile to ease the awkward moment. "Mostly now, though, I simply say, 'God, thanks that I'm alive.'"

"You're amazing."

He was looking at her like she was some kind of saint. "No, I'm not. I get grumpy and ungrateful and jealous, and . . ." Loose lipped. She looked at the half-empty bottle in her hands.

No wonder her head was buzzing and her lips were flapping.

"Jealous of who?"

"You know, I think I need to cool off," she decided. She hopped up and ran for the lake.

"Good idea," said Jason, coming after her.

He caught up with her at the water's edge and she saw he'd shed his shirt. And he was closing the distance between them like a man with a purpose. "Come here, you," he teased.

She stumbled backward and went down, tangling herself in the water lilies. She came up sputtering and he caught her.

He brushed her wet hair out of her face and chuckled. "I'm beginning to wonder if you're accident prone."

"Only around you," she managed.

With her drenched top plastered to her, she looked like a contestant in a wet T-shirt contest, the last thing on earth she wanted to resemble. She opened her mouth to tell Jason she needed to go home. Now. But he didn't give her time to speak. Instead, he pulled her to him and kissed her. Good and thoroughly, and all she could think about was how much she wanted this man. She shut her eyes, wrapped her hands around his neck, and binged.

Five minutes later, he was scooping her up and carrying her out of the water, laying her down on the bank. And then his hand was sliding up her thigh, turning her into a one woman Fourth of July fireworks display. If ever there was a time to say stop, it was now. But she couldn't.

Not until his hand started creeping up her midriff. The fireworks stopped instantly and she sat up. "I can't."

"Oh. Too soon. You're right."

"No, it's not that."

"Well, then what?" He sounded completely puzzled.

She kept her eyes firmly on the lake, dazzling in the summer sun. "I lost a breast."

"Okay."

He said it like he wasn't tracking. She let out an angry hiss. "You don't want to see me naked."

"How do you know?" He reached up an arm, trying to coax her down to him.

She inched away. "I'm serious. I had replacement surgery. It didn't go well the first time. The second wasn't much of an improvement. I'm scarred and imperfect." She came to a sudden stop, the tightness in her throat making it impossible to say more. She'd said enough anyway. Too much.

He let out a big sigh and sat up next to her. "Look at me."

She shook her head and kept her face averted.

He took her by the chin and turned her face to his. "Maybe I haven't made myself clear. I'm looking for the whole package in a woman. I don't want just a pretty face and a hot body."

"A body is pretty important."

"They come in handy when you're having sex," he said. "But I've got to tell you, if the only thing keeping you from wanting to be with me is this less than perfect breast, you can stop worrying right now. I'm a leg man." And to prove it, he grazed a hand over her thigh, starting the fireworks all over again.

"Every man likes boobs."

"Well, sure," he admitted. "But we don't care if they're fake or not. And who cares about some scarring?"

"I do," Hope insisted. She wanted to cry, and she wasn't sure whether it was from frustration or gratitude.

"You women worry about things that don't make the radar with guys," he said, giving her neck a gentle rub. "And, hey, you want to talk scars." He pointed to a long, white lightning bolt of a scar running along his upper arm.

It took up a lot of arm space. She wondered why she'd never noticed it.

"I got that when I was eleven. Ran through a sliding glass door." He shrugged. "Life happens."

Well, that was touching, but . . . "It's not the same."

Now he frowned. "The hell it's not. People get hurt or sick all the time. Then we need to get patched up. So, you had to get patched up. The important thing is, you're here. You're well."

"For the time being. But I don't know if it's gone for good."

"Well, I don't know if I'm going to fall off a roof tomorrow and end up in a wheelchair," he said. "But I'm sure not going to let that stop me from living my life right now. Here." Suddenly, he had the bottom of her shirt and was easing it up.

She tried to pull away. "What are you doing?"

"We're going to settle this right now."

"No!" Panic swamped her and she started to struggle.

"Hold still," he commanded.

"Someone will see."

"Okay, then."

He stood and pulled her up after him. Then he led her back to the house and inside. It was shadowy and cool compared to the sunny lake bank. She began to shiver. "Now," he said gently. "Come here."

There was no sense postponing this. Hope shut her eyes and let him pull the top over her head. She squeezed her eyes shut, feeling the tears sting her cheeks as he slipped off her bra.

Outside a robin was starting to sing. Inside the half-built home, there was nothing but silence.

"Hope."

He said it gently. He was going to let her down easy.

Her eyes shot open in amazement as he bent and kissed her scarred breast. "I want you."

And then she cried.

And then she took his face in her hands and kissed him, putting her whole heart and soul into it. It was a perfect kiss.

And a perfect beginning.

THE WEDDING BOUQUET

Why do brides often carry roses and baby's breath in their bouquets? Besides the fact that they look beautiful, these flowers speak the language of marriage. Baby's breath signifies everlasting love. White roses represent eternal love, red roses say "I love you," and pink roses stand for perfect happiness. Orchids are nice to carry with a small, white Bible. They stand for love and beauty. And every bride is beautiful in her own way.

"I DO"

*J*ason proved how much he wanted Hope when he proposed to her in August as her family picnicked on the site of what was going to be her parents' future summer home.

"It's about time," said Bobbi, hugging them both. "I want to do the flowers for the wedding."

But when they got married two weeks later, they didn't need flowers, other than the elaborate bouquet Bobbi and Jason planned together. Mother nature gave them plenty. The ceremony took place at the community garden, with family and friends gathered around. Altheus surreptitiously wiped his eyes as Hope stood among the blooms with Amber and Bobbi as her bridesmaids. Duke and Jason's brother served as groomsmen, and the looks flashing between Duke and Bobbi spoke of another wedding soon to follow.

The minister asked Jason if he took Hope to be his wife in sickness and in health, and Jason smiled at her and said, "Absolutely." And, when the minister told him he could kiss the bride, he laid a protective hand over her scarred breast and whispered, "I want you." And if the words weren't enough to convince her, the kiss certainly was.

They picnicked in the park, their feast of scones and tea sandwiches catered by Ty and Amber. They were about to cut the lavender cake when Amber nudged Hope and said, "Look."

A butterfly perched on the nearby vase of lavender, fanning its wings.

"I think Millie approves," Amber said.

"I think so, too," Hope said with a smile. Millie was right, life was short. And she was going to live hers to the fullest.

Center Point Publishing
600 Brooks Road ● PO Box 1
Thorndike ME 04986-0001 USA

(207) 568-3717

US & Canada:
1 800 929-9108
www.centerpointlargeprint.com